Frankie Teardrop

Bill Kte'pi

This is a ghost story, and only ghosts will understand it.

Frankie Teardrop

Copyright © 2015 Bill Kte'pi

First Edition, February 2015

ISBN: 978-0692391365

Published by Fey Publishing

http://www.feypublishing.com/

Cover Art Completed by Luke Spooner

www.carrionhouse.com

This work is a piece of fiction. All characters appearing in this work are fictitious. Any resemblance to real persons, living or dead, is purely coincidental.

For Caitlin.

"I haven't been able to close my eyes, not all the way, for a couple months," I told her. I have the kind of long eyelashes that get in their own way a lot. They were at it again, poking each other and keeping the corner of my eye open. Every time I washed my face or hair I could feel the water running right in. She reached up and did some kind of magic to detangle them. It really happened, but it's a metaphor too, you know?

ACKNOWLEDGMENTS

It's the out-of-character bits of a book that I always hesitate over. What to say, explain, or thank, in terms of the things that went into making it. Most of me thinks, even in this age of self-promotion, that the writer should be like a teakettle: shut up and work, whistle for attention when you're done. I don't even like talking about things I've written, even when someone asks me what a book is about, and I have the chance to interest them in reading it. The novel is the shortest expression of itself, you know? If I could fit it into a blurb, I would just write blurbs.

That said...

At a minimum I should acknowledge Kristen Duvall and Sophie Childs of Fey Publishing, present and past, and Gary Dreslinski for ushering me into the fold -- and for being a great sounding board for very different stories altogether, some years ago. There is a healthy dose of religion in this story, and therefore debts owed to C.S. Lewis, the books of Ecclesiastes and Job, and two of my former professors, Jerah Johnson and William Stiebing, both of the University of New Orleans, both monumentally skilled.

I could go on to point out the critical influences of Peter Straub and Jonathan Carroll in helping me, by example, figure out what kinds of stories I like to tell. Or that I watched Rio Bravo, Paris Texas, and Cool Hand Luke over and over again while writing Frankie Teardrop -- there's a lot of Paul Newman and Sam Shepard in both Frank and the Halloween Man -- or that I listened to Jim White, Richard Hell, Uncle Tupelo, Suicide, Wire, Ryan Adams, and the Meat Puppets whenever the movies weren't on. It's probably not important to let you know that -- it's probably an impulse held over from writing lyrics and band logos on textbook covers, from growing up in band T-shirts and loud boots.

If nothing else, I might as well tell you that the book was briefly called "It's Such a Gamble When You Get a Face," which may be its secret title still.

CHAPTER ONE

Under the droop of a yolky sun, the snow looked like so much rusting styrofoam, red-lit puffs of muffler exhaust on the horizon where the High Road led home to Cardenio, his shadow waverly like heat distortion. Half of New Mexico would have a white Christmas this year, and it was supposed to be even heavier up by Taos where near half a foot had fallen. Two toes, more or less.

Frank split a smile as he reloaded the pistol. He'd have to remember that, tell Philip that. <u>Grandma and Grandpa got two toes of snow!</u> Philip was the only one young enough to still laugh at his Dad's jokes. Ricky didn't laugh at anything that didn't have swearing in it, and Gina, hell, there was no telling what was in that girl's head. Out of nowhere that old Frank rose up in him, that blisterknuckle Frank from once upon a time, and he was pissed off for no reason. It spread like a spill he couldn't mop off himself, the way it had done a lot the last few months, especially when thinking about the older kids. He didn't like feeling it, didn't like himself for it or the specificity of its targets, but Ricky and Gina had drifted off to corners he barely understood, and somehow he'd finally let go of the balloon string conviction that it was something they'd get over.

Leveled his hands, straightened his wrists, peered down the barrel at the nail sticking in the post in the field across the deserted road, just an old post standing in the field to no real device. Some property marker from a time when the lots had divvied up different, or maybe something to show where a well needed diggin. Straightened up, liftin his shoulder blades away from the pickup he'd been leaning against, took a breath, exhaled as he eased the trigger, and watched splinters shed from the top of the post. Missed the damn nail by two toes if it weren't three. God damn. His aim was usually better than that, but in the reddening light the rusted metal blended in with the old wood. A little piss whistle of gunsmoke sank from the barrel, looking like some marble modern art for an instant as it caught the light, and disappearing no sooner than it'd feigned permanence.

The coyote who'd been loitering jumped at the sound of the gunshot, but didn't skitter off, no more'n he had with the last few shots. He was a city coyote, not much bothered by people, by noise. His ears never got their fill of hearing, his eyes never got enough to see. The crack of the pistol weren't any worse to him than a backfiring car, summer fireworks, the bass of some kid's stereo. All the same, the mangy thing lifted his head up at Frank no doubt hoping for food. He had that ranging look to him like he'd had more'n one meal from men's cast-offs, that blisterknuckle look.

Despite the snow and waiting for Kriste and the kids to pick him up, Frank was only just now getting cold. Always been like that, carrying his warmth around like a bear. Came in handy days like today, when caretaking one of the farmhouses out on Rory Calhoun Highway, just running the faucets so the pipes wouldn't freeze, clearing the gutters, checking things out for the owners while they were off at family for the holidays, led to a dead starter on the side of the road. He'd told Kriste go ahead and finish packing, drop by your church, pick the kids up, we'll get dinner on the road to your folks'. There was that pizza place Gina liked bout forty minutes out from Taos, the one with the green chile chicken pizza. Maybe that'd show to be one of her many exceptions to the vegetarianism she'd picked up at college, like bacon, Subway turkey sandwiches, and the meatball enchiladas Kriste had made at Thanksgiving.

First Christmas in who-knew that they hadn't spent with his Mom and Pop at home in Cardenio. Gina'd done a lot of sighing and eye-rolling at that, as though his parents had died just to disrupt her routine, but he held back, didn't say nothing about it. It was her thing to work out. They were young to be losing grandparents, especially ones that'd lived in town an' been there at every holiday, every birthday, every barbecue. He wasn't used to the void himself yet, that low dry gulch in his life that his parents had filled until the first Wednesday of November. Seemed like every day some new reminder popped up at him, some new sentence he couldn't form without their words.

People'd warned him the holidays were the toughest, but the truth was Thanksgiving had felt like an echo of the wake. You had family all round, you had food, the only real difference was the turkey, and so it hadn't hit him then. He'd thought he was old enough to be used to the idea of his parents dying, had friends whose folks had died plenty younger. But his parents weren't in the service; they'd been artists, taking turns every year, one of them staying home to work there and the other teaching the art and algebra classes at the middle school. Not real high risk work. Not real high risk people, when you came to it.

He thought about lighting a cigarette. Thinking about it made the pack on the inside breast pocket of his fleece jacket flutter like a heart. But he hadn't had a cigarette since his parents' murder. He kept putting the pack in his pocket, or tucking it next to his watch on the bedside table, and sometimes he fiddle fucked around with the lighter as if he was gonna light one. He hadn't quit but he was a long job getting round to lighting up.

For lack of anything else to do, he climbed up on the truck, a foot on the tire lifting him into the bed and another taking him to the roof of the cab, where he checked his cell phone again to make sure he hadn't missed Kriste's call to gunshots. Great reception out here: you could see the tower, poked up from out of the barrens to the south, beyond the post and the coyote and the snowy fields. On the other side of the road, those fields tumbled into hills covered with scrubby pines which got thicker to the east as they approached the Sangre de Cristo mountains. He took a breath and felt that old Frank that had ris up slunker back down, felt that smoldering twist of anger sputter out. Like he'd stepped up out of the mud it lived in.

The phone rattled against his chest as he was lining up another awkward shot at the nail, and he fished it out, flipped it open. Kriste's cell and the home phone were the only numbers he had set to vibrate as well as ring, so he knew it had to be her. "Hey hon," he said, feeling like a bank robber with the Colt in one hand and the Sanyo in the other. Everybody be cool, this is a robbery. Your money or your life. "We good for it?"

"Good as she gets," Kriste said, and he knew there was some story there, some drama with one of the kids. The ages they were at, probably one of them had wanted to spend Christmas with a friend instead of family, a fight that seemed to come up with one kid or another every year now. It was one thing with Gina, who'd spent last Easter with her boyfriend's family and gone to Disney World with another boyfriend for a Christmas in high school, but who were the families whose nine year olds, thirteen year olds, kept inviting friends to spend Christmas with them? He didn't think he was that much a stick in the mud, but it rubbed him wrong. Parenting was hard enough without other kids' parents getting in the way.

"Where you ridin?"

"We're about to turn onto Rory," she said, which put her a couple few miles away. "You hungry, Frankie baby?"

"Could eat, Kriste baby, but I'm not particular if it'll keep the peace."

"Good," she said. "Gina wants her chicken pizza, you know, from

3

--"

"Yeah okay, Capelli's. I thought she would."

"Ricky," Kriste said, in her campfire story voice, but the tone was lowered because the kids were right there with her, "would like a cheeseburger."

"A huhhhhwarr hwrrr!" the boy protested from too far away for the phone to pick him up.

"Yes," Kriste continued. "A Graveyard burger."

"The hell's that?" He regretted the "hell" -- the way Kriste'd been lately, it was dice if she'd give him shit for it or not. He wasn't sure she'd caught religion exactly, but it was at least a flare-up. The coyote wovered back and forth around the post, like Axl Rose in front of the mike, as though it knew Frank was talking about food.

"You remember," his wife said, in patient and explanatory cadence, and he knew it wasn't him the patience was needed for, "Graveyard burgers, from that all-night place we went to when we were visiting your brother?"

"That dive?" Frank asked. It'd been a hole in the wall, and they'd gone there so Mickey could play a few hands of cards in the back while the kids ate. "Honey, that's an hour out the way. Longer if we hit holiday traffic."

"I know, sweetheart," she said in that patient tone still. This had been the fight, then. "But Ricky agreed that we can go for pizza first since it's on the way, and not to complain that he's hungry. And he'll pay for it himself and take out the trash for Grandma and Grandpa while we're in Taos."

He could picture the negotiating that had gone on, the incremental offerings and compromises laid on the table. "Okay," he agreed. Between Gina and Ricky being in their teens and Kriste's on-again off-again flirtation with pentecostal churches and all that came with them, he'd learned it was best to make what you could out of what you could get. "That's fine. Way things are going, we may need a cup of coffee by then anyway, right?"

"Oh, you may," she said. "You're driving once I catch up to you. Me, I may need a cup of something-else-altogether, you know what I mean?"

"I'd say it's good odds anywhere with 'graveyard burgers' and poker in the back has liquor in the front."

"I'll show you liquor in the front," she said in an undertone, but not enough of one to avoid her daughter's distraught and disgusted, "Moommmmm!" Thank God, then. Kriste wasn't in her weird mood tonight. Maybe she didn't want to get into it in front of her parents, middle of the road Catholics who looked on Protestant things like speaking in tongues and laying on hands with deep suspicion.

"Anyway," Kriste said in that finishing the call voice.

"See you soon, babe. I'll call Bud to pick the truck up." He hadn't felt comfortable having the truck towed and leaving himself solo on the side of the road, and hitching with Bud into town would've ended up taking longer. It was safe enough, no one much came down this stretch of Rory who didn't live here.

He called Bud and then watched a moment for headlights, but there were too many on the High Road and the intermittent streets parallel to it for him to make anything out yet. The last of the light was falling, so sure and sharp it was like he could see the tail end of its arc, where darkness would gulp, and he turned a little, a foot dangling off the cab roof as he searched out that nail.

It was a blemish in shadow on the post, and he let his hands steady until the sights were at its center and fixing to stay there, and eased the Colt's trigger. The handgun was a .45 Defender Plus, which he told himself was the trouble. The piece was a deliciously light carry, and he liked the wraparound finger grooves, but the barrel was only three inches. For years he'd carried Pop's old steel-finish Series 70, which was two inches longer and a hell of a lot heavier. The Defender made more sense maybe, but he wasn't used to the loss of those two inches yet, and it made his aim sloppy, like a fucking Boy Scout's.

But finally, smack, he got it. He wasn't facing it dead on, so the nail didn't hammer right in. He hated that, had always hated when he hit the nail perfect but bent it because he should have been standing three feet to the left. But there it was. He'd taken a chunk of the post out but didn't reckon anyone would miss it.

"That's right," he said, holstering the Defender at his side. "That's damn right."

The coyote whined again, the whine becoming a moan. His eyes refocused in the near-dark, and he saw that it was not far beyond the post, and had sat down in the snow to paw at its ear, but shivered every time it touched it. He hopped down off the truck and crossed the street to get a better look, but wasn't going to get too close to a coyote, even a citified one.

He'd shot its ear. Just nicked it, but a chunk the size of a silver dollar had been ripped off of its long, triangular ear.

"Oh God damn," he said. "Oh, fuck, boy, I'm sorry. God damn why couldn't you move off? I told you I wasn't gonna feed you nothing!"

Frank approached the coyote slowly, trying to get a better look. If Mickey'd been there, at least he could've counted on having some alcohol handy, something to disinfect the wound. There wasn't a lot of blood splattered in the snow, all things considered, but the ragged end of the ear hung in three or four pieces, and that was a lot of opportunity for infection, especially if the coyote kept pawing at it like that.

"Lay off with that!" Frank said. "Damn, no way am I going to wrestle you down to clean that, wind up with your love bites for Christmas."

The coyote pawed at its ear again and yelped at the pain, snapping at the air between them. He took a step back, wondering if he could wrap his jacket around his hands to protect them, when light caught his eyes.

Later it would seem unlikely he'd seen the headlights and he'd have to wonder just which pair he'd seen, but nothing else explained why he suddenly looked up and west, to the intersection of Rory Calhoun Highway and Vegas Drive. A tanker trunk barreled up Vegas at what had to be thirty over the limit, fast, too fast, not so fast Frank didn't have time to wave his hands to the side as though to push Kriste's SUV out of the way.

Of course she didn't see him and she didn't see the truck either. Sure he would hear the squeal of tires, see the SUV tumble as she ripped the steering wheel to the side, he had barely looked up when the two vehicles collided. Metal twisted, folded, snapped, sprayed, tires left waketrails in the brown slush like fingernail scratches, and the tanker tipped on its side in flames.

The tank flinched off the ground, dragging the cab with it until the weight pulled it back down to the highway. Its northbound inertia still carried it along Vegas Drive, and the flaming husk of the tanker snapped the telephone pole at the street corner as the mass came to a stop. Behind it, the SUV had crumpled like an accordion and ricocheted into the middle of the street, laying lopsided driver side down, front axle broken like a crippled horse, wheels spinning uselessly, tires on fire.

He didn't notice starting to run. All of a sudden he was just on his feet flat out like he had the Devil on his tail. It was too far to see anything but the fire and the shapes of the vehicles, too far to be sure it was Kriste. He pulled the cell phone out as he ran, flipped it open, hit talk twice to call the last number heard from, but no one picked up. He kept running, shoving the phone in his pocket.

The distance went so slowly. Out here you could see things long before you could get to them.

When was the last time he'd run like this? High school?

He passed the edge of the fields, passed the intersection of Rory and MacLean, and his footsteps were illuminated now by the Christmas lights dangling icicle-like from the edges of flat roofs, by the spillover of light through living room windows, by the luminaria on lawns. People were coming out of their houses, people were at the cars, at the scene, "the scene of the accident," before he was even in shouting distance of them, with blankets and fire extinguishers, they were running around and waving hands.

"Frank?" someone called as he passed them, and he didn't turn to see who it was or why.

His lungs hurt, his feet hurt. He wasn't pacing himself. He wasn't aware of breathing.

He stumbled when his air ran out and his legs got tangled, and his palms skidded across the asphalt. Where were the sirens? Where were the fucking sirens?

Someone pulled him up and threw a blanket over his shoulders. He couldn't seem to hear anything. The sky lit up as flames burst from a gas tank, and the blanket provider ducked, hands over her head, but Frank just stood there, watching the fireball, and when it died down he watched its afterflash melt from his corneas. At the opposite corner of Vegas and Rory, someone had set their luminaria out in a strange pattern, or maybe the accident had just rearranged them that way. The little candles glowing from inside paper bags weighted down with sand formed a symbol across the gritty, stone-strewn front lawn, like two question marks at odds with each other and a hook comin between em.

He kept staring at the luminaria, knowin where he'd seen that sign before, and eventually passed out or went into shock. When he was paying attention again, the candleglow still lingering in his eyes, people were talking around him, holding his shoulders and keeping him from running to the smoking, flame-flickered remains of the SUV.

"Can't do nothing, Frank, can't do nothing, settle down man." That was Bud. Frank recognized his voice. The sirens were here finally, one of the fire trucks and two ambulances and two cop cars to boot. Don was directing traffic and waving people away. People were lined up, the few in the neighborhood, watching from their lawns, some of them from their windows. A couple of the women were holding thermoses, like they wanted to offer something to help and didn't know who to make their offer to. He recognized Karen there, and Inez's cousin maybe.

The paramedics started to carry people away from the vehicles.

The first two were so covered in burns, exposing raw tissue and bones badly broken on impact, that he couldn't make out any features, any human features. He shook and his heart raced while he counted, wondering if either of them was his wife, his daughter, one of his sons. A third was carried away zipped into a bag and he lurched against Bud's hands, but one of the neighborhood men had a grip on him now, too, and all he could do was twist between them.

7

A fourth stretcher, a second bag. The air stank of chemicals, smoke, and sick.

And the fifth and final, bearing someone obscured by oxygen mask and paramedics, clothes burned beyond the point of recognizability.

When he realized no more were coming, his knees started to sag, and it took both men to hold him up. "C'mon there, Frank," Bud said.

"C'mon man, stay strong, God bless, God bless." The other man was Alejandro McTavitt, who tended bar at the Beach. Frank nodded against him as though sense had been made, and realized Lobo was walking towards him.

Lobo's real name was Coby Davenant, but everyone had called him Lobo since he'd become the sheriff in Cardenio, after the old <u>Sheriff Lobo</u> TV show. The resemblance wasn't strong, but it'd been there in passing fifteen years ago, and it was just the kind of nickname that stuck.

Lobo took his hat off and held it over his chest. "Frank," he said.

"Aw fuck, Low, aw fuck don't say it."

The sheriff winced. Frank had gone to school with his little sister, had dated her two or three times. They weren't tight, but they were good. They were the kind of men who were never more than a conversation or two from becoming friends. "Frank, Ricardo and Gina are in critical condition," Lobo said. This wasn't going to be that conversation. "They're being taken straight to County General, and if -- once they're stabilized, the burn ward in Santa Fe has room for 'em."

Frank's shoulders hitched but he forgot how to make noise.

"Sheriff," McTavitt said. "What about Mrs Train and the boy?"

Lobo looked at the man and then back at Frank. "I'm sorry, Frank. Kriste and Philip are dead. It was quick. I know it don't count for nothing."

"Lemme see my boy," Frank said, and managed to shake off Bud and McTavitt, who had maybe lost the strength to hold on. "God damn lemme see Phillie."

"You don't wanna do that," Lobo said. "Later, you'll -- Frank, all you wanna do right now is come with me, I'm gonna take you straight to the hospital with me, all right, I'm gonna drive you there myself. Frankie T, c'mon, you gotta be with your kids right now."

"Go on, Frank," Bud said. "I'll get your truck home and replace that starter. You get with your family now."

"We'll pray for you, Frank," McTavitt said. "Anything we can do for you?"

Frank looked around. The coyote was visible in the distance, still wandering around the truck and the post. "Yeah," he said. "I shot that coyote by mistake. Get him fixed up. Take him up to the vet. Or the animal hospital, I guess, yeah, it's after business hours. Take him up to the animal hospital. Here, I'll pay for it --"

"Nah Frank," McTavitt said. He seemed happy to have something to do, gave Bud a glance like this evened them off. "Nah Frank, I got it, don't you worry about it."

"All right." Frank nodded. "All right then. Coby, take me to my kids, I wanna see my kids."

Sheriff Lobo led him to his patrol car like you'd lead an old man to the bathroom, and the world felt hot and hard around him.

In the hospital, he didn't sleep and didn't touch the coffee that was brought to him. He sketched idly, drawing question marks chasin each other in a circle. One of the nurses commented that it looked like a brand, but not a useful one: there was no way to refer to it, no Double T or Bar S, just squiggle thing. Almost like crossed scythes

Gina Marie Train held on until 4:53 a.m. on the morning of Christmas Eve, before succumbing to pulmonary failure and trauma as a result of extensive third-degree burns.

Although he would require a skin graft to replace tissue on his right arm that was lost to an eschar, and his forearm was splinted to treat multiple fractures, Ricky Train survived. As did the coyote with the ragged ear.

CHAPTER TWO

Bile crawled on Frank's throat and sweat washed his forehead when he realized he knew the phone number for Yazzie & Son Funeral Parlor without looking it up. It was the Son who answered, Andrew, and Frank didn't need to introduce himself. "Mr Train!" Andrew said, with the mild surprise of the professional he had made of himself. "I hope nothing is wrong? Not a problem with your parents' stone, is it --"

"No," Frank said, and now his tongue was dry. He had thought he could do this all on autopilot. He had thought, having just buried his parents and been principally responsible for the care of their estate, that doing the same for his wife and children would be as simple as talking in his sleep. "No, this is new. I --"

"Of course," Andrew said smoothly. "What can Yazzie and Son do for you?"

"My wife," he said. "The kids, two of them. Gina, Philip, Philip's the youngest, he _was_ the youngest, he's eight. Was eight. There was a car accident, they're, they're still at the morgue, I haven't." Words dissolved into breath.

Andrew paused, but to his credit, not for long. "Dios mio, Frankie," he said. "I'm so sorry. Of course we can do it. Do you want to come in, do you want --"

"No," Frank said. "No. I have a lot I need to do. I haven't even, I need to call Kriste's parents."

"Do you want us to do that?"

"Jesus no!" Frank said, sounding angrier than he meant to, more ragged. "Sorry. Andy, no, we were supposed to be there last night, oh fuck, we were supposed to be there last night and they must've tried to call. I gotta talk to them myself."

"Sure. Listen, I'll call the morgue for you, all right, I'll take care of that. I think Bobby's on duty right now, I know Bobby. You come in when you can, we'll work out specifics --"

"We already, talk to your dad, we already picked out caskets me and Kriste. When we were taking care of my folks, it got us thinking you know. About what we wanted. I guess, I guess that worked out. For the kids -- uh, fuck, Andy, I trust you, just, I don't want to think about it --"

"Don't," Andrew said quickly. "Don't think about it. Do what you need to. We'll do what you don't need to. That's the motto here."

But there was a lot he needed to do, and not just calling Bruno and Inez. He'd been through this with his parents, the process, the mechanics of afterdeath. Not just letting family know. You could phone tree that, one person would call another, get the word out. There was the bank to deal with, the schools, Kriste's job. Magazine subscriptions to cancel. Cell phones to shut off. The life insurance, the lawyers, the coroner's office to have them send death certificates to the many people on the other end of the line who'd ask for copies. It was Christmas Eve. Many of the places he had to call would be closed the next day. He'd have to call them now, have to get the ball rolling, do what needed to be done. It was like for this wild moment, some stuffed shirt buried inside him liked the roteness of it, the chores he'd need to do, liked knowing he'd be able to be more orderly and informed about it than he had when his parents had died. He knew how to do it now. He knew how to ride this thing. It wasn't much different from caretaking.

Cowboy's like the land, his father used to say. Arthur Train Junior might've been an artist, but four generations before him and maybe more had lived and worked on horseback, and he'd supported himself and his wife on cowboy dollars when they were in school. A cowboy's like the land, stomped on, kicked down, rained over, shit on, stormed on. Don't matter what kind of shape he's in when it's all over. Whatever happened, he's there, grateful to still be above snakes.

As long as he didn't leave the room, the kitchen with the phone cord coils tangling the air from the wall to his seat at the table, his back to the doorway into the living room, his eyes on the address book with its stratified handwriting, its fifteen-twenty years of accumulated names and numbers and scratchouts and corrections through pencil and ink and smudges and the way her lower-case f's were different last year than when they got married but her s's were exactly the same --

As long as he didn't leave the room, it was like she wasn't dead. Philip was just at a friend's. Gina was back at school. And Kriste, Kriste was anywhere but dead.

He turned to the CONTACT NUMBERS section of the address book, more consistent in its handwriting, more recent in its vintage, and after a moment's consideration of the hour, shaded his water with a little whiskey. Phone still in hand like a tether, holding his hand up high so its coils wouldn't catch on the tops of the chairs, he started a pot of coffee. His compromise for drinking before noon.

As it began to drip, he dialed numbers.

He swallowed cooling coffee in throat-swelling mouthfuls and put his Stetson on, shrugged his winter coat on, before grabbing the address book and heading out to the bank. The more got done, the better. When his parents died, he'd dealt with a little bit every day, and it'd ruined every one of them. This time he meant to push through.

Bud had fixed the truck as promised, and left a hand-printed note that just said "Call the house if you need anything," with his home number. "Call the house" was married man code, Frank knew it well. It was a way to say "I care, but I usually delegate emotional matters to my wife, so if you call, you'll probably be dealing with her."

The truck started smooth as sunshine, and he headed up Rio Bravo Road towards Center Street. Cardenio wasn't a large town, but with the farms and small ranches around it, it was big enough to keep a couple few restaurants afloat and some snack-and-sandwich stands besides. It was more developed than when he'd been a kid, but maybe not much bigger. There were still plenty of houses made of spare tires and aluminum cans, and even more of the stuff tourists loved to take pictures of if chance or bladder brought them by: coyotes painted on the sides of businesses howling at the moon, cartoon-cute wooden snakes set out like sculpture, ram skulls with neon tracing the horns, whatcha'd call Santa Fe Tacky.

The Loker girl caught his eye when he got to the bank, and nodded towards the back. She'd been the one to answer the phone when he called about opening Kriste's safe deposit box. Probate would go faster if he got that done now, in case she had a recent will stowed there. One of the many things he'd learned about the practicalities of all this shit.

"'Lo Chelsea."

"I'm so sorry to hear about your family," she said. "I remember babysitting for the kids when they were younger."

"Thank you," he said. "I appreciate your letting me do this today. You get the paperwork?"

She nodded. She looked so grown up now in her work clothes and everything. He remembered when she had hair cut like Dorothy Hammill and too much eyeshadow. "It won't take long. In and out. After the holiday you can come back and take care of your accounts and mortgage and so on."

"Okay," he said. "Great."

They went into the room with the safety deposit boxes, and Chelsea and a guard removed #383, which Chelsea unlocked and opened and rifled through. There was indeed a will there, which she put face down in a manila folder.

"I know you can't show it to me," he said, "but can you tell me the date on it before you send it to the court?"

She nodded and glanced at it. "It's from 2006," she said. "Sound right?"

"Sounds old. She's updated it since. But go ahead and send that in, I'm sure you have to."

"We do. We can leave you alone now. Just let us know when you're done."

"It's okay," he said, and bundled everything together. Papers mostly, some heavier things that would be gems and gold they'd bought when they were worried about other investments. "Need me to sign for anything?"

"Here," she said, taking a form out of the manila folder and putting it on the table. "And here, if you want to close the box instead of transferring it to your name."

He hovered over the second form and shook his head, after signing the first. There was something too final about it. "No," he said. "No. Not today, Chelsea."

"Of course, Mr Train. Is there anything else we can do for you?"

He shook his head. "I have a lot more to do before, you know, before the end of the day. And Christmas."

She leaned forward and gave him a little one-arm hug before kissing his cheek. "We'll pray for you, sir. My family will. We'll light candles."

"'Preciate it."

The bank was downtown. Center Street was the main drag in Cardenio, at least for ordinary daylight activities. You'd want to take Burns into Swayville if what you were after was a little gambling or a little whiskey, and the teenagers stuck to River on date nights. But here, it was Christmas Eve day, and people were doing last minute shopping, buying ristras of dried red chiles and produce at old Tuck's grocery, hams for Christmas dinner at the meat market, fresh hot tamales from the tamale ladies whose carts were a fixture on Center Street from Halloween through Valentine's.

All these people milling around, people he'd known or known the families of all his life. The Barelas, the Lokers, the Meeres, there were the Playforth girls, the McCartys and the Archuletas. The Garcias Kriste was related to and the ones she wasn't. They were all around him, and not more'n a handful knew he and Ricky were the only Trains left. With the holidays and all, word woulda traveled on short legs. Bud and his people would know, anyone living out on Rory and whoever they told, but most people, most people were busy wrapping presents and putting tinsel on scrub pines and replacing the candles in their luminaria.

Frank stepped out of the way of people going in and out of the bank getting those rolls of dimes for Christmas stockings, those savings bonds for grandchildren, and held Kriste's papers against his chest and closed his eyes, bowing his head so the brim of his hat cloaked him and made it look as though he might be studying something on the ground. He imagined that if he stood perfectly still, surrounded by people who

13

thought he was the man he used to be, the man he was wouldn't catch up to him.

CHAPTER THREE

Ricky looked peaceful despite the bruising and bandages covering his arm, the IV on the other wrist. Behind the blotches he was pale, malnourished. The system shock, Frank reckoned. He didn't look much like Frank had at this age. He was gentler-looking, more fragile. This was his first broken bone. He'd only been to the hospital to have his appendix out. He wasn't a perfect kid, but he was a good one, rebellious in ways that were annoying or frustrating more than dangerous. Not like teenage Frank at all, not a kid you lost sleep over.

"Mr Train?" A doctor leaned over the doorway clipboard first.

"Yeah."

The doctor came in and closed the door. "Dr Archuleta. Ricky's going to be fine."

Frank relaxed a little. He hadn't realized he was still worrying. "Can he come home tonight, or do we have to wait till morning? I mean, it's Christmas."

"I'm sorry, he's going to have to stay here for at least a week."

He sank into the chair. "Oh, come on."

Dr Archuleta tapped his clipboard. "We didn't know at first. There are two kinds of skin grafts in cases like this: a split thickness skin graft, where we use a dermatome to remove very thin slices of skin from the patient and reposition them where they're needed. A split thickness graft starts to heal the first day. With Ricky, though, the eschar was just too deep. When we removed the burnt tissue, we realized a full thickness graft would be necessary, one that includes a little underlying muscle and blood."

"Christ," Frank said.

"It's okay. It sounds gruesome, but it isn't a difficult procedure. It's just important to let it heal, because fixing it is expensive if it heals wrong, and if there's no risk of infection, your insurance won't cover it. We're looking to avoid significant scars here. Last thing the boy needs."

"All right. But if he stays in the hospital, he'll be fine?"

"He'll be fine. We're watching him like hawks for infection, and even on the off chance he developed one, we'd treat it immediately. He needs to keep that arm as still as he can, but with the fracture to the ulna, that's not going to be hard. No stretching for six weeks. No running or upper- or full-body exercise for ten weeks. When Ricky's ready to go home, we'll schedule some follow-ups, so those are just guesstimates."

"Uh huh. Is there anything I need to sign, fill out?"

"The nurse will bring that for you. Do you have any questions for me?"

"When's Ricky likely to wake up?"

"Another hour, two hours. He'll be groggy until about dinner time. I'd like to keep him on a liquid diet for a day or two because of the anesthesia."

Frank nodded, and the doctor left him in the room, where he started sorting through Kriste's papers. The gold and gems he immediately put in his pockets, for lack of anywhere safer just yet. He wasn't sure about the stones, but the gold had to be ten grand worth. It had seemed like more when they'd bought it.

Most of the joint paperwork was kept in his safe deposit box. In Kriste's, there were bank records and tax forms in there going back forever, just in case they were ever audited; old car paperwork he supposed she just never got rid of; certificates of deposit and savings bonds, in her names as well as the kids'; some letters he'd sort through separately; God, a photo from before they were married, when they were just kids dating for a few months; and, tucked into the mess, a medical form that took him a moment to read, as though his eyes had to focus through the jargon. The single sheet was smudged with pencil marks and rippled places where something had been spilled on it.

It was dated 1998, when Ricky was a baby and Gina was just starting school. Kriste's name was listed under MOTHER, after the official masthead and some abbreviations he couldn't figure. Under CHILD, Ricky's name was listed, and Frank's own name came soon after, SUBJECT. The RESULTS were NEGATIVE, said the form.

Ricky's breath hitched, but he stayed asleep, just twitching in his sleep, and it registered on Frank that this was a paternity test, and that it claimed he wasn't Ricky's father. Pencil marks lingered around FRANK and NEGATIVE, and she had doodled thick angry swirls in the margins, most of it nonsense, static: but in the middle was a dark and deliberate circle broken by a bent line travelling through it.

He didn't know how long he stared at it before the door opened after a knock and the floor nurse led Bruno and Inez in. "Frank!" Inez said, and grabbed him hard, like she was going to fall over. He shoved the papers back into the folder and put them on his chair as he stood up into his mother-in-law's awkward hug, nod-waving to Bruno over her shoulder.

16

"Ricky's still asleep," he told them. "He's going to be fine, he's just had a skin graft. They need to keep him here for a week or so to make sure he doesn't get an infection."

"Ohh," Inez said, while Bruno just stared stoically at the sleeping boy. "Oh, no, he'll miss Christmas and New Year's both."

"We'll make it up to him," Frank promised. "Inez. Bruno. I'm sorry --" Inez hugged him again, and Bruno clapped him on the back. They had both been crying. He could tell from Bruno's eyes, Inez's voice. "I'm glad you're both here," he said. "Did Anita not come with you?"

The floor nurse quietly brought in chairs for them. She must have known that Ricky's room was a place for more than just one person to recover. "Anita's at the house," Bruno said. "Your house. We stopped by there first, those friends of yours told us where you were, she stayed to, well, to make calls."

"Phone calls," Inez clarified.

"Okay," Frank said. "I took care of, you know, arrangements. The bookstore, the college, insurance, that kind of thing. And the, the service."

"Already?" Bruno asked.

Frank nodded. "Got it done. You know? I wanted." He glanced at Ricky, unsure how much the boy could hear. "I wanted that all straightened out before he wakes up. Listen this is the thing."

"Oh, the poor boy," Inez said. "Poor sweet Ricardo."

"Named after my uncle, you know," Bruno said with sad pride. "Uncle Ricardo was the smartest God damned Garcia ever lived, I swear."

"I know," Frank said. "I know, and the last thing my boy needs is, well, I feel it even in me, you know, the way I'm thinking, everything going on, we don't want him to wake up and feel like everyone's ignoring him because he survived. Like all our attention is on, on --"

"Yeah," Bruno said. "Yeah, okay."

"Don't you worry," Inez said. "We'll have Christmas right here. Right here in this room."

"I dunno how the nurses are going to feel about that," Frank started, but Inez gave him a look, and he imagined the nurses trying to get through that look. "Hell, the floor's 'bout empty. I've got -- the presents are at home, I'll bring them."

"We'll stay here in shifts," Bruno said. "Ricky's not going to be alone for a minute until they let him out. Maybe we can get them to bring a cot in."

"Grandma?" Ricky said faintly. "Grandpa?"

"Hey trooper," Frank said. He focused on keeping his voice steady.

"Did I break my arm?"

"Yeah. Yeah, you busted your wing, and got burned. Ricky? Do you

17

remember, do you remember what happened to your Mom? And Gina and Philip?"

The boy's eyes fixed on him and there was something there, some deep knowledge. "No ..."

Inez and Bruno brought their chairs closer, and Bruno touched Frank's hand, met his eyes in a way that conveyed his willingness to take this bullet. Frank shook him off. "It was a bad accident, Rick." He forced himself not to stammer or falter. "It's God's own luck you even made it."

"They're _dead_?" Ricky said, and he tried to get up. Bruno held him down, and Frank worried whether he was doing so gently enough. But the pain seemed to do the trick. Ricky gasped and fell back, despite the morphine drip. "They can't be dead. That's fucking nuts. That's fucking wrong --"

Frank felt like he was standing outside the room watching himself and everyone in it, watching Ricky piling up them sandbags of denial to build a bridge between the mind and the heart. Soon he was asleep again, and Frank took the first shift on the cot the nurses provided, as Bruno and Inez left to lend a hand at the house. Inez left some cash on the table and insisted he get dinner when he woke up, like somehow he was gonna claim to be broke in order to get out of eating. No one knew how to act, and they pieced shit together from everything else they'd done in their lives, quilts to cover up in.

Hospital rooms never get completely dark. The light came in from the hallway, from the dials and displays on the machines, from the moving shadows outside, and Frank lay in the dark watching Ricky, wondering who the boy's father was. In his house on Borachon Creek, relatives who weren't his family tended to the business of burying the relatives who were. With his parents and children dead, his blood thinning from the world, it was like being orphaned, being adopted.

CHAPTER FOUR

You read much C.S. Lewis, Frank? he'd been asked once. *He said: all that seems Earth is Hell or Heaven. Lord, open not my weak eyes to this too often.*

At the northern headwaters in Colorado, the Rio Grande was a rushing and thrashing thing barely buckled to its gorge, a snake that twisted in the pinch of rock and earth. The slice of the river that passed Cardenio by was calmer, flatter, its might skimmed by the trout streams that trickled through the pine barrens. Broad as a highway and as light as a bedsheet, silver-still for long stretches and then roughed up by ripples, broken against rocks and dips.

To the south its waters were sucked up by a bosque that followed its shores for two hundred miles past Santa Fe, a ribbon of forest that faded into desert when it reached the nadir of the water's reach. Mesquite thrived there, hackberry, palo verde, a cottonwood or two like a thick clump of hair. The thick green, the muck of organic sediment along the riverbed, the quicksand of those places that were neither river nor forest but loved by both, all made for a scar of swamp in the middle of wasteland.

But here, delicate limens of ice two days after Christmas extended the banks into the bed, cracking squeaking as the water passed beneath. Fat-bellied cormorants and dagger-nosed godwits perched long legs in the water, stabbing at fish and tilting their heads back to snorfle them down. Terns overhead bid their time, and when they swooped down the ice would crack in fragments so glass-thin they dissolved before the gentle current had anywhere to take them. These were the birds that had stayed, birds too stupid to leave or too full of faith that this year's cold would be short and kind.

The coyotes and javelinas hunted along the river, taking down badgers and prairie dogs when they could. East of the Grande was the Santa Clara Indian Reservation on the Santa Clara Plateau, the Valley of Wild Roses where Arthur Train Junior took his sons camping when they were children, bought the tobacco a Tewa-born cowboy had introduced him to. When Arthur was a child, his grandfather had brought him camping on the same land, and he wouldn't have been surprised to find out his family had been visiting that land since before the act that made it a reservation, since the hills ran wild and the river still thought for itself. There had been men and women like the Trains on this land for as long as the land had been real, since the days when wild gods still danced in the shadows and the ravens had not yet stolen the moon from the other side of the world.

From Santa Clara, the road led to Chimayo and the High Road, a series of connected roads, mostly State Route 76 in this part of the stretch, which led from Santa Fe to Taos through farmland, Spanish villages, hills overlooking forests. The High Road formed the boundary of what people considered the outlying areas of Cardenio, although the town limits actually ended a few miles east of it, and the farms which abutted it sometimes continued on the other side like they were politely ignoring the traffic. This land had always been fuzzy that way, like the road had been drawn with a shaky hand that didn't quite manage to stay inside the lines, and had trembled this way here, that way there, missing the nooks and crannies of the real world beneath the blue highways, the unpaved world.

The farms west of Cardenio raised mostly corn for animal feed, syrup, cornmeal and cornstarch, biofuel. The biggest commercial farms were owned by the Wilata, Meere, and Rodriguez families, who between them produced a glut of summer jobs for teenage boys from towns all over. The Meeres grew nothing but animal feed, silage slowly fermenting in the tall silos. You could smell the stink of it like sour mash brewing in a haystack at the roadside farm stand the Meeres' neighbor ran, and any time his business went poorly he blamed the Meeres. There was bad blood between the Meeres and Wilatas, disputes over land, disputes over daughters and bastard babies. The Rodriguezes worked the land along Borachon Creek, a tributary of a tributary of the Rio Grande. Sweet and flint corn, chiles, limes, mealy but shiny apples, chickens for eggs and meat and fighting.

The only cattle around were kept for dairy, and only half of them belonged to commercial dairy farms. The Lazy 7 Ranch where Arthur Train Junior and Rafael Antonio Guiberto Mondragon cowboyed had been out of commission since Frank and Mickey were boys, and they only saw it once, at a rip-tearing hoot-n-holler farewell party thrown by the owner's son for whatever former hands wanted to show up. Frank had his first beer at the Lazy 7, the bottle warm from the too-near campfire but the beer inside still Coleman-cool. It made him burp hot dogs the rest of the night. Mickey insisted he touched his first tit that same weekend, when he talked a drunk fourteen year old tomboy into believing he was thirteen instead of nine.

The hills around Cardenio looked like ant-hills or burrow-wasp nests, like fists bunched under oilcloth. In the winter, with the snow still blanketing the ground and hiding the edges of everything, the few sheep let out to wander under the watch of their boys were near about invisible. They looked like motion, like wind, like a river current.

Some of the old farms were sold off and turned into housing lots after each World War, became neighborhoods imprinted over unsold farmland. The land on either side of Pond Drive was the Barelas' subsidy land. They cashed regular checks from the Department of Agriculture as a reward for not growing one thing or another, for the sake of the market. The pond didn't have a name except on the Geological Survey, and folks just called it "the pond" or "the fire pond," since it'd been officially designated as that last one in 1974, excusing the Barelas from paying property taxes on it.

Past the Barela place were the fairgrounds, which'd fell to disarray in the last few years. Not only had they not seen a carnival since Frank's boyhood, but the October rodeo had been cancelled in the 1990s, and every year people predicted the same thing happening to the April one, which would only leave the Fourth of July. Rodeo business brought in more tourists than anything else, though some years there were plenty of new faces at the cockfights, people who'd just read in some newspaper article, some internet thing, about cockfighting still being legal in New Mexico.

Like most small towns surrounded by mapless spaces, from the sky Cardenio looked like a tight cluster spilling frills. It hadn't been built according to any plan, but had accumulated the way clutter will in a living room. Most of the town was laid out along Center Street, River Drive, Burns Road, and Church On Fire Lane, that last named just how it sounded, a church that'd caught on fire ages and ages back, all the men in town forming a bucket brigade that fought it all night, dumping bucketful after bucketful of creek water on the flames. Took long enough to put out that men from the neighbor towns, from Cabredo and Periquet and Lonely, had time to get there and pitch in.

The snow was heaviest in the nameless places, powerful places free of buildup. There was nothing under the sun to melt it, not a thing to mar it except the tracks of animals. A white crow pecked at the snow, letting it melt in her mouth.

That same someone'd told Frank, You know what William James said about the supernatural? About proving something's out there that ain't quite normal? He said in order to show that not all crows are black, it ain't necessary to show that no crows are black. All you gotta do is find one white crow. Just the one.

The lines of the town, the streets and footpaths and secrets, were melted down by traffic, standing out like circuitry as the crow flew over them. Borachon Creek twisted through the southern half of town, trickling away in the southeast. Snow made Cardenio look more like a town anywhere else, hid its name under the sun, behind the moon. In one corner, far from River and Swayville and the dodgier parts of town but a ways from Center so that no one would have to be confronted with it while shopping, the lines had become deeper, clearer, from the heat of funeral traffic. The Yazzie & Son Funeral Home was downtown, on Mercy off Center next to the Loan Gunmen check-cashing/title loan/pawn shop and the Taco Casita. But the cemetery where they did their most public work was on the outskirts, the mirror image of Rory Calhoun Highway. There were old timers who might still call this stretch the Graveyard, or Graveyard Road, but once upon a whenever somebody'd thought names like that were too damn depressing, and officially now this was Tom Mix Circle, a neighborhood without any inhabitants, named for a dead fake cowboy. It had the only lawns in town that never went yellow.

The wake had been at Frank's parents' home, because death had made their place tidy and his a sort of waystation for casserole dishes, enough green chile to fill his freezer, lasagnas he'd never live enough lives to eat, Hamburger Helper with everyone's individual touch. The funeral service had been at St Catherine's in town, and the procession had left from there. The graves'd been dug in advance and Frank found himself wondering in one of them abstract trains of thought how that worked way up north, where it was cold long enough for the ground to freeze deeper than just a layer of icy mud on top. Did they wait to bury their dead till spring? You'd think you'd hear bout that kinda thing in movies.

Thank God they never moved anywhere like that.

Mickey and his latest wife Jessie had come in from wherever Mickey was living now. Their cherry red Trans Am they called Colorado stood out like a lime in a bucket of lemons, with a bumper sticker that said God Was Drunk When He Made Me (But I Forgive Him!) They both stood next to Frank, on one side, with Inez and Bruno and Anita on the other, like Frank was the only lynchpin left joining the Train family to the Garcias. Ricky was in the hospital. They could move Christmas to his hospital bed but not this.

Frank had approved one thing after another for the service, some cousin reading a poem for Philip about childhood innocence, another reading a diary entry about Gina, things he couldn't remember, things that washed over him. He shivered like the cold was the only thing he could feel, and watched the white crow dart back and forth in the air overhead, never landing, like she was waiting for someone to drop a crumb of something. He guessed that was what crows saw people as: things that sometimes produced crumbs, other times went to yelling and firearms.

The priest running the show was from St Catherine's, Father Michael, not anybody from Faith Rising or any of Kriste's other weirdo churches, and he didn't have a shred of guilt about that. It wasn't just her funeral, and by God and by damn he wasn't gonna bury his children to the words of those snake-handlers. He got angry just thinking about it, found himself composing all the things he'd say to her when she bitched at him for being disrespectful to her new religious feelings, and his throat hitched up like cartoon Ichabod.

Even the coyote with the ragged ear was here. The vet had called yesterday morning, wanting to know what he should do with him, and Frank had let a long silence go by before answering, as though he'd hoped someone else would get on the line and solve it for him. "Bring the old boy here, I reckon," he'd said finally. "We got room for one more." The coyote looked a world different with his fur groomed and shampooed, glossy from eating food he hadn't had to scavenge or kill, and Frank hadn't reckoned what to do with him yet.

The coyote didn't have a name yet and roamed around the cemetery, avoiding the crowds as surely as they avoided him. People took him for a dog of particularly low breeding, especially them out of towners, but didn't like the look of him even so. Frank kinda liked that. This need for hospitality, this need to be calm for everyone like he was on display. It made him remember the old days when he'd been a rat caught in the storm of the world before being napped up by Kriste and dried out in the warmth under the sun. No, Ricky wasn't like teenage Frank at all. Teenage Frank would've got himself killed by now, beat to death or drunk to death or maybe he would've gotten into the harder drugs, the rockstar drugs. Maybe he would've lived just long enough to discover meth and not much longer. Maybe he would've beat Kriste to the punch and wound up scattered across the highway.

He watched the crow fly because he didn't know what else to look at, and it did finally land, perching on the shoulder of a man standing off to the side along with much of the rest of the crowd. Frank recognized him, had seen him with the crow before, and frowned. The man was in a cheap Mexican suit and a plain red baseball cap. He was gaunt enough that his ribs would probably have shown clearly if he'd raised his shirt, and his several weeks' growth of beard showed a good dose of grey. He didn't look up and meet Frank's eyes, but was looking off somewhere else. Maybe at the coyote, that damn coyote.

Soon Mickey nudged Frank in the side. "Hey Frankie boy, who is that guy anyway?"

Frank didn't blink or move his eyes away from the man in the Mexican suit, towards whom the old coyote had wandered. "That guy who?" He spoke in an undertone, though he realized the services had ended and people were just saying their little things, their little delay things because they couldn't all pull out of the parking lot at once.

"That guy there, the one you been staring at. I still can't place him. What's he, Kriste's cousin?"

"What?" Frank asked. "Still when? Who?"

"Uh, what?"

Frank frowned and found a sentence tucked beneath his tongue. "What do you mean, 'still'? When have you met him before?"

"He was in the hospital," Jessie said at Mickey's other side. "When we went to see Ricky, he was just leaving. Mickey didn't recognize him, so I figured he must be from Kriste's side of the family?" There was a dubiousness in Jessie's voice that wasn't in Mickey's, like she'd picked up on Frank's vibe, whereas the Mick probably hadn't picked up a damn thing since the weekend that was less than eighty proof.

"No," Frank said dully. The man in the Mexican suit was looking back at him now. His eyes were dark and set deep and as unblinking as Frank's own. "You saw him in the hospital? He was seeing Ricky?"

"He said he was family. That's what the nurse said."

"He fucking isn't," Frank said, and felt how bad his legs wanted to jolt across the cemetery, felt his fists clench, felt the fabric of his suit jacket tighten across the shoulders where he knew he shoulda had it let out but didn't reckon on having to use it again so soon after his folks' funeral. "He fucking isn't family, I'll tell you that goddammit. He fucking isn't!"

Somehow he'd made his way to shouting, but before he fell another step to running, the man had flinched and rabbited off. The crow was gone, the coyote growling in the direction the man had darted. Frank had no idea what he'd say if he caught up to him, what he'd do or how.

And oh how Kriste would have been mad at him if he made a scene.

"He just isn't," Frank said quietly now, and that white crow she swooped overhead, like she'd just been by for the show and would be happier riverside now it was done.

"All right, Frank," Mickey said just as quietly. "All right."

"Jesus, Frank," Bruno said in disapproval, but no one was looking at them. Everyone was very careful not to.

CHAPTER FIVE

In the aftermath of the funeral, everything dissolved slowly like Christmas vapor, like breath hanging in cold air. People wandered off the cemetery grounds bit by bit, spending the interim talking in smaller groups and circles, many of them saying hello to people they hadn't seen in years or since the last funeral. It was like a convention held for people who'd known Kriste, Gina, and Philip, and two things struck Frank, hit his anger as sure as the funny bone spot on your elbow.

First, that Ricky wasn't there. As though being hurt had excused him from the family for a week or two or more. Maybe worse, like surviving had singled him out, like he was lucky enough that he should just be grateful for that. No one was saying that, and in fact everyone talked about how terrible it was for him, but still, there was that vibe, that "well, the Ricky problem is taken care of" vibe, like as long as he wasn't dead everything would be fine.

And second, that the attention ... no ... the grief. The grief wasn't equal. It was a triple funeral, but more people were there for Kriste and Gina, more people knew them, Philip was just a little kid who had had plenty of school friends but who was only known as "a kid" to everyone else. He hadn't been old enough yet to relate to adults, to make an impression.

Philip deserved as much mourning as the girls did, should be mourned exactly because nobody knew him as well. That was the tragedy, that was the fucking thing right there. Snipped shut before he had a chance to become a person. Oh, no one wanted to see it that way, no one wanted kids talked about like that, but even Gina had still been on the road to filling in all her Mad-Libs, no more an adult than spaghetti on the boil was dinner. Philip, he'd still been dry pasta in the box.

And now Frank was doing it too. The three of them dying together, being mourned together, hell, they ended up being compared, like if one of them had led more or less of their life than another, their death weighed different, left a different footprint. God damn it.

Soon there was no one left in the cemetery but him and the workers shuffling around, them and the coyote. He really ought to leave that coyote here, but he'd shot the thing, for Christ's sake, and it didn't like the man in the Mexican suit any.

"All right," he said. "Boy!" he called out. "Here boy! You coyote you!" He pronounced coyote with two syllables like Pop would have, what he thought of as cowboy style. Arthur Train Junior's voice had always taken on a certain cadence, a certain deepness, when he told stories about his days cowboying at the Lazy 7 with Rafe Mondragon, who wound up his brother-in-law. They were wild back then, Frank suspected, a wildness Frank and Mickey had both got a portion of and put to different uses.

"Heel coyote!" Frank called again, since the thing was obviously watching him, ears perked. He slapped his palm against his thigh and it bolted towards him, following him to the pickup and, at the cue of his snapping fingers, leaping up into the back, where his claws scrabbled on the metal bed before he settled down on some tarp Frank used to keep tools dry.

ooo000ooo

In the room with Ricky, Frank kept feeling like he was standing over his own shoulder and watching himself -- looking back and forth between him and Ricky, wondering at all the things he used to think the boy got from him. Hadn't he thought the kid took after him? Hadn't he said his boy had his eyes? Had the Train forehead?

Ricky'd always taken most after his mother. Gina was a Mondragon through and through, like Frank's mother's genes had used him as a conduit to get to the girl. She had, she'd had, that long, glossy hair, that morena complexion, even the Mondragon smile which you could see in photos from the 1920s of Frank's great-aunt or great-great-aunt or whatever she was. And Philip had been young, but he'd been a young Train for sure, the spit and image of Mickey at the same age. Everybody talked about how handsome he'd be when he grew up.

At least Mom and Pop had lived to see Mickey married again, he thought. That'd been important to Mom especially. Pop had always embraced the Bohemian artist bullshit that went with spending half your time with paints or chipped marble, but Valerie Mondragon Train had reverted to old school Catholic propriety as soon as she became a grandmother, and hadn't liked it at all that Mickey had been not only divorced but scampering around with any skirt that swished his way. One of those memories suddenly snapped into focus the way they had been since Mom and Pop died, this Kodak Carousel of images he didn't look for but couldn't stop from coming. His mother in the kitchen as it used to be, her hair tied back with a ribbon, singing along to Joni Mitchell on the hi-fi in the living room, pale green walls she'd painted with daffodils, a

26

big red mixing bowl of something just as pale, just as green. Watergate salad? That's what they called it, right? It was the other half of the seventies, not the wheat germ part, the encounter group part, but the pudding mix and mini marshmallows and canned pineapple all mixed up into a delicious glop he could almost taste now.

The image passed as quick as it came on. In Frank's mood, he saw things never woulda otherwise, twigged to nuances you miss in the moment: the way Ricky looked at the young, attractive aunt he hadn't known long enough to think of as family, the way Jessie looked at both Ricky and Frank, a kind of sympathy other people weren't giving 'em, and Frank realized it was cause of Mickey's kids. Paris and Tex hadn't shown, and neither had their mom. But Daphne had divorced Mickey a long time ago, and her kids hadn't seen their father much. Frank understood that, understood that whatever a family tree might say, he was a more distant relative to them kids than a cousin's cousin. But Jessie didn't see it that way, and felt bad for him on account of it.

"So you think you gonna hold up all right, buckaroo?" Frank asked Ricky in a lull. He knew he sounded awkward, abrupt, and both Father Michael and Jessie gave him sad, comforting looks. He was out of sync with everyone now.

"Still hurts," Ricky said. "I just sleep a lot. There's nothing on TV."

"Yeah," Frank said. "I know, pal, I'm sorry. Look, I'll come back and check on you later. I gotta get to work."

"What?" Jessie said. "Frank, can't it wait?"

"People pay to have their places caretook. This time of year especially it ain't something can be slacked. I farmed it out the last two days, but work's work, it's gotta be done." And they needed the money. Sure, he could get people to cover for him. People he'd feel obligated to split the money with, but even if they didn't let him, other folks would hire him for less because they wouldn't want to burden him with work. With Kriste's income gone, that kindness would put him and Ricky in the poorhouse.

"Seriously, Frank, I think you should take some time off --" Mickey started to say, and Frank gave him a look that said shut it down. Mickey nodded, held up a palm. "All right, man. Whatcha gotta do. Anything we can do?"

"Hang out as long as you like," Frank said, meaning stay with Ricky, look after my boy.

"We got nowhere to be, Frankie Furter," Mickey said, meaning you got it, hoss.

When Frank when outside to the truck, Lobo was sort of wandering around, like he wasn't really waiting for Frank. But he nodded to the coyote still sitting in the back, when Frank got in earshot.

"You got a permit for that, any chance?"

27

Frank laughed. "What, the coyote?"

Lobo nodded, hitched up his belt. "Yep. Looks like you're keepin it, don't it? Or you want me to call animal services?" Animal Services was one woman, who ended up keeping most of the strays she was called in on, them that weren't rabid or violent.

"Hell, no need to call Marcie. I guess I'm keeping him. I need a permit for a coyote? You serious, Lobo?" Frank opened the door, but didn't get in yet.

"It's what the State of New Mexico calls a permit to possess an exotic pet, Frank. Like ferrets and snakes and things like that, you know?" Lobo nodded, waited a moment, then added, "I'll fill the paperwork out for you, float that through, don't worry about it. Call it a Christmas present, I reckon."

"All right. Thanks then, Lobo."

"Uh huh. Uh huh." Lobo didn't look inclined to leave just yet, so Frank stood there with the door open, waiting. "Real sorry about everything, you know. I mean ain't that a fuck in the pisser."

"Yeah. Thanks."

"Ricky holding up?"

"Holding, anyway. You know. He's a kid. They bounce back."

"Yeah, yeah they do. I was about his age when my Pop died."

Frank took a breath. "I forgot how long ago that was. I guess you were. Guess I don't need to worry none about Ricky, seeing how you turned out."

Lobo cracked a grin and spat a loogie of tobacco on the snow. "Uh huh." He slapped the side of the truck, and the coyote's ears perked up. "Well you take care now, Frank. All my best to you and yours."

ooo000ooo

The coyote stayed put the whole time Frank worked. The McGreavy place at the end of Pond Drive had raccoon tracks all around the winter coop, and they hadn't got into the chickens yet but them coons were clever and if he hadn't been by to put up more chicken wire, bury a few poisoned corn cobs in the snow, they probably might've.

The problem with flat roofs was weeks like this, winters like this, when the snow came harder than usual and the cold stayed long enough to freeze it over. When people wanted to go on vacation for Christmas, go to Grandma's in Colorado or a sister's in Texas, they called Frank, and so did some of the ones who didn't go nowhere at all, just didn't want to get up on their own roofs to shovel. He spent the evening shovelling snow off roofs, piling it into mounds at the corners of each house. It was colder than raking leaves, heavier, and a few hours in he could feel the soreness in his back starting a bloom.

"Careful up there, Frank!" a voice called up to him late in the evening, as he heaved a shovel full of snow over the side, careful not to step more than he had to on the tarped-over soil on top of the roof, which would serve as someone's rooftop garden in the spring.

The coyote howled from the pickup's bed and then laid down and whined, covering its ears with its paws. Frank looked down to see the man in the Mexican suit in a patch of moonlight, the snow bone-colored around him and untouched by footprints. It was one of the first things Frank noticed, the complete lack of footprints in this virgin expanse of snowfall, and the man standing in the midst of it like the world'd just fallen in around him. There wasn't a car in sight he coulda driven in on, neither.

"We been introduced, partner?" Frank asked, peering down. The Colt Defender was holstered under his jacket, as it always was when he was working. Never knew when you might run into a drunk or someone trying to break into a home they know ain't occupied for the week.

"Now don't be like that, partner," the man said, tossing the word back at him. His voice was a little shaky with age, the voice of a smoker halfway down the road to emphysema, but it was a snake oil voice all the same. Warm like a Santa Fe hooker's thighs just after dark. "I can't see how one name's more Christian than another anyway. Ain't it true Jesus and all his posse was a bunch of Jews?" The man tugged at his suit and snowflakes fell off it. "Whoo-wee, I don't know, just what I heard." He grinned, and his tongue flicked out quick between his teeth. "Don't you fall now, you dim drunk fuck."

"What was that?" Frank asked, and as he took a step closer to the edge of the roof, meaning to be threatening, to be imposing, use his high vantage over the man to convey a threat, his foot skimmed along snow that had melted and refrozen over a metal pipe, a sprinkler used by the summertime gardener. His leg lurched forward, and his weight canted too far to the side, but he leaned away in time, caught himself, and managed simply to look foolish.

"Whoa, want to be careful about that," the man said, and pulled a fifth of something or some damn other out of his pocket, taking a sip and grimacing. "Want a pull?"

"Don't reckon. I'm on the job. Have we met before, Mr -- ?"

"Marlowe," the man said. "Name's Josh Marlowe. We wouldn't be much in the way a partners if we hadn't met before." He rubbed his nose and pulled his fingers away from it before thrusting his shoulders back. There was a weirdness to the way he moved, like an actor, a clown, a marionette.

Frank watched Marlowe, who looked back at him. "Heard you visited my boy in the hospital."

"I don't recall that I did," Marlowe said, looking up at him over the booze. "You got a boy in the hospital, do you? On top a all that family that died? Powerful shame, Frank." He slapped his stomach and shook all over, nodding to himself.

Some click of body language, some ttch of mannerism, had fallen enough into place that Frank placed him. The suit hadn't been enough. Who the fuck didn't have a cheap Mexican suit in the closet? He'd known, he'd figured, all along, not consciously, fine, but he'd fucking known all right, the way a dog knows a stranger. Whoever this Josh Marlowe was on an ordinary day, whatever it was he did, Frank had met him before when everything was different.

He was the Halloween man, the scarecrow man.

"What's this all about, Marlowe?" Frank asked, and without reaching for it he felt his gun at his side, became more aware of it. "Kriste cheat on me with you, is that what all this is? You got some fucked up way of doing your thing, having your little moment with the cuckold, is that what you're about? You think you're Ricky's father, don't you. Telling the hospital you're God damn family."

"You wanna come down from there so we can talk, partner? Or you want me to keep breaking my neck like this while we play shoutsies for the neighbors?"

"I want you to break your fucking neck. Stop dodging me and answer a God damn question. You think I don't know you? You think I don't remember you? I fucking know you without a name, Marlowe. I fucking remember you all right."

Marlowe held his hands out in mock amazement. "You <u>know</u> me <u>without a name</u>. Well shitfire and save matches, Frankie Train, you could save me a ton of money in therapy if I believed in that shit! I don't have to go to confession ever again, do I? I can just have you do it for me, seeing you know all there is to Josh Marlowe."

The coyote moaned again from the back of the pickup, parked a dozen feet or so away in the driveway.

"You gonna answer any questions, or you just gonna sit there barking all night?" Frank asked.

"You're sounding all tough again, aren't you?" Marlowe asked, and smiled a shit-eating smile. Two of his teeth were stained grey. "Like the bad days. The old days."

"Before Kriste? You didn't know me then, pal. And you wouldn't want to. You best pray them days is over. Now you just tell me. You're him, aren't you? You're the fucking guy from, from Hosteen and Texas. The guy from Halloween."

"I got no idea what that is, Frank. Sorry. I mean, I know what Halloween is, but I got no idea what you're yapping about." He even looked sincere. But if he wasn't the Halloween man, who the fuck was he, and what the fuck could he want?

God damn and fuck it.

Frank pulled his gun and flipped the safety off, making sure Marlowe saw him do it. "I want you to answer some questions, Marlowe. You understand me?"

Marlowe put his hands up slowly but didn't look worried. "I reckon I will when you ask 'em."

Frank nodded. "Who the fuck are you?"

"Josh Marlowe. I live in town now. In Cardenio."

"And before that?"

Marlowe shrugged. "Here and there. To and fro. I wander until I find a job, mostly. You sure you need that gun, Frank?"

"What were you doing visiting Ricky?"

"I wanted to look in on him. See if he was okay. It was a bad accident. The burns --" Marlowe shook his head. "He was in bad shape. I worried."

Frank's throat hitched at that. "He your son?"

"Is he yours?"

"The fuck you mean?"

"Wasn't asking about a fuck, Frank, but it sounds like you were. I'm asking, do you love the boy? Do you raise him like you would your own son?"

"God damn you." Frank's finger twitched. "You're asking me if I love my son? When we lost everything else --"

"Oh, Frank." Marlowe shook his head. "Be grateful for what you got, my boy. Be grateful you got Ricky, and Mickey and Jessie, and Newt and Dove and all them family you got in so many places. Be grateful you got Cardenio and a good job and all the world. There's always so much more to lose, Frank."

Frank shook, took control of his breath, forced it into a rhythm. "I'm grateful. But I ain't Ricky's father, not biologically, not if you believe those tests, and I'm asking you, are you?"

Marlowe met his eyes and said coolly, "You better hope I am."

Frank almost shot him right there. "What the fuck is that supposed to mean?"

"It means if I ain't, Kriste did us both a wrong. Don't it?"

"Oh, God damn you."

"It was a long time ago. Don't remember her like that. Don't do that to her."

"You fuck. You slept with my wife?"

"You're in the wrong movie, partner. Get your wits on. Man up. Don't do this to her."

Frank levelled the gun and found Marlowe's forehead with the sight. "Did. You. Fuck. My. Wife?"

"Oh, yes," Marlowe breathed. That cartoony hick voice he wandered in and out of was gone now. "Oh, did I ever. Do you want to kill me now, Frank? Do you want to kill Ricky's father? What if it turns out I'm not? What'll you do then? How many men are you willing to kill before you're all the boy's got left?"

"Fuck you."

"Do you want the details? Do you want to know how many times we did it? Do you want to know how she liked it? Do you want to know who was better? Is that what you want? Do you want to know if she ever had us both on the same day, if my come chased yours out and that's why Ricky's not your own? Is that what we're at on this fine winter day? Or are you gonna come down from there and stop putting her name through all this?"

Headlights bathed the road with white as someone drove down the road. Frank looked up briefly, and when he focused on the end of the gun again there was nothing beyond it. Just a clutter of footprints where Marlowe had been standing.

He searched around, his eyes needing to readjust to the darkness, and saw Marlowe at the edge of the lawn for an instant, and then he was gone again. And now there he was, past the end of the road and half-covered in darkness as the approaching car passed the last of the neighbors' houses and turned into the driveway.

"Why did she do it?" Frank yelled after Marlowe, trying to get a bead on him. "Goddammit, you son of a bitch! Why won't you admit who you are?" He didn't know which question was more important.

But he couldn't find the man again, there was nothing beyond the end of the road but shadows, noise, snow, and the car came to an idle as its driver rolled down a window and called out, "Mr Train? Is everything all right up there?"

Frank waved the gun around helplessly, aimlessly, and couldn't find anything to shoot. He had only just got it reholstered before everything went bone-colored, and he slipped on that frozen bit of faucet, tumbling like a snowflake onto the hard, cold ground. The coyote was at his side before the man was, but he could barely register either of them.

All he could think about was how he'd had the Halloween man in his sights and been too chickenshit to shoot him while he had a chance.

CHAPTER SIX

Fog hung over the fields like a shelf under the sunset for the sky to sit on. It was a warm Halloween and it had been a hell of a wet October, one of those months when the weather was a below-the-fold headline every day. Weather of Biblical proportions, they kept calling it on the Santa Fe TV, and made a big deal out of showing how there'd been enough consistent rain that there was new growth in the Rio Grande bosque, little sprouts and twiglets on the verge of the wasteland -- the forest expanding while it had the water to do so. Mostly the rain wasn't heavy, but it just kept coming, two months after the usual wet season.

El Nino, people kept saying. La Nina. The Day After Tomorrow. Global warming. Storms over to the Gulf. Tsunamis in the Pacific. When Frank was a kid, it was the Russians they'd worried about, the nukes. Los Alamos wasn't far away, and everyone knew someone who'd claimed some tie to the Trinity project or the later bomb tests. They'd seen a mushroom cloud, they collected a mysterious check every month to keep their mouth shut about rads they'd soaked up, or they said it was all just a hoax to cover up aliens. Everybody took nukes serious when Frank was a boy, and fuck, it wasn't like they weren't out there anymore, wasn't like they'd just disappeared when the Soviets turned Russian again.

These days you didn't worry about countries, he guessed, so much as you did the world going sour. Terrorism seemed a much vaguer threat, something you looked for when you were in its territory like you did muggings and malaria. But weather? Everybody got weather.

Ricky was taking Philip for trick-or-treats. Frank hadn't been sure he would, Ricky getting older and all and maybe Philip even getting old enough not to want to be with his brother, but too young as far as Frank and Kriste were concerned to be out on his own. It might be Cardenio, it might not be the city, but every year you read about those razors widged into apples, that bubble gum laced with strychnine, and who knew what they might think of next. You worried about the world going sour.

Besides, you couldn't get as much candy on foot or bike. If you wanted the loot, you had to get in the car and hit another few towns. Ricky had a learner's permit. Kriste might flip out if she found out Frank was letting the boy drive without a license, with his kid brother to boot, but fuck if the kid weren't responsible as all hell and a natural driver at that. Some of his friends had been driving farm equipment since they were twelve, and he pitched in at McGreavy's at harvest.

Anyway, Kriste was manning the house to pass out pinon fudge and Dum-Dums, and Frank had his rounds to make. He had the usual stuff and a few jobs that couldn't wait without making em considerable harder. The way the rain'd been coming, it'd gotten muddy in the low-lying areas, and Jessup's old silo had started to list to one side. Sort of thing a man ought to take care of himself if he's gonna farm, but Jessup only took up the business his father'd left him cause it meant not having a boss, and he was as lazy a farmer as ever made it through a year.

Out south of Borachon Creek, you found a lot of unincorporated townships and farms floating amidst the waste like islands, grit that oysters'd never built into the pearls of real towns, places a hundred, two three hundred years behind the curve on that graph. Rumor had it there were meth labs out here, and there was a whorehouse or two, but mostly you just had old lands and the people who lived in them.

They got their mail in Cardenio mostly, if they got it at all. In this part of New Mexico, this was where you had your rural crazies, the ones hadn't been to school in three generations and lived off land no one knew for sure if they owned. They shopped in Santa Fe or drove out further than that if they were among the old-timers who more and more saw Santa Fe as having gone bearshit crazy, a neon and pastel southwest version of San Francisco, Atlantic City, Hong Kong, the kind of place you might go for a honeymoon when you were kids but wouldn't do nothing serious in.

Most of these folks, if they needed something done they called Frank. Leaky faucet? Frank Train. Satellite on the fritz? Frank Train. Need an extra hand fixing the barn roof? Frank Train. He'd picked up the business from Dude Borachon, who'd retired at the edge of forever, and it was the kind of thing that took him way out of his way for the steady, low maintenance stuff, but paid off when someone used him as a middleman to contract day labor for harvests and fast-paced repairs, stuff he kicked to the usual suspects for easy money finders fees.

Today after lending a hand with Jessup's silo, it'd been terracing some tomato plants for the Widow and tracking down a wandering colt for that cranky son of a bitch Hank McCarty, who was a hundred and forty six if he was a day and lived out in the middle of nowheres mumbling to himself and rolling coins into rolls. He always paid Frank in rolls of change, usually quarters these days and sometimes silver dollars.

The cold hadn't been easy to find, not with all that land to range and the time between McCarty seeing it was gone and Frank getting there, and it was too late for him to get back home in time for dinner since they wanted to feed the kids early before trick or treats, fill them up with some real food so they wouldn't binge on Snickers and Sour Patch Kids. He'd called Kriste, told her to go ahead without him and he'd get some other work done while he was out here.

Dinner was a green chile cheeseburger from Rocky's Cinco y Dime, a white square general store visible for miles away by its red Coca Cola sign and the complete lack of anything else around. Pink burger juices and driblets of green chile sauce had stained through the bottom bun and slicked the wax paper wrapping, and he'd washed it down with a beer, a warm sopaipilla wrapped around a Reese's peanut butter cup, and finally a few inches of Wild Valley Cactus liquor dumped into a half-empty longneck of Sprite.

It was a warm, clingy Halloween, and All Saints was bound to chase that warmth off till March or April. The kids and Kriste were set, and there wasn't nothing critical he had to do the next day. He was fixed to treat himself to a drunk.

He parked the truck in the driveway of an abandoned housing development from the 80s, at the crossroads of Hosteen and Texas, and turned the radio up. Used to be he never could get anything to come in out here, but Kriste'd got him an XM radio for Father's Day and within a couple channel flips he had the Allman Brothers on.

There was a scarecrow hanging from a pole catty-corner to him and Frank got out, stood in the bed of the truck, and started swaying, kinda dancing, between slugs of tequila. It was Halloween, just any other night except for all the reminders of Things He Didn't Do Anymore: didn't trick or treat no more, didn't smash pumpkins, didn't toilet paper nobody's house, didn't put mice in mailboxes, didn't go down to the creek to get high and drink beer and screw. No parties and no costumes.

And maybe that was some of why he was getting drunk, shit maybe he was overdue for a mid-life crisis. Mickey'd never had one but never stopped acting like a twenty year old, so what'd that prove? And today, well, today at the Widow's he'd done something he felt kinda guilty about. Maybe he shouldn't cause he didn't do nothing wrong exactly. But it was uncomfortable all the same.

Everyone called her the Widow but she wasn't old. Her husband'd died when she was 22, 23, somewhere in there, and that was only fifteen years back now. Somewhere along the road she'd turned the family farmhouse she'd inherited from her late hubbie into a whorehouse. They still kept the bigass garden and the chickens, and more often than not that meant some of the johns would volunteer to pitch in a hand and do chores for em, cause whether they was paying for sex or not they didn't feel right leaving a woman to do all that.

What they didn't do, Frank did, and had done since Dude retired to

Arizona. The Widow had three girls working there these days, and of course any time he went out to fix something or build something, they flirted with him, offered him discounts or freebies, asked if he was sure he didn't want to take his fee in trade instead of cash. And every time he flirted back just enough not to be rude or standoffish but was never specific, never implied anything, always declined offers and mentioned Kriste.

Today, though, when he was leaving and the Widow had said, "Sure we can't offer you a tip, Mr Train?", he'd said, "Not today, but you never know."

Still wasn't anything <u>wrong</u> exactly, but he hadn't told Kriste about all this flirting to begin with, and this "you never know" business wasn't something he'd thought of ahead of time. It bothered him that he'd broke the routine like that, cause routine, well, it was <u>routine</u>, it was habit, it was automatic, and you gotta figure when you break it without thinking about it it's cause deep down south you been doing more thinking than you thought. And the truth was that wasn't all that bothered him. Kriste had been changing lately. Oh, not just lately. God, it'd been before Philip was born, maybe as far back as when she was pregnant with Ricky. But it'd been so gradual he didn't see it at the time, not until she started going to a new church, and then another, and then churches that weren't even churches, they were just in somebody's home. She started praying at restaurants before dinner, and he'd learned not to talk politics around her anymore, because he knew she was on a lot of wrong sides but he didn't have the patience to do his homework and actually argue with her on it.

Oh hell, he may as well be honest about it. He was getting pretty sure Kriste was cheating on him. All this holy roller shit, he didn't know if it was connected or not, but there was something about the way she looked at him sometimes, something about the way she looked when she didn't know he could see her.

Somewhere in the midst of that reflection he got tangled, and shrugged as he took another gulp of Wild Valley. The amount of money he spent on booze stayed pretty much constant through his life, which'd meant he bought less now and bought better. Figured that was a good way to do it. Didn't do the kids any harm to see you could have a drink without getting fucked up, and the drink didn't have to be jug wine or plastic bottle vodka, but it didn't have to be French champagne or hundred year old Scotch whisky neither.

So he drank and he danced and he watched that old scarecrow. Who the fuck put a scarecrow up in the middle of nowhere? Weren't even any crops to safeguard and hadn't been since he was a boy and them guys who were growing up to work computer customer service now were still hay farmers, running combines all day and hitting the Beach with their farmers tans. There was a pumpkin at the scarecrow's feet, a face carved in it but no candlelight burning, so Frank reckoned it was somebody's why-the-hell-not idea of a Halloween decoration.

"You poor old scarecrow," he called out, and his voice warbled some, slurry. "Ain't even got a light to see by, and it'll be darking soon. Not even anybody to give you tricks or treats! You want some tequila?" He took another sip. The Sprite had gone flat in the muggy air, but the tequila still had its bite. "It ain't really tequila, but your mouth don't know."

"Yeah, I'll have some," the scarecrow said, and Frank fell stupidly over, landing on his ass on the opposite edge of the bed. The scarecrow's voice was perfectly reasonable and conversational, and the fabric where a mouth would have been had moved when it spoke, so he was pretty sure he didn't imagine it.

"Uh," Frank said. "Is there someone in there?"

The scarecrow stretched its arms from where they'd hung limply splayed as though on a rod, and straightened out first one leg, then the other, before hopping down off the pole. "Yeah, over here," he said, rolling his shoulders one by one like he had kinks to work out of em. Most of his face was drawn on sackcloth, but there were holes cut for his eyes, shaped like diamonds on their sides. His wide-brimmed floppy hat hung low, keeping his eyes in the shadow of the last of the sun.

"How long you --" How long you been there? he was going to ask, which was stupid. "What the hell are you doing out here? Who are you?"

The scarecrow shrugged, brushed its face through its mask. Straw stuck out of its sleeves, and it wore gloves, but when its arm stretched Frank could see skin showing in the gap between the sleeve and the glove. "I think I fell asleep. Crazy, right? I thought this would be a good costume. Looks like my candle burnt down, though." He crossed the street, actually looked both ways before doing so and came across the diagonal, crossing Hosteen and Texas at the same time, and put his hand out. "Drink?"

"Yeah, all right," Frank said, and the scarecrow crawled up into the bed as Frank passed him the bottle. The guy's boots clanked on the metal as he got in, and that was reassuring too. Call him a superstitious fuck, it being Halloween an all, but for a minute he thought the scarecrow might really be, well, a scarecrow. He watched as the guy ripped a small slit in his mask, right between his lips, and carefully drank from the Sprite bottle.

"Wooo-whee!" the scarecrow said. "That there ain't half an hour bad, is it? C'mon, don't let me stop you."

"Stop me from what? You from around here?"

"From dancing, man. Ain't that the best, dancing on Halloween? C'mon, I'll bet you were a hell of a rhythmic rascal when you were a kid, weren't you? Check this out, check it out right here and now boy." The scarecrow took another long sip of the drink, sucking in the cheeks of the Sprite bottle, and then wiped his mouth with his straw-stuffed sleeve, handed the bottle back, and flipped backwards out of the truck. He landed in a decent but imperfect split on the street, hopped back up, and did a little jig, pumping his hands and feet as he tossed his head back.

Frank laughed. "Looks like the God damn Snoopy Dance, fella."

"What, you think you can do better? I've got all this straw to work with here, c'mon. Show us your stuff, old pup. You're the spit and fucking image of Dean Martin, you're telling me you ain't gonna dance?"

Frank sighed and wondered how to get rid of this weirdo, but what the hell, right? He felt almost high, that's what tequila could do you. And then "Staying Alive" came on the radio. "Oh man," he said, hopping down from the truck. He wobbled, almost fell over, caught his balance. "This was so huge when I was in school. We all loved that movie. We all got into whoever's truck had room and went out to the old drive-in outside of Lonely, what the hell was it called?"

"The Mid-Nite, wadn't it?" the scarecrow asked. "The Mid-Nite Revue."

"Yeah, that was it. They showed blue movies after midnight on Wednesdays, we went to one once, wasn't nothing but a few women taking their clothes off in black and white and sitting on those old couches, those divans, while guys with handlebar mustaches kissed them."

"Porn's come a long way, I reckon. But man, listen to the music. C'mon, show me a strut. You musta had a hell of a strut back then."

"Did I fuck," Frank said, and did the little thing he used to do at the school dances when this song came on. He could remember the feel of the leather jacket he wore back then, the one he'd gone to Santa Fe to find in a secondhand so he could afford real leather and not fucking vinyl like Trevor and that fuckwad Davenant. It had felt like someone else's skin for the first month until it accepted him, molded to him, like he'd had to wear it long enough to get the taste of its last owner out of its cowskin mouth. "I never wanted to like this song," he said as he danced-strutted-strode along the road. "I was into more, you know, Joe Cocker, Meatloaf, Springsteen. Darkness on the Edge of Town, that shit was cool. But damn, it was catchy, and the girls liked it. I think I got to third base for the first time to this song. Or maybe it was something by the Talking Heads, I dunno."

"Every song's a good song for exploring all Eve's hollows," the scarecrow said, arms folded in amusement as he leaned against the truck. "Am I right or am I right?"

"Brother you ain't wrong," Frank said. "Man, that kinda took a lot out of me. Getting old, you know? Hey, I'm Frank, by the way. Frank Train."

"Glad to meet you," the scarecrow said, and it was his second opportunity to give a name but it really didn't occur to Frank until later that he never did so. "You dance a mean groove, Mr Frank Train. You sure your name ain't <u>Soul</u> Train?" The scarecrow did a little pirouette followed by another split, and tossed himself back to a standing position in a way that made it look like he really was full of straw.

Frank laughed, grabbed the bottle from the bed and drank most of what was left. "So what the hell you doing way out here beyond the beyond, pal? Ain't like you're gonna meet up with any trick or treaters here."

"Ran into you, didn't I," the scarecrow said, but then shrugged, pinching his nose again and rolling his shoulders. "Wanted a good costume. What better?"

"But no one <u>sees</u> it!"

"Don't make it any less a one," the scarecrow said, and his voice sounded like he was grinning. "But you know, you know what William James said about the supernatural?"

"Man, who the fuck is William James."

"You remember. A shrink from way back when. Anyway, he said in order to show not all crows are black, it ain't necessary to show that <u>no</u> crows are black. All you gotta do -- well, whatchoo think?"

"All you gotta do is find one that isn't."

"One white crow. Just the one."

"So you're, what, you're scaring off the white crow, huh? Like for Halloween."

"I reckon it could be something like that. Plus, lookit where we are."

Frank looked around. Empty fields, the trickles of blacktop where that housing development was gonna go in but never did, the driveway, and the truck. "Yeah?"

"Crossroads, pard. We're standing at the crossroads at Halloween, practically midnight."

"Hell," Frank said. "It ain't nothing near midnight." But the sky'd come darker than it oughta, not a hint of day at the edges, and the glistening bulge of the moon'd passed over most of the sky. "Even if it were, I don't follow."

The scarecrow crouched down on the road, looking back and forth and spreading his hands out parallel to Texas, an old farm road that was repaired too seldom for truckers to bother it as a short-cut and led from a quarry at one end to Lonely at the other. "Crossroads, my friend. Where everything's something else for a minute. Where old worlds ain't gone to dust yet."

Frank belched, and felt like if the truck rolled away he'd just float. "Lost me, doc."

"They used to put phalluses at the crossroads. Big stone dicks. For real," he added, laughing when Frank did. "Your guess is as good as mine, old pup, but tricksters used to live at the crossroads, too. Them elves who helped the shoemaker, right? Rumpelstiltskin."

"Pleased to meet you," Frank said.

"-- hope you guess my name. Uh huh, crossing the streams now, but everything's peaches but the cream, Frankie dog. Everything's peaches but the cream."

"So what'd they do at these crossroads? What, they just live there, hang out there?"

"It's like, if you own one road, right? Let's say you own Texas."

"Fucking A I own Texas," Frank said, head back and watched the sparks starkle, or some other way round. "My middle name's Sam Fucking Houston."

The scarecrow shook himself like he had ants in his pants and chuckled. "So you own Texas, right? And I own Hosteen. Who owns this? Where we're at?"

"Both of us, I guess."

"Or I own it going east and you own it going north, huh?"

"I dunno. I guess."

"I try to do something there, you're all 'hey, that's not Hosteen, it's Texas.' I pull the same if you try anything. So it's nothing, you know? It ain't got a name. Ain't Texas, ain't Hosteen, but neither of em's whole without it. That's powerful, is what I'm saying. You know some people think the Devil's got the run of the world? The physical world. Cause of the fall of Man. They used to get all religious about maps, cause maps got names. Maps make space into places. And the crossroads, it's a space inside a place, you see what I mean? It's a real, physical thing you can go to, but it's an idea, too. It's neutral ground, man. A little bit a me and a little bit a you."

"But what would they do?"

The scarecrow stood up and took the bottle of Sprite but didn't drink. "They'd make bargains, old pal of mine, old palomino. You wait long enough at the right crossroads? Midnight on a Hallowed Be Thy Ween? Sure enough the devil'll stop by eventual, and then you can make your deal with him."

"Aw yeah," Frank said now, nodding. "Sure, now I remember that stuff. Man, you know all them old ghost stories I guess. Me, I think I forgot em when stuff like Friday the 13th came out."

"Friday the 13th is just superstitious bullcrap," the scarecrow said irritably. "We're talking old power here, big power. What do you think, would you do it?" He leaned forward, looking at Frank, and his mouth was drawn into a grin on that ashy sackcloth. "Would you sell your soul, Frank Sam Fucking Houston Train?"

"Sure," Frank said, chuckling. "For a six foot cock and a million dollars, right? Or wait, I'd wish for more wishes."

The scarecrow huffed a little, and neither of em said anything for a time, as the moon passed a little further. "Well, I think it'd be a hell of an opportunity to pass up, you ask me. Do you even know what your soul's good for?"

"Goes on to Heaven," Frank said reflexively. "That's the part, you know, when I die that's the bit left."

"Sounds dodgy. You read much C.S. Lewis? The Narnia guy, he wrote a lot of religious stuff too. He said: <u>all that seems Earth is Hell or Heaven. Lord, open not my weak eyes to this too often.</u> He didn't want to <u>think</u> about it, you know? If Earth is all of that, soul ain't going nowhere at all. That's what Mr C.S. Lewis said, when you come to it."

"Huh." <u>All that seems Earth is Hell or Heaven.</u> There was something creepy to that, but it didn't seem to add up the way the scarecrow said. "I don't know, it's late for that kind of thing, you know."

"C'mon, don't give me that. Like you never stayed up all night stoned talking about the nature of the universe."

That'd pretty much been Frank's every Friday for a few years, if he didn't spend it fighting or screwing. "Yeah," he said, remembering them old days, them all or nothing days. "Yeah, you know what, I'd do it."

The scarecrow nodded. "I know, man. I know you would. I mean, how can you not, right? What a fucking deal. I think about it sometimes. You ever think about how you'd spend the lottery, or what your three wishes would be?"

"Yeah, sure, everybody does. Man, I'd go to Disney World. I never been. Get a big house with a lawn, like a serious lawn. Irrigate it with fucking Perrier, you know what I mean? And the baddest fucking ride." The words could be straight out of 1980. Paying for the kids' college didn't even occur to him.

"Disney World's badass," the scarecrow said, and he sounded younger now. Sounded like T-Bone practically, one of Frank's friends in high school who'd died in a hit and run a few years after graduation. "That'd be a good way to spend that cash, for sure. With the soul thing, it's more like the wishes, you know? Be a rock star. A fucking rock star. That'd be cool. Or marry the hottest chick on the planet. I mean, you look like a married man, I'm sure your wife is fine --"

"Kriste's great, man," Frank said. "Gave me a new lease on life. Didn't even know what that meant before."

"Yeah, that's cool, that's cool. So maybe, I mean, there's immortality and things like that too, you know?"

Frank laughed. "Oh, that'd be a tricky one, good thinking! Sure, Mr Devil, you can have my soul when I die! In exchange, I just want never to die."

The scarecrow rubbed his chin, and Frank thought he might be laughing. "You don't get to wait till you die, Frank. You sell your soul, that's it, it's gone then and there."

"Oh." He thought for a minute. "That don't make no sense. You sure?"

"Sure as cotton. It's just how these things work. Ain't no point otherwise, right? Devil don't play no 'pay you Tuesday for a hamburger today' shit."

"Yeah, all right, I see your point. Well, fair's fair."

"Fair's fair."

Another silence settled, and the scarecrow seemed gidgety, so he got up, grabbed the bottle of Sprite. "So hey hey, it's Halloween, right? Midnight on Halloween! Ye cats and bowsers! I'm thinking, let's do it up, let's do the crossroads thing. Oughta be a kick in the head."

"What, you want to sell me your soul?" Frank stood up only because the scarecrow was. He hated sitting when someone was standing next to him.

The scarecrow belly laughed. "No no, you sell me yours. You wouldn't want mine. Come on, how about it, chum?"

Frank waved a hand. "Sure, all right. Listen, I gotta head home. You need a ride?"

"No, I'm fine. Let's finish this before you go."

"You sure? I don't see a car. How'd you get here, anyway?"

"Frank. Focus. Shake my hand." The scarecrow held out his hand, and Frank took it. His new friend's hand was warm beneath the glove, and he had a powerful grip, keeping Frank's hand there as he poured the last of the contents of the Sprite bottle over their clasped hands. "Do you give me your soul in trade, Frank Train?"

Frank laughed a little. It was Halloween all right. "Yeah, you got it. It's all yours. As is, you mind! No refunds, no returns."

"No refunds," the scarecrow said with no hint of a smile in his voice. "No returns. And what would you like in exchange for this trinket of yours?"

Frank shrugged. "I don't know. I'll wait on Disney World until I win the lottery, I reckon. Let the honor system take care of it. Take a penny, leave a penny."

The scarecrow tensed and tapped a foot. "Be ... specific."

"You know, whatever strikes your fancy. Like Secret Santas. I leave it in your hands."

The scarecrow bent his head down and Frank thought he could catch a glimpse of teeth through the mouth slit in his mask. "Oh my. Oh, Frank, isn't that something. You do manage to surprise me after all." He pinched hard on the handshake, and a spot of blood appeared in the bridge between Frank's index finger and thumb, stinging in the tequila, before the scarecrow pushed his hand away. "It's done!"

"All right," Frank said, irritated now, and he climbed into the cab of the truck. He was wobbly, but he wasn't going to hit any traffic for a while, and if he was having trouble then he'd just pull over. "Catch you later, pal. Happy Halloween."

"No no," the scarecrow said, dancing daintily down the road towards Hosteen. "Happy Hallowed <u>Day</u>, Frank! Happy All Saints Day to you and all your own!"

Frank turned the truck around, and as the headlights swept the road, they found no trace of the scarecrow or the man who'd worn the costume, although the pole was there and the pumpkin beneath it. He must have gone back the way he came. Must've had a car nearby Frank somehow hadn't seen.

The drive home was slow and troubled, and he felt a growing sense of shame for staying out so late, for drinking when he said he'd be working, for what he'd said at the Widow's. He'd been acting like a kid, like he used to, and fuck he really couldn't afford a mid-life crisis. That was the last thing he needed, he'd wind up knocking up some itty bitty thing in town like Marshall had before he quit his job at the bank so his wife wouldn't be able to garnish his wages.

All that crossroads shit, he knew he'd heard that before, it'd been on a <u>Twilight Zone</u> or <u>Outer Limits</u>. Why'd he been feeling so weird, why hadn't he remembered it at first, why'd he been thinking so sluggishly? He hadn't had Wild Valley lately, maybe this year's bottling had something ginchy going on in it. He'd felt almost drugged, like someone'd snuck a morphine drip onto him. By the time he got to Cardenio, he couldn't remember much of what he'd done unless he thought it through, and he told Kriste he'd had an old-fashioned drunk like his old man did sometimes, and she'd shrugged and peered in the womanly way and they left it there.

<u>Lord, open not my weak eyes to this too often.</u>

CHAPTER SEVEN

"There's only been one execution in New Mexico since the death penalty was reinstated," District Attorney Martin told him. "So I'm telling you right now, we're not even going to ask for it. I'm sorry."

Frank took a sip of the coffee the DA's secretary had brought in to the mostly empty conference room. The room smelled like percolator coffee below the current of the ventilation system, and the heavy oak door muffled the sound of Lite 101.9 playing on the speakers in the reception area. His suit felt uncomfortable and too much, but being around lawyers always made his jeans and workshirts seem inappropriate. "You're not going to ask for it?" he asked carefully. He thought he understood the basics of the criminal justice system pretty well. TV told you a lot, and he'd talked to one cop or DA or lawyer after another since his parents were killed. But he wanted to make sure he didn't misunderstand anything here. This wasn't television.

"Look, we're not going to let him plea it down. But we're going to go for what we can get. With a life sentence, he won't even be eligible for parole for thirty years, and in a case like this, they hardly ever get it the first time."

Frank sat very still. He hadn't dealt much with cops since he was a kid, and a DA was still a cop when you came to it. But he was still used to flipping back and forth between resentment and timidity. "But you mean a life sentence for each murder, right? All the ones in Colorado? The, the mass murder in Wyoming?"

Martin got up, pacing back and forth at the side of the table, tapping his pencil against his thigh. "Here's the thing, Mr Train. We can't prove any of that. We can't put a good enough case together for it."

"But you were so sure. That's why it was so random, my parents, because he'd done it before, killed so many --"

"We were sure. I still have, let's call it, a strong suspicion. But we've got nothing to take to trial. If we charge him with all those murders, what if it turns out one of them wasn't him? We'd never be able to nail the person actually responsible. Trying him for those murders would hurt our chances of charging someone else for them. Without more to go on, we've got no way of knowing if any of them are copycats."

The rest of the conversation became background noise as Frank weighed this over, giving the appropriate responses where he needed to. David Lucas Hanion, the man who'd killed his parents, was barely thirty. He had waited in a Santa Fe parking garage for who knew how long, beneath the Trains' Range Rover, and when Pops had gotten close enough, the guy had sliced the hamstrings of his feet, rolled out from under, bludgeoned Mom with a chunk of concrete identified as part of a parking space carstop, stabbed Pops in the throat.

The police had leveled with Frank after a few months of the usual empty talk. They'd picked up Hanion on genetic evidence, and danced around for a couple days because they couldn't find a motive. He hadn't taken anything, hadn't tortured or raped them, and had only driven the Range Rover as far as a nearby industrial park where he'd probably had his own car waiting. When they recovered digital photos of the Trains on Hanion's camera, taken days before the murder and then deleted, they tagged him as their man, and with the FBI's cooperation, connected the hamstringing and short-distance auto theft to a series of unsolved and otherwise unconnected murders in other states.

But if Hanion was a serial killer, he was the disorganized type, just a guy who kept killing people for who knew what reason. It made him hard to figure out. The deaths seemed to be meaningless even to the killer. The closest thing to a clue, an indication, just a fucking tatter of what had gone on in Hanion's head was something he had carved in the dashboard of the Range Rover with the same knife he had used to slash Pops's tendons: a circle with a bent line through it, exactly the same as the one Frank later saw formed by the luminaria at the corner of Vegas and Rory, the night of the car accident. The one Kriste had scribbled on the paternity test.

He'd mentioned this to Martin and the other cops, but after some poking around at it, didn't pursue it further. None of the insurance photographs showed a clear shot of the luminaria: what they did show didn't contradict the idea of them having been arranged in that shape, but didn't confirm it. There was no apparent connection between the family on the corner, the Ibanezes, and Hanion, nor the Trains or Garcias or truck driver, for that matter.

He knew they figured he'd imagined it the night of the accident, and why not? The Ibanezes didn't seem to know anything about it. Why wouldn't he imagine seeing that brand the night his family died, after seeing the photos of it from his parents' murder?

The symbol, whatever it was, hadn't shown up in any of the other murder scenes. Frank figured that was a good part of why they didn't think they could win a serial murder case against Hanion, and that Martin wasn't bringing it up cause he didn't want to upset him, remind him of the car accident. They'd had some heated words about it.

Now everything that was hot had just gone numb with time and tedium.

ooo000ooo

He did some shopping out of habit. Santa Fe had always meant shopping to him, buying whatever it was he couldn't get in Cardenio, which had been pretty near everything once and was still a long list. There was always something Ricky would want from the record store too, some import or single. He'd given Frank a list, written in pressed-hard pencil on a sheet from the notepad they used for grocery lists, the one with the magnet on the back and the ducks on the front. He'd been sullen about it, had wanted to come to the city too, but Frank was adamant. The kid was having trouble enough these days, no fucking way he was coming to hear lawyers talk about his grandparents' murderer.

Gina would have had him loading up a cooler with vegetarian frozen meals, all those fake burritos, fake pizzas, fake hot dogs. You could get some in Cardenio now, and if you ever wanted to hear an old man complain all you had to do was bring up soy cheese crumbles or tofu burgers.

He got everything on Ricky's list because it was easier than stopping to think about what to deny him. Pinback, Between the Buried and Me, Underoath, The Bled, Fear Before The March of Flames. Frank couldn't stop himself from asking, "These are band names?" Kriste would have gone on about it. Frank remembered fielding comments like that from his pop, and tried to be the cool dad. But sometimes he couldn't tell the difference between a band name and an album name.

He grabbed a handful of magazines from Hastings, from Ricky's list, almost a hundred dollars worth, most of them with punk rockers or tattoos on their covers, but at least the kid was reading. Frank hadn't at that age, nothing more than stroke books and National Lampoon.

At the grocery store, he skipped the vegetarian section but got a couple packs of Orangina, a couple bags of salt and pepper potato chips, because he couldn't remember which kid had liked them. The casseroles and Tupperwares of green chile were finally starting to dwindle, so he was cooking more, he and Ricky baching it for permanent now, so he got some racks of venison ribs, wild turkeys cause every Train man knew how to roast a turkey, Boboli pizza crusts and sacks of pepperoni, and a case of brick chili, which you couldn't find almost nowheres anymore. Arthur Train Jr had raised his sons on weekends of brick chili, a relic of pre-refrigeration days: a box of chili con carne with all the liquid squoze out, leaving dried beef, chiles, and marjoram, a brown square you'd boil

46

in water and serve over canned beans and Fritos.

The meat sat in the big camp cooler in the truck, with the coyote with the ragged ear sitting guard over it, and Frank did a little sightseeing cause truth was Santa Fe still wowed him a little, still struck him silly with being so big and so citified. Now, he'd been to Orlando, Florida, for Disney World, been to New York, New York, when he was thinking of going to college there, and El Paso, Texas, and Denver, Colorado. All of them was bigger'n Cardenio for sure, and bigger'n Santa Fe too. But what got him about Santa Fe was how it still looked like it was meant for this part of the world. Tackier'n Cardenio by a sight, but still more or less the same people, same kinda buildings.

New York'd been bagels and falafel and a hundred things he never heard of before or since. Disney World'd been hot dogs and carnie food. El Paso, mostly burritos. But Santa Fe, Santa Fe still had green chile cheeseburgers at the McDonald's, the waitresses still asked you "red or green?" when you ordered a bowl of chile, and if he answered "Christmas" they'd know to give him some of each. Everybody had ristras up, and in Christmas they'da had luminaria too.

Santa Fe was like Cardenio grown up a little unfamiliar. Like when a friend's brother leaves town for a few years, comes back talking about things you haven't heard of, listening to music you don't know or friends you ain't met.

He drove through the Barrio Analco on East De Vargas, Santa Fe's oldest neighborhood. Lots of "oldest this" "oldest that" touristy stuff because the Indians had lived here eight hundred years ago before Santa Fe was even called that. He'd always liked it, and all its adobe-style square buildings that you could imagine being there since the headwaters of time. When he was a kid and they'd gone on field trips to Santa Fe, he'd been the one telling his friends to hush so he could hear what the guide was saying.

The oldest church in America was in the BA, Mission San Miguel. He parked on the street alongside it and hopped out of the truck, giving the coyote a reassuring scritch on the neck. The animal didn't like the noise and smells out here in the city, although he'd kept calm just fine while Frank was in the courthouse.

The Mission always made him feel good. He'd seen pictures of them cathedrals in Europe and New Orleans and all, and they were nice in their way, and the stained glass in New York, same thing. But they never seemed church-like to him. The Mission was dark brown adobe, square and simple but elaborate compared to the neighboring pueblos, and below its plain cross was a large empty chamber where the bell used to ring.

Frank pulled the tailgate down at the back of the pickup and sat on it to eat his lunch, unwrapping the green chile bacon cheeseburger he'd picked up at McDonald's and washing it down with a strawberry shake, just like when he was a teenager. He'd been hungry for that kind of thing lately, and maybe it was because of all the damn well-meaning casseroles or maybe it was just cause Kriste wasn't around to plonk peas and carrots onto his plate. When he was done with the burger, its grease still clinging to his fingertips, he dipped his fries in the shake. He'd had a girl did that in high school so he'd done it too when they were out. Wasn't till after she said you were only sposed to when the shake was chocolate. But fuck it. He liked strawberry better.

The Mission had become pretty much a tourist thing, you had your camera-necklaced northerners wandering in and out taking photos, and some of em snapped pics of him and the coyote, which he just shrugged about. Go to Hawaii or something, you want to see exotic life. This was just New Mexico, fuck's sake. They wound up in the gift shop, of course, buying rosaries and cross pins.

There was another fella didn't look like a tourist, though, more like a downtowner wandered over from wherever he'd been being crazy. His hair was scraggly, not just unwashed like a regular homeless but like he spent a lot of time pulling at it. Grey and stringy and uneven, and his beard the same, patchy and ragged. His clothes were obviously pieced together from whatever Goodwill had available: a striped shirt like a damn Frenchman and another shirt peeking out from underneath it, Army jacket, jeans too baggy.

The guy started to approach the tourists, and Frank sighed, felt obligated to keep him from bothering them folks. "Hey fella," he called over, not threatening, just howyadoin. "You wanna share some fries with me?"

The guy looked at him a minute, shuffled over. "I ain't looking for change, mister," he said.

"That's fine," Frank said. "But you want some fries?"

"Yeah, all right. That your coy-ote?"

"Uh huh." Frank moved over so the guy could sit down if he needed. He didn't smell bad, at least. Just a guy down on his luck and most likely more than a little crazy. Church woulda been the right kinda place for him to be if it hadn't gotten all touristy.

"I'm Terry. What's your coy-ote's name?"

"Ain't got one, but I'm Frank."

Terry gave him a canny look, then pinched a few fries and ate them absently. "Power in namelessness, ain't there Frank. You doin him a favor there, not naming him? Or you just waiting to take your power when you need it?"

Frank frowned. "He just ain't a dog, is all. Ain't got a collar, ain't got a name."

Terry grinned and tilted his head back like to swallow the moon, singing, "I ain't got a home! I ain't got a name! I'm just a lonely dog! I ain't got a home!"

"Something like that," Frank said. "What're you up to today, Terry?"

"Oh, you know me, Frank," he said, staring off at the distance. "You know how I do."

Frank shuffled a cigarette out of a pack of Luckies, passed one to Terry too, and then lit them both with his pop's old Zippo. "We met before?"

"I don't know if you have, but me, I got a long lived kinship with 'before.' Well don't I hell."

"Uh-huh," Frank said, taking a drag, and when Terry reached over with his nonsmoking hand for more fries, he caught a look at the tat on the back of his hand. It didn't show up as well as it mighta otherwise cause it was yellow but it was that damn fucking circle with a broken line through it, from 10:30 to 5:00. Frank grabbed his hand without thinking about it, and Terry yelped like a chihuahua. His hands felt older than he looked, frail, crackly, like they'd been broken and healed a few times.

"What the fuck is this?" Frank asked. "What's this mean, this brand? This tattoo?" But maybe brand was right. The lines were raised, much more than an ordinary tat woulda been, like the ink had been laid down over scar tissue. And hadn't he been thinking of it as a brand since the night in the hospital? Hadn't that been what ever'body called it who seen him sketching it?

Terry yanked his hand back, and stumbled backwards away from the pickup. "It's just a tattoo, mister!"

"I know that," Frank said, and stood up too, trying to stay calm-sounding, not sound crazy. "Look, I need to know what that means, what that symbol is. It's important, Terry. Come on." He reached for his wallet. "I can pay you. I can pay you for the information, all right? No biggie. I need to know."

"It doesn't mean anything," Terry insisted, "it's just a tattoo I got. Like people get Chinese on them. I gotta go." He dropped the fries in his hands and backed away quickly before breaking into a run, the back sole of one of his shoes flopping broken and tongue-like as his feet slapped the ground.

Goddammit. Frank froze for a sec, debating getting the gun out of the glovebox where he kept it when he was in the city, and then thought, fuck, that's nuts, I'm not chasing some crazy homeless guy through downtown packing a pistol. But in those few seconds of indecision, he lost some ground on the guy, who was leaner, faster, and just plain damn crazier, which was enough to put a block between them.

The coyote ran ahead of Frank like he knew what was up and as Terry rounded a corner down a sidestreet on the dumpster end of a taqueria, the coyote pounced him from behind, knocking him down on his stomach.

Frank caught up a moment later, regretting the cigarette. Couple few people'd seen 'em running, and a boy in his twenties peered around the corner like he was expecting a mugging and something to play hero with. Frank gave him the deadeye and pointed a finger at him, shaking his head. "Don't sniff around trouble, kid, we're all good here."

The kid looked from one to the other, and Terry rolled over, sat up and waved the kid off. When he'd left, Terry looked up at Frank, and at the coyote still standing attentive next to him. "Shouldn'ta lied, Frank. We ain't neither one of us good, is we? That's what you're asking about, huh. You're asking, have I touched him too?"

"Just tell me 'bout the tattoo, Terry. Good, bad, I don't give a shit about the rest."

Terry rubbed his arm like he'd hurt it when the coyote knocked him down. "That your coy-ote Frank, for real?"

"I reckon he's his own coyote and got nothing to do with this."

"We ain't nobody our own, Frank. We all belong to something or somebody, and me?" Terry leaned forward, held his hand up to show the tattoo. "Me, I belong to <u>him</u>, and that's what that means. And I guess you know why."

"I guess you better tell me. I seen that brand a few places, that's what I'll say. Seen it when my parents died. Seen it when my family died."

"And one other time too, I guess. Didn't you?" Terry sounded sympathetic now, but like he was making an effort, too. Like he was straining something. He stood up slowly like to see if Frank was gonna stop him, and when he didn't, held out a hand. "Could I get a cigarette? Didn't have a chance to finish the other 'un."

Frank lit them each a fresh butt and passed one to him. "One other time?"

But it came back to him. Halloween, the scarecrow had had it sewn into his shirt with yellow thread. It hadn't made much of an impression then, but it'd clicked later, eventually. "When you made the deal," Terry said. "He was wearing it, wasn't he."

"Josh Marlowe," Frank said.

Terry shrugged. "Ain't a name I know."

"The scarecrow."

Another shrug. "Don't mean nothing to me."

Frank paused, leaned against the wall, and exhaled smoke. "The Halloween man."

The coyote whined, and Terry nodded, pointed first to his nose and then to Frank, and shivered. "Oh yes."

"Did he put the tattoo on you? What did you give him? What did you do? Dammit, I told you, I seen that symbol when my family died. I

50

need --"

Terry looked slackjawed. It wasn't a change in expression. It was just like a flip had switched inside him, shut him off. The cigarette continued to burn, hanging from his lower lip, and ash drifted from it, but a line of drool slipped down too, breaking when it struck his chin. "Uh," he said a moment later.

"Terry?"

The older man's eyes still looked dull, but he turned towards Frank. "You're still here."

"Dammit, I'm waiting to hear what you know! Don't you understand how much this matters?"

Terry looked at him, looked past him, his eyes almost milky with age. "Do you know what the raven told the sparrow when the Great Forest fell, Frank? She said this is a ghost story, my love, and only ghosts will understand it."

"I don't. That doesn't help me."

Terry shook like he was suddenly cold, and tip-toed across the thin street. "He didn't put nothing on me. It just showed up, burning and sore the morning after I met that man, that Halloween man and all his angels. I guess the rest you know. What I paid. The symbol's his, and so'm I, so'm I oh Lord. He left me enough to live on, I reckon. Oh sparrow mine. Oh moon and sea, oh carry me."

Terry's voice was coming over slurrier, higher pitched, and as he walked he became erratic like a drunk.

Frank looked down at the coyote and pointed at Terry, but the beast just covered his head with his paws like he was hearing something he didn't like. "Terry, wait," Frank said. "Let me buy you something to eat, let's get some dinner, we'll talk about this, I need to know more --"

Terry laughed, twirling around in a pirouette before he faced Frank again. His eyes now were as blank as paper, covered over entirely in matte whiteness. "It's almost sundown, Oedipus, my time is running thin. Another time, my brother sparrow, another time again."

He sang to himself as he trip-toed out of the alleyway, an old skip-rope song. "Cinderella, dressed in yella, went downstairs to kiss her fella. Made a mistake and kissed a snake, how many doctors did it take? One, two, three, four --"

Frank jogged after him, but on "four," Terry was gone, nothing but cigarette smoke wisping where he'd stood, and the faint smell of liquor on the air.

CHAPTER EIGHT

Friday nights Frank took Ricky to the Beach, a block down a nameless street from Burns in the part of town they'd called Swayville long enough that even Pops Train hadn't known why. The Beach was a bar, and not some pink and green plastic cactus bar like you'd have in Santa Fe, not some sports bar with ten kinds of buffalo wings and twelve kinds of microbrew, but a plain old God God damned bar, wood floors and green vinyl. There were five, six kinds of beer, which was more than there'd been when Frank came of age, and if you wanted something to eat you had a burger cooked on a hot plate with beans from the crockpot, or you went cross the street to the Archuletas' spaghetti joint.

Two doors down from the Beach you could play cards or dice at the Harvey Girl Bookswap, and word was one of the girls working the door there would take you upstairs for the price, but Frank had heard rumors like that about girls at the Harvey all his life and knew at least half of them was gump. There were other places around to gamble, but the Harvey was traditionally the respectable joint, the white joint, where you'd find a doctor and a banker as often as a farmhand or longhauler.

Once in a while someone'd give Frank a hairy eye look for bringing Ricky in, since the boy wasn't sixteen yet even, nevermind eighteen or legal, but cause it was Frank the bartenders didn't have a problem with it. McTavitt had known him all his life, and they'd both come here with their own fathers as boys.

Ricky, the first couple months after the new year he'd been timid about being in the bar, sorta hunkered down over the same beer all night, which he drank with his hands on both sides of it like he was hiding the mug. Lately he'd loosened up, gone on to two beers sometimes if they stayed long, even asked if he could have a shot of whiskey, which Frank told him fuck no he couldn't and not to push it. The waitresses liked him cause he was a good looking boy, a boy raised good and not trash, and he'd made a good impression being all shy and everything.

Tonight he'd flirted with Lisa Davenant some, who waitressed there, just that little bit of flirting you do when your pops is right there and the girl's six years older'n you and the sheriff's daughter to boot. Frank gave him some space to work. It was like kissing your babysitter, you had to get your practices somehow, get your game up and ready before the real thing come by.

So he and Lobo sat back, each of 'em with an eye on their kids, while they jawed and chawed, spitting lobs of tobacco juice into a spitoon on the floor between 'em. They were a few drinks down the ladder, and on Lobo's favorite topic, The World's A Shitter.

"It just ain't nothing but frustration," Lobo said now, thumbnail worrying away on the label edge of what they'd always called Johnny Fuckyou Walker cause of some joke neither of 'em could recall no more. "It ain't nothing but a lot of huffing and puffing."

"Yeah, I reckon," Frank said. "What's that?"

"Everything under the sun, Frankie bo. Everything under the sun." Spirit in the Sky was playing on the juke, somebody's country-fried cover of it with a lot of steel guitar, and both Lobo and Frank tapped their fingers along to it without realizing what they were doing. "It's just a lot of worry about, a lot of fuck you daddy, you know?"

"What, parenting?"

"Parenting. Exactly." Lobo levelled a grimy finger at him, the nail torn at the edge. Even at ten, eleven at night, he was dressed pretty nattily for a guy who could stand to lose thirty pounds. But his fingernails were dirty like a park ranger's. "Don't matter what you do, they do whatever the hell they want. Whatever the hell. Good Dad, bad Dad, don't matter, do it? Look how we come out, pretty much the same. Your dad was a pretty good guy by you, mine was shit. Didn't matter, did it."

Frank kept his own counsel on that. "Ricky ain't been the easiest kid since the accident, but he's got some more teen years yet to go so I guess it'll get worse. Gina wasn't too bad. Argumentative, that's for sure. Picky, whiny. But hell, we all was."

Lobo snorted. "That one there," and he nodded to Lisa, "I needed to spend some of my Christmas money taking care of a problem for her. Be thankful it's a boy you got now. Aw. Hell, you know what I mean. There's certain kinds of problems a boy don't gotta deal with, you see what I'm saying."

Frank looked at pretty plain Lisa Davenant, who'd probably plump up like her father before she hit 30, and took another drink. "I guess maybe he oughta if he's raised right, though."

"Yeah, you'd think so, wouldn't you." Lobo knocked the rest of the bottle into his glass and his glass down his gullet. "Ain't like it used to be, you cain't be your kid's only parent no more. Or one of two, even. Nah, they got the schools now, they got the government telling you what you can and can't do, they got television and movies and fucking rap music giving em all these damn ideas. Can't do your job no more."

"I dunno," Frank said. "Reckon our folks had the same problem. Shit, Lo, we used a listen to Black Sabbath, Judas Priest, and smoke dope and save up money for whores."

Lobo gave him a sour look. "Things ain't what they used to be."

"Well, no, no, they ain't. I ain't arguing that, no doubt."

The sheriff nodded, mollified, and continued his canoe on that crick. "We've strayed from the way of our fathers. Or their fathers before them, anyhow. Maybe theirs before them others."

"Yeah, how you figure? I mean, I still spanked the kids. I ain't one of these fucking softie fathers wants a let 'em bang pots and pans all the day so's they express themselves, giving 'em goldstars for painting Betty Crocker frosting on the walls."

"We ain't godly men no more, Frank," Lobo said, and looked across the bottle at him with saggy dog eyes. "We ain't a godly race. We gotta get back to Jesus."

Frank nodded out of habit, and then sat back, the whiskey swimming in his head like mating goldfish as he watched his boy flirt with Lobo's girl. "Well now, Lobo, people been saying that for two thousand years or so, ain't they. Maybe Jesus was the problem to begin with. Might as well get used to it and start enjoying life while it's there."

Lobo grunted, stared at him for a second, and stood up unsteadily. "Sugar," he said to Lisa, "I'll see you later. Don't lead that boy on none, and when you get off work, you come right home. Your ma'll know if you don't."

"Geez, Pa," Lisa said, ducking her head so she could flash Ricky a can-you-believe-it look. "I'll go home, don't worry so much."

"Take it easy, Lobo," Frank said, waving a hand, and the sheriff just grunted at him in response, hitching his belt up and bunching his shirt in fists as he walked out of the Beach with a careful and deliberated stride.

Ricky gave Frank a look like he knew something'd pissed Lobo off, and like he in turn was pissed about it, but Frank just shrugged, dug out some bills to pay for the drinks. He may as well pay for Lobo's rather than get it left on the sheriff's tab. Never really paid to have the sheriff pissed at you if you could avoid it, and it was easier to treat for the drinks than apologize for disagreeing with some stupid "things ain't as good as they used to be, we ain't a godly race" argument.

He'd barely paid it and finished his own drink off, though, before Lobo was back through the doors. The sheriff cast his eyes loosely over the room, not at Frank in particular, and said, "Anyone interested in the well-being of Mickey Train prolly oughta poke a nose into the Harvey Girl." He spat once, letting the brown stain land on the floor, and turned around, slamming the door behind him.

Well God damn.

Mickey and Jessie'd moved back to town on an indefinite sort of basis, living in Ma and Pop Train's place. Mick said it was so there'd be more family around, you know, not so spread out. Frank got the feeling maybe he'd had some bad business somewhere, too, something he wanted to leave behind.

He'd always been a gambler, never losing big or winning big without cancelling it out soon enough. But it wasn't like him to be in the Harvey without so much as coming into the Beach for a drink. He knew Frank and Ricky'd be here.

"Mac," Frank said. "Wonder if you can do me a favor."

McTavitt grunted noncommittally.

"Let Lisa off work for a bit so she can give Ricky a ride home?"

The bartender clicked his tongue, and nodded. "Yeah, all right. Lisa?" He had to repeat her name because the kids were engrossed in their own back and forth. Frank wasn't sure they'd even heard Lobo.

"You mind giving Ricky a ride home, Leese?" Frank asked her.

"Oh, sure," she said, and Ricky grinned wide as Moon River. "What time you want me to put him to bed?"

"Just see the boy home, girl," Mac said gruffly, and Frank nodded to him.

"Rick," he said. "I'll be home later. Won't be too long, but you don't have to stay up."

"Yeah," Ricky said. "All right, don't worry. See you later, Pops."

The kid was so engrossed in the girl he didn't ask where Frank was going at eleven o'clock at night, so maybe he'd heard Lobo and maybe he just didn't care.

The Harvey Girl Bookswap'd been named for the Harvey Girls who used to wait tables at the restaurants along the rail lines back in the day, giving travellers a nice bite to eat in a respectable joint. The Harvey'd probably been one of them restaurants once, but Frank didn't know if it'd ever been a bookstore.

He stepped down into the split-level joint, passing the woodburned sign, a year or two old, that said NO TEXAS HOLD-EM, and the neon pink dice that lit up the cash register that was only used if someone bought a beer, a coke, or a pack of smokes. The girl running the register had been a grade or two ahead of Gina, Brittany Rogers, blonde hair she was still doing nutty things to, a face that'd prolly look twelve until it woke up on the other end a forty. He'd taught a year of Sunday school in his church phase, and she'd been in the class, drawing pictures of the animals on Noah's ark and writing lists of what she could do to be a better Christian.

He knew the rumors about Brittany and was sure they weren't true but hoped they never became so neither. Kids these days, they thought about sex different. Maybe they didn't think it was a bad thing to be a whore now. Gina'd read all those books, written all them essays, about sex empowerment and sex positive and whatever. "Hey peanut," he said. "What's good?"

"Everything's peaches but the cream, Mr Train," she said with a wan smile. At twentyfuckall she was already tired, but he'd chalk that up to Friday nights. "Don't see you in here much."

"Never been a cards man, even these days with the teevee. Mick around?"

"Yeah." She bit her lip. "Yeah, I didn't know if that's why you were here. He's in the blue room. I think you better take him home, Mr Train, you don't mind my saying so."

"Don't mind a piece," Frank said, and paused for a sec. "Britt, you find yourself thinking that again when I ain't here, you feel free to call me and say so, all right?"

She nodded as he stepped away from the register. "Just dint feel it was my place, sir."

The front room, a couple steps down from the register, didn't have a name. There were a couple tables there, a couple video poker and video blackjack machines, a TV and the beer-and-cokes fridge. The TV was on ESPN, where a west coast hockey game was playing in silence. The room was smoky with cigars and cigarettes, and the hopsy smell of cheap beer permeated everything, made the tabletops tacky with their accumulated condensation and spills.

Frank nodded to some of the guys he knew, and felt eyes on him as he walked around the edge to the blue room, the middle stakes room. All the rooms looked the same, no red or blue to be seen, but it was just what they called stuff.

The blue room's door was locked, so he knocked, waited, and someone opened it, peering out at him and then nodding like he was expected. Inside were three tables, one of them empty. Mickey was sitting at the nearest with Blackie Davenant, Will Traum, Pete Angler, and Lincoln Train. Linc was their cousin on Pop's side. Blackie was Lobo's brother. They were all playing, but sullenly, only as much talking as was necessary, and Mickey's lip was swollen.

"How's the game, fellas?" Frank asked, looking around. No idea which one of them popped Mickey, if any.

"Think it's bout time for you to take your brother home," Blackie said, not looking up from his cards. "He don't know when to fold."

"Uh huh," Frank said, and walked around the table a little, nodding to Linc, patting Pete on the back. He took a burning cigarette from the ashtray and took a drag off of it. "How about it, Mickey, you ready to head out?"

"Not yet, Frankie Frank," Mickey said, his voice thick with drink. "Gotta win my fucking money back from these fucking faggots."

"Easy," Frank said, and Blackie had stiffened in his seat. "Which one of 'em pop you, Mick?" He leaned down, took a long drag of smoke, and blew it past Pete Angler's face before putting the cigarette out. Angler was about six, seven years younger'n him, a snot-nosed kid who used to draw pictures of naked ladies on playing cards and try to sell them outside school. These days he owned half the Pump-n-Go with his father-in-law. Pete gave him an angry look but didn't say anything yet.

Frank didn't look up but heard Mickey's chair push back, the feet scraping against the floor before he answered. "Well now, that was Blackie."

"What I figured," Frank said, and backhanded Blackie Davenant hard across the face. Blackie was leaner than his brother, more wiry. When his little brother who nobody had called Lobo yet joined the police force, Blackie'd made a big deal out of signing up for the Marines, then been kicked outta boot camp for reasons unknown. During the first Gulf War, he'd left town for most of a year and sometimes claimed he had spent the time in the field, had "been called back up."

Sadass loser or not, he was the kind of guy who'd fight till his fists turned soft, if you put him in that sort of position, so Frank didn't. Blackie lunged at his midsection as he got up, pushing him against the wall, and Frank brought a hand down hard inside his collarbone, jerked a knee up in defense, pushed Blackie away and hit his jaw as hard as he could manage at that angle.

Teeth scraped against each other in the bigger man's mouth, a crown popping loose even as bruise bloomed on his already red face, and Frank's knuckles split like blisters. The look of hurt, fear, nervousness in Blackie's eyes sent a brief, nostalgic thrill through him before Will Traum grabbed him by the back of the shirt, and Blackie's fist pounded into his stomach, knocking the wind out of him and filling his throat with a choke of bile.

Will wasn't a big guy, and Frank twisted away from him, elbowed him, and then stopped when Blackie pulled a knife, one of those long curved ones like you got at the Lonely flea market or the Army Navy store.

"Whoa there," Linc said. "Blackie, now them's my cousins, remember." Lincoln Train had his uncle Arthur's cowboy ruggedness but a mean streak like his father Butch. He'd terrorized Frank and Mickey when they were kids, before he got bored with 'em and moved on to girls.

"Telling me I can't fight back just cause they're your kin? Fuck that!"

"Blackie," Lincoln said firmly, and nothing else. Blackie and Will both backed up.

Frank straightened his shirt and nodded to Lincoln. "Come on, Mickey. It's time to cash out."

Mickey hesistated, and then grabbed his chips in a clean and easy grab. Even drunk and socked around, he was graceful, but Frank didn't overlook the fact that his brother had remained seated while he was being sandwiched between Blackass Davenant and Will Traum. Nor that as soon as Mickey was up, he put his younger brother between himself and the rest of the room.

Frank pushed him out the door first, towards Brittany and the register and the couple hundred bucks he could get for the chips, and Lincoln called after them, "Don't forget now, Michael, you'll be owing me some money."

"The hell's that about?" Frank hissed when the door was closed, while Brittany carefully counted out eight twenty-dollar bills and six ones.

"Aw, I ran short," Mickey said. "Linc spotted me some. I'll make it good soon enough."

ooo000ooo

Mickey had called Will Traum a cheat and Blackie Davenant a jarred fart who'd spend his life in the shadow of a little brother who himself weren't nothing but a tin-star with his hand in the cookie jar, and that's when Blackie had laid into him, with Traumie kicking him in the side while he was at it.

"Well," Frank said, as they sat by their respective vehicles in the Train folks' driveway, "you shoulda told me that and I would've popped Will one too." He hadn't especially wanted Mickey to drive home, but sure as hell wasn't going to leave that Trans Am in the parking lot where one of the boys might decide to key it or do for its windshield. "Whaddaya mean about Lobo, anyway? And shit, you should know better than saying that bunk to Blackie."

"Ain't bunk, but yeah all right. I get so fucking steamed when I've been knocking them back, you know how I do. Lobo's got a hand in a lot of things around town, little brother. Surprised you don't know that, thought you two were tight in your way."

Frank shook his head. "Not since we was kids, and not then either. We were around each other a lot, but I don't know you'd say we ever liked each other. We're just used to each other."

"Yeah, well," Mickey said. "Maybe he's not the best guy to be used to, Frank. It's a good thing I'm back in town. You still need looking after, don't know the white hats from the black."

"Reckon," Frank said, and lit a cigarette, eyeing the house, where Jessie was sitting in the lit kitchen, conscientiously not watching them. "'Jarred fart,' Mick?"

Mickey grinned, showing a tooth that'd need to be capped. "I liked that too." The grin faded, and he rubbed his chin with regret. "Wish he hadn't socked me so soon, though, he got me in mid-sentence when I was telling him to shut his cock holster. I thought that was pretty good. Better for his brother, though, cock holster."

"Cock pocket would be better. The rhyming."

"Cock basket."

"Cock scabbard."

"Good 'un. Cock pestle."

"Pizzle?"

"Pestle," Mickey said. "Like a mortar and pestle? Like some guy's gonna put his pizzle in the pestle."

"I thought the pestle was the pizzle. You're thinking mortar."

They both smoked in silence until the tobacco had burned down to the ends, and then Mickey shrugged as he moved away from the cars to their parents' house where his wife waited. "Well, I don't really cook."

ooo000ooo

It was past midnight when Frank got home to his house on Borachon Creek Road, and like with his folks' place, light bled out of the windows from someone waiting up. He caught a glimpse of movement as he came around to the door from the driveway, and stopped, watching.

Ricky and Lisa were on the couch. Through the window, in that light, everything Frank shoulda straightened up, tidied, got underlined. There was a crumpled-shut bag of corn chips on his chair, an empty beer bottle next to it, magazines left here and there, laundry he hadn't bothered sorting. The kids were blind to it, of course, being at that age, even Lisa.

He'd figured maybe there was a chance the kids would get to necking even though Ricky was a fair lot younger'n the girl, but they'd gotten past that: Lisa was laying back on the arm of the couch, one leg splayed along the back of the cushions and the other on the floor, with Ricky still half-sitting but leaning into her. Her shirt was pulled up and her bra pulled down, and Ricky had a hand on one of her breasts and his face pressed into it, his head moving back and forth just slightly as he sucked her nipple.

The girl's eyes were closed, her head back on the arm and sometimes abruptly twisting one direction or the other as she stroked the back of Ricky's neck with her fingers. Frank didn't mean to watch, but was just caught up short by the surprise of it. Just before he turned away, Lisa opened her eyes and lifted her head a little, like she knew he was there. But with Ricky having all the lights blazing, and Frank in otherwise total darkness out in that New Mexico midnight with not a streetlight for miles, there was no way she could see him.

He walked around the other end of the house and sat by the

workshed. Weren't no way he was gonna burst in on the two of them. Let Ricky have his fun, it'd never again be as intense and stupid as it was when you were 15.

He tried to remember if he'd ever been like that with Kriste, just drunk on sucking her tits on the couch and so stupidly into it that he wouldn't even bother dimming the lights, drawing the curtains. He guessed not, guessed he hadn't been. But they hadn't been together when he was that young. And he'd never had Ricky's timidity. It wasn't until he was older that he'd ever been impressed with a girl, shocked by her. Wasn't something he'd learned, exactly, more like something he'd lucked into.

They'd gone to the same school, him and Kriste, but she'd been a couple years back of him and he didn't remember paying her much mind. He'd been a wild kid like Lobo. Feeling girls up before he asked their names. Crashing parties in Lonely, Cabredo, even Taos back when the hippies was still all over the place like they didn't know the echo had finally died down from Woodstock.

It was like he'd all of a sudden noticed Kriste after she got out of high school, and he sure as hell hadn't been looking for "settling down," hadn't had any damn interest in sticking to one girl, but they got serious when she took pregnant, and though he'd fooled around before that, he never touched another woman again after. He mighta been wild, he mighta been lawless, but fuck a duck, he hadn't been without honor.

He didn't feel like the boy who'd done that, not anymore. He didn't know if he'd do the same thing if it happened again.

But it couldn't. Kriste was dead now. She'd been his door. He'd gone from wild kid to working with Dude Borachon on a reg'lar basis instead of the bullshit piecework he'd done when not working on cars or fields, and before long he was a father. You weren't a father till your first kid turned three or four, he reckoned, cause that was the point where you had to start answering questions and setting examples, but before that you were basically a janitor.

Fatherhood had opened everything up. Made a man out of him. He'd felt more possibilities than ever before, like all of a sudden he could pick which Frank Train he wanted to be, even switch between 'em. You help a kid with her science project, like you know something about science; you read more books to kids than you've read for yourself in your life; you watch different TV, listen to different music, and yeah, he'd started to drink different too. Maybe one a the differences between him and Mickey was Mickey never had his kids around very long.

He watched the moon pass the sky, waited for Lisa Davenant to go on home, thought about how Kriste'd been his frontier, and now here he was with nowheres left to explore.

60

CHAPTER NINE

The night before Easter, Ricky didn't come home. He had gone out with his friends, "just out," a deflection Frank didn't press because he knew damn well a specific answer, even if honest, wouldn't a stayed right for long. They'd start out at the movies or something, head to someone's house whose parents weren't paying much attention, go down to the creek, who knew what else. Not everything'd changed since he was a kid.

It wasn't like Ricky to stay out all night, and Kriste'd grounded him the one time he had, even though he'd called. Or maybe especially since he called, since that'd opened the window to direct disobedience.

And so maybe, Frank figured, that was why he didn't call this time. If he didn't call, Frank couldn't tell him to come home, Ricky couldn't disobey. It was stupid logic, yeah, but teenage stupid. And like he'd told Lobo, the boy hadn't been himself since the accident, and he was getting to that wild dog age anyway.

Frank baked a pan of Pillsbury cinnamon rolls like they had every Easter, half of 'em burning on the bottom cause he'd replaced the non-stick pans he'd accidentally fucked up with cheap aluminum ones, and scrambled some eggs with green chiles and tortilla strips. His mother had made migas every Easter, or her mother did if it was a year the Mondragons were visiting. He reckoned he ought to have called them, see if they wanted to have Easter dinner, but he wasn't any good at planning out family stuff. Kriste'd done that, of course, and he felt a bit stupid every time he realized there was slack he hadn't picked up yet from her dyin'.

When he'd ate and had some coffee and got his church suit on, he left a note for Ricky and put his Easter gifts on the kitchen table next to it. The old wicker Easter basket had been Frank's when he was a boy and was still woven with purple and yellow ribbons (Gina, for her part, had got Kriste's old pink and blue basket). It was filled with a bed of green plastic grass, a big dark chocolate bunny cause Ricky liked it better, some Twinkies and Little Debbies. Wrapped in boxes next to the basket were some Black Sabbath CDs Frank thought were worth a gamble, a card confirming a subscription to one of the magazines Frank'd picked him up in Santa Fe, and tickets to a UNM Lobos football game in the fall, the home opener. They'd make a weekend of it, Frank figured, the road trip to Albuquerque and everything.

Mickey and Jessie got to St Catherine's for Easter mass not long after Frank did, and sat next to him in the pew the Train family'd occupied for twenty years. Mickey was visibly hungover to anyone who knew the signs, and hell, maybe still a little tipsy from a hair of the dog, but he was cleanshaven, his suit immaculate, and there weren't no doubt who to thank for that. Even if it didn't work out in the long run, Mickey ought've married Jessie twenty years ago, woulda done him the kinda good that mighta lasted.

Jessie squeezed his hand when she sat down, and was probably about to ask where Ricky was, when the Mondragons arrived just behind them: Frank and Mickey's maternal grandparents, their uncle Rafe and his wife, his kids Newt and Dove and their spouses and kids, and Dove's baby grandson. The pew filled rapidly, and Frank's grandmother leaned over Mickey and Jessie, demanding of him, "Donde esta Ricardo?"

"Ricky couldn't make it, Nana," Frank said, wishing he'd prepared something else to say.

"Nana," Mickey said, "Jessie doesn't speak Spanish, remember? Let's stick to English in front of her?"

"Absurdo," Nana said, continuing in English even so. "It's Easter, we in church! Quieres hablar ingles en iglesia?"

Her husband pulled her back over laps and murmured to her, scolding or calming her, who knew. She muttered a few more things in Spanish, and soon enough, services began. Frank sang when he needed to sing, and mostly just nodded along, listening to the same hymns and homilies he always had. Nana Mondragon kept shooting him critical looks, or maybe they weren't aimed at him as much as at the spot where Ricky woulda sat, so he did his best to look like he was at alert attention, or sometimes frowning in deep thought at the state of his boy.

"Brethren," Father Michael said, reciting the reading from the Epistle of Saint Paul to the Romans, "know you not, that so many of us as were baptized into Jesus Christ were baptized into his death? Therefore we are buried with him by baptism into death: that like as Christ was raised up from the dead by the glory of the Father, even so we also should walk in newness of life. For if we have been planted together in the likeness of his death, we shall be also in the likeness of his resurrection: knowing this, that our old man is crucified with him, that the body of sin might be destroyed, that henceforth we should not serve sin. For he that is dead is freed from sin."

Yeah, Frank thought. Too bad for Ricky he ain't dead, that'd free him from grounding for sure. He regretted it right away, shame blushing from his temples to his neck as though someone had overheard him. It felt like everyone in church was looking at him, not just looking but seein': seeing that even though he was surrounded by family, there were gaps there, big gaps, Ricky alive but unaccounted for, his kids and wife and parents dead in the last half year and half his grandparents dead long before that, leaving him holding this one unbalanced branch of the family tree and trying not to be toppled by it.

They'd all figure him a failure for sure, Ricky not even showing up for church, and why should he, why should he heed? Wasn't like Frank was his real dad.

He woke up in the cold of the night sometimes wondering who else knew that, wondering if people had suspected. Put 'em side by side and they looked nothing alike, he thought now. He'd just fooled himself all along, fooled everybody. Kriste'd known, obviously, but had she really gone all that time without telling nobody? Not her folks, not her sister, not her friends?

Did the father know?

Did <u>Ricky</u>?

Maybe everybody under the sun had known except Frank himself.

Frank still wondered if Josh Marlowe was Ricky's father, which he'd as much as implied. Marlowe'd visited Rick in the hospital right off the bat, presented himself as family. What'd they talked about? Frank hadn't asked. Didn't want to think about Ricky calmly saying, "Yes, my real father visited me in my hospital bed."

Was Marlowe really the Halloween man, or just someone like Terry, someone who knew him, got "touched" by him?

"Easter's not as popular as Christmas," Father Michael said when his sermon began. "The kids don't get a week off from school, people aren't as likely to visit their family to celebrate it or come home from college for it. They don't have after-Easter sales, or Easter movies, or a month's worth of Easter TV specials. It's easy to think Easter just isn't as important as Christmas.

"But that's not the case. If Christmas is a promise, Easter is its delivery. If Christmas is an engagement, Easter's the wedding, and which do you celebrate the anniversary of? Well, some of you young newlyweds may celebrate both, but ask your fathers and I'm sure you'll find it's only the wedding anniversaries they even remember." People laughed at that, and knew when to. You could always tell from Father Michael's tone of voice and body language when he was gonna tell a joke, although they were never very funny. He could be funny in person. But as a priest, he was only sorta funny. And sorta funny was about all his parish wanted.

Out of habit, Frank scanned the other pews of parishioners. Easter was like Christmas, you saw the folks who you didn't see any other time, especially since the real diehards, the real candle-lighters, woulda gone to Easter Vigil the night before. He was surprised the Mondragons hadn't dragged Mickey and Jessie off for that. His mother's family had always been devoted, old-school Catholics, and one a his uncles woulda been a priest if he hadn't died in a rodeo accident when his mother was just a girl.

"Christmas, it's all about gifts, isn't it? Oh, not really, I know. We celebrate the birth of our Lord and the miracles that surrounded it: but when you leave this building, when you go home, one way or the other it ends up being about gifts, like the ones the kings of the Orient brought to the baby Jesus."

Frank tilted down towards Jessie and whispered as quiet as he could, "How's Mick doing?" She just shrugged in response, wiggled her hand back and forth in a so-so way.

"Easter? What's your gift on Easter? Some chocolate bunnies, some jelly beans, and the end of your Lenten sacrifice. But really, it's not even about that: it's about grace. Your gift is salvation by the grace of God, and you don't get that on Easter, you don't get that at the dinner table, you get that every day, friends."

He was sure everyone was staring at him. Every time he looked across the aisle at another pew, the folks sitting there were looking back at him, steel-eyed as jackals. A memory hit him again out of nowhere, but this one wasn't real, couldn't be, as sharp as it was. Walking in on his father in the bedroom, looking out the window with his pants pulled down and his cock in his hand, hard and red. Arthur Train Junior's hand rested against the window frame, and outside was some kind of parade, some kind of commotion. He was breathing hard and there was a fresh cut on his ear, wet and dripping.

"Easter's been celebrated since at least the second century. It's the oldest Christian holiday, almost as old as celebrating the Sabbath on Sunday. Easter isn't a Christian holiday. Christianity is an Easter faith. The resurrection of Christ from death, after His sacrifice upon the Cross for Man's sins, that is the essence of the faith. Those days when He remained on Earth after death before ascending to Heaven, those days when even His disciples doubted Him, those are the days we live in still."

Two rows ahead of him, a little girl had turned around in her seat, kneeling on it as she peered back at him. Her eyes were cold and deep, and her hair had fallen out of the careful Easter hairstyle her young mother'd arranged, giving her a curtain to gawk through and hide her whites. She opened her mouth like she was going to stick her tongue out at Frank, but it just hung there, empty, gaping, a line of spit falling from it onto the velvet accents of her Sunday dress.

He smiled at her, and all she did was drag her index finger down cross her forehead from her hairline to the tip of her nose. She didn't smile, didn't blink, and Frank looked away like losing a game of chicken.

"Grace isn't something we deserve. It isn't something we've earned. It isn't that record you might buy your son for doing a good job in his math class, it isn't the free meal you get for winning the taco eating contest at the Fourth of July, it isn't even like a birthday present. You did nothing for it, and you get it anyway. "

Jordan Heath was sitting in the front like he always did, with his grey old mother and his two daughters in immaculate white dresses. Jord's wife had disappeared off somewheres twelve years ago when the twins was barely out of diapers, and rumor said either he killed her or she run off with a rodeo worker, depending on which way the wind was blowin'. Could be both was right. He turned around, arm on the back of the pew across the shoulders of both his daughters, and leaned his head back to look at Frank.

His neck was bent at an angle it shouldn't be without breaking, and his tongue was dark like the meat of a good rare prime rib. He brushed crust from the corners of his eyes as he looked at Frank, and it flaked to the floor behind him at Mrs Esther's feet like dry leaves. When he rubbed his eyes again, they crunched like pork rinds, the dry skin around the bony sockets raining in a fine dusty mist and leaving broken, oozing wounds behind.

"Grace is why we can be redeemed despite our sin, why our souls can be made whole again.

"Now don't go thinking that just because you don't have to earn it means you can't <u>lose</u> it. Grace is part of your soul, but it's more like gravity than mass. It doesn't just sit there. It reacts. You can't stay in a state of grace when you're sinning. When you commit a mortal sin, the Holy Spirit departs from you. You have to earn that grace back, but the fact that you <u>can</u>, the fact that you can be forgiven, that's the gift."

Everyone in Saint Catherine's was looking right at Frank, everyone except his family, both those in the pew with him and the cousins and whatevers strewn around the church by marriage and other distances. They didn't blink or say anything, and Father Michael seemed oblivious to it. Frank glanced at Jessie, at Mickey, at the Mondragons, but they looked unaware of anything unusual. He tried not to meet anyone's eyes, and any time he did, there was nothing there but deep darkness. If he looked closely he could see red rimming the flesh of their eyes like from sores, the kind you get from rope burn or a cheap hooker.

"None of our works, none of our good deeds, make up for our sins. We do more bad than good. The gift we're celebrating today is that through Christ's sacrifice on the Cross, the world is allowed to live in a state of grace despite that."

Through the remainder of mass, Frank looked at nothing but Christ on the Cross and his own warbling reflection on the crucifix's gleamed surfaces.

Afterward, he waited his time to talk to Father Michael, knowing that he was making the family wait for him in turn, cause showing up alone meant he'd gotten himself attached to them, like a rogue oxygen molecule floating around until hydrogen snatched it up. But he stepped his distance from them, and nodded when Father Michael looked up at him.

"Hey," Frank said. "Good sermon, Father."

"Thank you, Frank. I see we have the pleasure of your mother's family this Easter."

"Yeah. They're staying with Mickey at the house, I think." How old would he be, how long would he have had his own house paid off, before his parents' house stopped being the house? "Listen, your sermon today, there's some things, I wondered if I could talk to you. About, well --"

"Grace?"

"Yeah." Frank nodded. "I guess so. And the soul. The immortal soul. Christ, I don't know, now I'm saying it, it doesn't make any sense. I don't know what to ask."

Father Michael paused for a minute and asked, "Is Ricky feeling okay?"

Frank shrugged. "He didn't come home last night."

The priest nodded as though this solved something. "It's Easter, you understand. I do have plans, and it doesn't sound as though this is a crisis in any sense but the existential."

"Sure, yeah. Yeah, I know, I know."

"Don't get me wrong, you're welcome to join me." Father Michael grinned. "I don't spend every Sunday having tea and sandwiches with the Catholic Ladies Society of Cardenio, you know. Today Hank McCarty is coming into town, coming to have dinner with me in the rectory."

"For real? Old Hank never comes into town no more."

Father Michael nodded. "I think he may feel his time runs slim."

Mickey poked his head between the two. "Mind if I join?"

Frank hadn't realized he'd been listening, and gave him a look that said as much, but realized his brother was looking for an excuse to break from the Mondragon herd. He sympathized with that sure enough, but didn't know about dumping the clan on Jessie.

Father Michael, though, simply nodded, after glancing at Frank for signs of dissent. "Of course. I'm sure your grandparents will understand a little mens' business."

A glance at the Mondragons, who prided themselves on the stubbornness and fierceness that family legend said had kept one of their number alive in the Crusades, made Frank wonder. But, feeling like a kid again and figuring Mickey felt the same, he decided that there wasn't much they could do about their displeasure if he wasn't around for it.

66

Jessie would be stuck with 'em, but inspiration struck Frank right in the nick. "Jess?" he asked, and she nodded, obviously hoping to be asked along or something. "I'd appreciate it to hell if you could go by my place, keep an eye out for Ricky?"

Nana Mondragon crossed her arms in a standing huff, and Jessie, with all the grace that'd gotten Mickey to marry her, managed to split a grin that still stayed solemn enough for church.

ooo000ooo

As four men sometimes do on Easter, they wound up shooting cans and bottles in the barrens behind the rectory.

Old Hank was in his Sunday suit even if he hadn't gone to mass. It was black and old-fashioned and the kind of thing you'd figure someone'd be buried in, but it fit him well and he didn't look half bad in it. Shooting was his idea cause he said he hated sitting still. Frank had his Defender, which McCarty just glanced at and shrugged, saying "A Colt's a fine gun, anyway." Mickey and Father Michael borrowed pieces from McCarty, who carried a disturbing amount of hardware in his truck.

"I prolly shouldn't be driving anyway," he said by way of explanation. "So maybe I'll crash sometime and get holed up somewhere in a storm. Never know."

Mickey wasn't a steady shot and probably hadn't held a gun in years, and Father Michael wasn't paying enough attention to the shooting, so Hank and Frank split most of the hits between them, exploding bottles into glass fragments that showered the pine stumps where they sat, and knocking holes through cans until they were too bent-over and hunchbacked to make good targets.

"Not bad, Frankie," McCarty said after a while of this. The coyote with the ragged ear had taken to him, and McCarty gave him a scratch on the back of the neck. "Your pops teach you to shoot?"

Frank nodded as he pegged off a freshly emptied can of Michelob. "Me and Mickey both."

"You knew Pops, didn't you Hank?" Mickey asked. "I remember him mentioning you once or twice in a passing familiar way."

"Really?" Frank put his handgun down. "Now I didn't know that."

Father Michael had brought lawn chairs over, their feet making harsh noises in the grit of the ground as they were dragged and then sat upon, and he seemed fine just listening, as though he'd arranged some match here with the Train boys and old man McCarty.

"Yep," Hank said, and fired a shot so exact the pull-tab flinged away from the can without the can falling over. "Long time ago when Arthur Train Senior, your grandfather, was still alive, they called his son Junior. He was a good boy, Junior. Sharp but not too talky. Didn't miss a trick.

Got me out of a jam once, but I don't know if he realized it."

"When was that?" Frank asked in surprise. He heard very little about his father's life in Cardenio, before leaving to work the ranches and marrying the sister of a fellow cowboy. Arthur Train Senior had died a long time ago, and to Frank it had always seemed as though his father didn't become real until he met his mother, or had before then been only a lonesome, silent cowboy, the sort you'd see in cigarette ads and postcards.

"Long time gone," McCarty said, "and today ain't the day to tell the tale, young Train. But he was a good boy. Troubled, but the best of them always has been. Lot to be troubled with in this world. All the streams and creeks of the world run into the sea and it ain't ever full."

"Speaking of which," Father Michael said. "Frank, something troubling you enough to risk the Mondragon wrath?"

They were four, five beers in. Had Father Michael wanted Mickey and McCarty to be part of the conversation, or had he bid his time once they were included, so Frank'd be tipsy enough to be loose-tongued, not mind being a little more public about things? Who knew.

"I've been having a hard time of it," Frank said slowly, and all three men nodded, Mickey adding a late and slurred "Amen."

"No one expects you to have it easy," Father Michael said. "Especially not with raising a teenage boy on your own now, and being strong for him."

Was there any kinda rebuke there? It was hard to say. "What you were saying about divine grace, I reckon," Frank said slowly. "What you were saying about the soul."

"Yeah, that part was good," Mickey said, and everyone paused for a sec before Frank continued.

"Well, you said grace is a part of our soul, right?"

Father Michael nodded. "Grace is the means by which the soul is redeemed, as long as we don't slip from that state of grace. You can lose it, if that's what you're asking. But you can get it back."

"Without grace, there ain't no salvation. Right?"

"As surely as there's no coffee without a pot. Can't just put beans in a cup of water."

Frank leveled his wrists in front of him and waited for his vision to steady before squeezing the Defender's trigger. A brown bottle of beer burst into wet shards and the last bit of clingfoam. "Well, what if you lost your beans? What if you lost your soul? You can have a soul without grace, and get the grace back. Can you have grace without a soul, and get it back?"

Michael didn't say anything for a moment, just frowned, and then said, "That's not really how it would work, but there's no losing the soul. Frank, why don't you tell me what's really bothering you?"

Ricky ain't my kid, and that's why he's still alive. All them closest to me been dying. Even the cousins, the distant aunts and uncles, there's been more of them dying lately than normal, and is that coincidence? My wife cheated on me and died before she could explain. My little boy, my only real son, died just a kid. My girl died with a whole life in front of her she was just learning to live. My folks were killed by a nut. And all maybe cause I gave my soul away to a stranger at the crossroads of Texas and Hosteen. That's what's bothering me, padre.

"That is what's bothering me," he said, and didn't look at any of 'em. "I think I lost my soul."

"Check the bottom of the bottle," Mickey said wearily. "S'where mine usually ends up."

Father Michael came over and rested a hand on Frank's shoulder. "Son, I understand how you feel, but it's still there. Your soul's still with you. It's just hurting now. I'd tell you it'll pass, but it's a lie. You never stop missing a loved one. All you can do is learn to live with the loss."

Frank shook his head. "I ain't talking metaphorically! I mean I literally. Fuck. I'm saying I think I got no soul. It's--"

"It isn't something you can lose," Father Michael said in calm, reassuring tones. "No more than you can lose your personality or your thoughts. They can get out of control but the soul's there, it's your essence, what the Catechism calls the spiritual principle."

"But I gave it away," Frank shouted in frustration, and his eyes felt hot and wet, his gun hand shaking enough that he had the sense to holster the piece, just like reflex. His shoulders trembled, and Father Michael's hand left them with a flinch.

"All right," McCarty said behind him. "Why don't you two go on inside and have some lemonade."

"Hank," Father Michael said, "this is a spiritual matter, I have it in --"

"Go inside, Michael," McCarty said. "Git. Me and the boy gonna jaw." The old man's voice'd come over all steel, and his hand inched just that tiny bit like he was gonna slap leather.

"All right, Henry, all right," Father Michael said, and glanced at Mickey.

Mickey slapped Frank on the back. "Stay strong, little brother. We'll talk when you get inside, all right?"

And in a moment, Frank and McCarty were alone in the barrens, Father Michael bringing the lawn chairs in with him. McCarty drained the last bottle of beer, tossed it at a stump, and blasted it out of the air. They watched the glass sprinkle the dirt, and the old man turned to him.

"What you done, you damn fool?"

Frank shook his head. "I shouldn'ta brought it up, Mr McCarty. It's just hard for me lately, with the family and all. And this being Easter."

69

"Fuck that. That ain't what you said." McCarty leaned up close to him, real close, took a sniff. Looked him over. "Roll up your sleeves."

"Mr McCar --"

The gun poked him in the ribs, and McCarty's upper lip curled skywise. "Roll 'em up, boy, so's I know we can be nice to each other when I see you ain't got his mark."

Frank's stomach sank, and he rolled his sleeves up, turning his arms back and forth before the old man nodded. "The mark like a circle," Frank said. "Like a brand."

"With a broken line through it."

"Oh Jesus. McCarty, you gotta tell me what you know." He had the old man's shirt bunched in his fists but didn't remember grabbing him. "You gotta tell me."

McCarty pushed him off. "Boy I don't got to tell you shit. The Hollow Man ain't the kind of thing nobody wants to talk about." He twisted his mouth shut, fretting. "Goddammit, boy. Your daddy wouldn't be too pleased about this at all. Goddammit. Where the fuck you run into him?"

"The Hollow Man? I been, I been thinking of him as the Halloween Man, the scarecrow man, it was at the crossroads of Texas and Hosteen --"

McCarty blanched. "Fuck, kid, that's not far from my place!"

"Yeah, it was on Halloween. I'd been out by yours --"

"Last Halloween? Fuck!" McCarty paced back and forth. "Fuck! Did he say anything about me? Did he ask you about me? Did you, what did you tell him? Was he looking for me?"

"You didn't come up! I swear your name never got mentioned."

"My name, maybe not," McCarty said, and then shook his head. "Nevermind. If he didn't talk about me, he didn't talk about me. God damn, what the fuck was he doing out there."

"Striking a deal, he said. Waiting at the crossroads for midnight and a bargain."

"Yeah," McCarty said. "Yeah, I guess he would be."

Neither of them said anything, watched the scrubby bushes in the distance, and the coyote darting after a sparrow.

"Who is he?" Frank asked. "Josh Marlowe. I run into a guy later, says his name's Josh Marlowe. I think it's, I think it's him, the Halloween Man."

McCarty snorted. He seemed old suddenly, all the way old. "Sure could be, but I don't know this Marlowe fella. He been around, your Halloween Man. All us old men, we got a lot of names, you know. The Hollow Man. The Hallow Man, maybe. Pass Christian. Walter the Skinless. Jack Dust, the sorcerer who rode with the Mechanicals until it all went bad for them."

"Man I met didn't seem like an old man. Josh Marlowe definitely ain't."

"Never does," McCarty said. "And maybe he ain't one."

"I don't get your meaning."

McCarty shook his head. "So you did the deal with him, huh."

"Right at midnight. You did the same?"

McCarty nodded after a pause, and then nodded again. "A long, long time ago. I was young and fucking stupid and wanted all the wrong things."

"So what'd you get for it?"

The old man cocked an eye at him as sharp as a pistol. "Son, that's near about as personal a question as you can ask a man next to what his wife's pussy tastes like. What'd you get?"

"I don't know. Fuck. He's real, ain't he? What do I do? What did you do?"

"I just lived. I ain't got good words for you. You done a terrible stupid thing, and terrible stupid things is gonna happen to you for it. But you deserve it, you hear me?"

His face burned, his throat felt sore. "But dammit, McCarty, my family. They didn't. My folks getting killed. My wife and kids."

"Rotten luck."

"His brand showed up both times. You know?"

McCarty grunted. "I guess I don't know what to say about that 'cept I should probably slap you silly if you really been so stupid all them people had to pay for it for you."

Frank barely heard him, and just kept spitting out things he couldn't tell nobody else. "In church, I was seeing things. Things I ain't sure was real. People looking at me."

McCarty sighed, but there was relief in it. "I ain't been to church but twice since I shook hands with Walter the Skinless in the water of the Pecos River. I ain't eager to go back till they bury me. It ain't the only place you'll slip, just the worst. Or you better hope."

"You been living with this a long time, I guess."

"I've stayed above snakes. Ain't got a choice in that. Others been luckier. They died."

They watched the spring sun cast shadows from the rectory. "I feel like a little fucking kid," Frank said. "Finding out the boogieman's real, the bad man."

"We're the bad men, son," McCarty said. "What scares me, what really fucking scares me, the older I get? Thinking maybe he ain't the bad one."

CHAPTER TEN

That wasn't the last night Ricky went missing. He'd show up the next morning or sometime after school, sometimes obviously hungover, other times clean as a whistle and freshly showered, but every time no matter what, he was sullen as a misfed cat. Frank stopped taking him to the Beach, and when Ricky was suspended for three days for grabbing the art teacher's tits while very obviously drunk in class, Frank did what his own pops had done when Frank'd been caught joyriding.

He called a favor into Lobo and had Ricky locked up in the otherwise empty holding cell for them three days.

It made him sick to do it, but hell, he couldn't let the boy see so. So he slipped Lobo some cash to cover things and had Ricky's meals sent in from the Rockinghorse Diner across the street. Eggs and biscuits for breakfast, green chile mac-n-cheese for lunch, hamburger steak for dinner. Every day he had his own lunch in the diner so he could hear back from the waitress how his boy was doing.

"Aw, Ricky's fine," she'd tell him every time. "He's a cute kid. So lonesome in there."

And Frank'd nod to that, finish his coffee, and head out to work, fixing this, tinkering with that, touching up the other, until it was time for dinner, which he'd been having with Mickey and Jessie at the house. He thought about Philip, about some time a year or two ago when the other kids were off doing their things and Philip was in the kitchen with the grown-ups while Mickey was visiting. Frank had handed him a can of beer and then held his glass out, saying, gimme a fill-up, Philip.

"Hate to say it, Frankie," Mickey said on the last night. Frank was planning to pick Ricky up from the cell in the morning and drive him straight to school, and was half tempted to hang around and make sure he fucking went. "But this ain't gonna do the trick for the kid, you know that."

Frank spooned cheese on top of the chili Jessie had made. It was chili, not chile. She'd mixed ground beef and sausage and tomato and onions and beans in with them chile peppers, with sour cream and cheese and avocado on the side, and it was good and all, but it was the kinda thing he was only used to getting at Wendy's, as different from chile as them burgers they flipped out at the Santa Fe Horse Show with the pineapple and the barbecue sauce. "I dunno, Mickey," he said as he watched the cheese melt. "What else'm I gonna do? I ain't sending him to one of them kiddie boot camps, those things are fucking sick."

"Yeah, my sister went to one of those," Jessie said. "Drugs," she added when Mickey gave her the brows. "My parents just bout lost it, cause I hadn't given 'em much more to worry about than being out late a few nights, so when Cesca found cocaine, well, off she went to boot camp."

"Did it work?" Frank asked. If it had, then maybe, if Ricky didn't shape up soon...

"Christ no," she said. "She fucked one of the 'counselors' and didn't get off coke for another three, four years. That shit's like those commitment retreats where you're supposed to rediscover your marriage, or those tent revivals. It's a brief, intense experience where you make brief, intense promises, and once one fades, so does the other."

Frank nodded. "'Bout what I figured, but that's put pretty good."

"Yeah," Mickey said, "she's a sharp cookie. And Frankie baby, this jail shit, it's just the same thing, you know. Smaller scale, but what're you, trying to put the fear of God into him by making him piss in the corner for half a week? Did it work for you when Pops did it?"

"Well, I ain't stealing cars no more," Frank said defensively. "I guess that's an improvement."

"Yeah, but did you stop then?"

He had, but he knew that wasn't the point. He'd kept up with the drinking and the whoring and the partying, and did until he met Kriste. His father's jail brainstorm hadn't had a thing to do with it. Frank sighed and washed a bite of chili down with cold beer. "So what the fuck do I do, then, I wait for him to grow out of it? What, I just sit back and say 'oh, boys will be boys,' and let him walk all over me?"

"Fuck if I know, man, that's why my kids live with their mother."

"Christ, Mick," Jessie said irritably, and he put his hands up in defense.

"Hey, it's a shitty situation! I'm not gonna pretend I've got the fix. Frank grew out of his shit, maybe Ricky'll grow out of his."

They all ate their chili in silence, and after a slice of pie and an episode of Breaking Bad Frank got up to go. "Well," he said, with that here-I-go-leaving tone.

"Hang on," Jessie said. "Mickey?"

"Oh yeah," Mickey said. "I mean since you're just going back to that empty place and all, well, you don't have any work to do tonight, do you?"

"Nothing I gotta, I guess," Frank said. "Gotta check on the Widow sometime this week."

"Oh, the old whore can wait," Mickey said, and Jessie slapped him on the shoulder as she cleared the dishes. "Anyway, look, I was thinking we could go through some of Mom and Pop's stuff, you know? I mean we've been putting it off, all of us, on account of not selling the house, but shit, it shouldn't be just a museum. It shouldn't all just sit there."

Frank grunted. He reckoned Jessie'd had a hand in this notion too, but maybe they needed that kick in the pants from somebody who wasn't family in the same way. "All right, yeah. Yeah, I can help with that."

"I was, we was thinking one night a week, you know, until everything's sorted."

"Can't promise I'm available the same night every week, you know how work is."

"Yeah yeah, that's fine." Mickey nodded, got up. "I thought, the studio? I'll grab some trash bags for any paint that's dried out or ... whatever. You wanna grab some of the boxes from under the stairs?"

"Sure thing," Frank said.

Jessie brought Mickey the trash bags and asked, "Do you want some help, or should I let you have some brother time?"

"All the same to me," Frank said, and when he saw Mickey was hurt, added, "But if it's all right, yeah, wouldn't kill me and Mickey to have some guy space."

In anyone else's house, "the studio" would have been just a large unfinished basement, maybe a secondary family room, but the elder Trains had long since installed a high-quality ventilation system and a Sharper Image ionizer to deal with paint fumes and other problems. Frank still remembered that summer, when his mother's NEA grant came in. It seemed like the sounds of workmen had gone on forever, spoiling the lazy mornings of his school vacation.

It smelled musty down there, stale, and it was too silent.

"I'm used to them working down here," Frank murmured to himself, and Mickey nodded.

"Yeah, it's weird, isn't it? Always seemed like one of them was down here at all times, or not gone for long."

"There were always bowls of soup getting cold or drying out, that Pop didn't bring back up to the kitchen."

Mickey grinned and shook his head. "Not soup. That was Pop's 'chile.' Remember, he'd take the Campbell's condensed tomato soup --"

"And add the brick chile. Yeah, shit, I forgot he added the soup to that. I can't believe he gave us shit for liking Velveeta."

They both laughed, and after a moment Mickey said, "You know, I've actually got some of the brick chili."

"Yeah," Frank said, "I picked up a case in Santa Fe." They laughed again, and it trickled away when they remembered what he had been in Santa Fe for.

Basements were a rarity in Cardenio, and the fact that the house had such a large one would have been a big factor in its resale value, if the housing market hadn't gone to shit. Even if you had something worth a lot didn't mean anyone was around for buying it.

The studio was divided into two rooms separated by an open doorway, in addition to the little nook where the water heater was. The floor was concrete that could be frigid in the winter but stayed cool in the summer, and made footsteps louder. Nothing decorated the walls, not even wallpaper, because they were so often covered by canvases or dropcloths. Expensive diffused ceiling lamps made up for the lack of natural light, although one of them critics who came up from San Antone had said that Mom and Pop's "distinctive use of color as a result of their working conditions" was part a their signature.

There were several workbenches arranged seemingly at random, a more business-like table covered in sculpting tools and painting supplies, three easels, and a couple of endtables for elevating still lifes.

Still lives?

"So how should we do this?" Frank asked. "I mean, I don't want to, uh. I don't want to throw anything out if it's art. You know?"

"Yeah," Mickey said. "I figure, the things that were in progress but not finished, we oughta mark those somehow, right? And anything done that isn't drying anymore, or needs to be sprayed. You remember doing that?"

"Yeah, man, we fucking complained to shit about the smell." One of Frank and Mickey's chores as kids had been spraying finished paintings with sealants to protect them, a minor deed of a few minutes' work which they'd treated like it was hard labor. "We were little dicks, when you think about it."

"Maybe yours is little," Mickey said. "Anyway, the stuff that's finished, we ought to store that somehow, shouldn't we? We don't want it just heaped. And maybe, I don't know, maybe we ought to think about selling some."

"Yeah, I guess," Frank said, but didn't really want to be thinking about that yet. Mom and Pop had always sold their stuff, obviously, but he didn't know what they would have asked for anything, if they cared which pieces were sold and which weren't. Seemed invasive, was all. "One thing at a time, Mickey Mick."

"Uh huh, Frankie Frank. So let's get it going."

The trash was the easiest. There were tubs and palettes of paint which had only been covered with Saran wrap. Fine for the short term, but months later they were thick and dried out. Likewise there were doodles, preliminary sketches, notes and such, the kinda things that wouldna been detailed enough to keep even if Mom and Pop Train had been Pablo Picasso and Salvador Dali.

The things that'd been finished and been drying, they were long dry now, even the thick oil paintings. Now, some of 'em, even Frank could tell they woulda had more added to 'em later but there was nobody gonna finish 'em now, so Mickey went ahead and sprayed 'em, laid 'em out on a workbench to dry another coupla days, and then worked on figuring out the sculpting area. Mickey'd always understood sculpting more'n Frank did. He'd played around with Mom's clay when they were kids, the way Italian kids probably played with pizza dough.

Frank got cracking on the paintings. Both Mom and Pop painted. Both of 'em, for that matter, sculpted, but while Mom had been about clay and marble and like that, the sorts of things you thought of when you thought "sculpture" and "statue," Pop had gone for bent wires and melted plastic and weird shit like that where you didn't really know what you were looking at. Really that'd been the divide, Frank supposed. His devout Catholic mother, a Mondragon in a long line of Mondragons, had been the realist. Arthur Train Jr, that wrangling cowboy poet who could go days without saying more'n howdy and good night and then spend a hour talking nothing but brick chili and what was good about it, he was the one spent his time on abstracts, on expressionism.

He tackled his mother's paintings first for that reason. It'd be easier to tell what state of finished they was in. He pulled the dropcloth off the wall where she often worked when she was doing triptychs and what-all, and immediately gasped, coughing on the smell of oils and turpentine, suddenly sharp as cheese. There were four canvases on the wall, strung up so she coulda seen 'em easily, reached 'em easily all at once, with the paints at the ready to the side of her. It was how she liked to work sometimes, didn't like having the canvas on the easel, all tilted and below her.

The four paintings were of the crossroads at Hosteen and Texas.

In the first, the streets were near empty. She'd painted with oranges, reds, browns, and Frank could almost smell the mesquite and hackberry burning in some harvest season wildfire in the Rio Grande bosque. The roads formed an offset cross, almost a T with the continuation of Texas barely visible in the corner. In dark browns muddied with red, she'd sketched the shadows of two men standing at the joint of the roads, leaving most of the scene blank, lonely as a coyote's heart.

The second and third showed the roads from other angles, not just positioned different on the canvas, but the vertical angle changed too, like the "camera" had been moved way way up for the first one, looking down at a man walking up Texas while someone waited for him on Hosteen, and way way down on the other, so that the intersection was dominated by giants looming up into the sky.

That second one looked finished, but who knew what details might be missin'. There was a grey cast to it that mighta been the first inklins of what woulda been rain, clouds, stormlight, one of them late thunderers that part of the area got a lot after summer'd set. The third one, though, in the third one, the roads themselves were just sketches, maybe not even recognizable if it weren't for the other paintings around them, and it was the men who'd been detailed, down to the wrinkles alongside Frank's eyes, the seven o'clock shadow he always ended the day with, and that lip-lick look on Josh Marlowe's face.

It was Frank and Marlowe in painting three, not the scarecrow, but Marlowe, and Frank felt a rush of blood to his face, the thump of trapped fists in his temples, because somehow -- somehow, oh God, somehow, this here was validation, this was the first connection anybody but him had made between the Halloween Man and Marlowe.

It wasn't a connection, not exactly, not all spelt out, but God damn, it put ... it put what, exactly?

It put Marlowe at the scene of the crime. In someone else's mind, anyway, and not just anyone, but his mother, goddammit, his mother who died at the hands a somebody using the Halloween Man's brand.

In the painting, Frank looked old, sickly, the kinda sick you get when a fever's burned too long, when maybe there's an infection you caught somewhere, something that needs to be cut out. His teeth were gritted ino a smile, the hair by his ear matted with sweat. Little touches of red made his eyes look bloodshot, and there were tubes of paint still nearby labelled carmine, alizarin, rust, like this was what she'd worked on last, before that day they went shopping in Santa Fe.

Marlowe looked nondescript. Any old fella with dark hair and deep eyes, and it mighta been he had a scar real close to his lip or that mighta been shadow. That expression, though, kinda hungry, kinda excited, kinda .... well kinda sexual. There was no

it's why he wears a mask

mistaking that. It was why he'd been a scarecrow. Cause nobody seeing that look, nobody would do no kinda dealing with him, 'specially not over a soul. It wasn't a crazed look, it was all too sane. It was the kinda look'd make you realize the fella was serious and not fooling around.

The fourth painting showed the crossroads empty 'cept for a shadow, and it was hard to tell just whose shadow it might be.

"Hey," Mickey said from behind him, and Frank realized he'd been staring at the paintings for who knew how long, just zoned out and whitepaper. "Been a while since I been around regular, but didn't Mom and Pop trade off?"

"How do you mean?" Frank asked, not yet turned around.

"Take turns, you know. Mom would do the heavy art stuff one year while Pop taught, that kinda thing."

"Yeah. It was Pop's turn to teach. He said he didn't mind this time, he didn't have much inspiration anyway."

"Well I dunno about that."

Mickey had uncovered the opposite wall, where rough-cut pieces of canvas had been tacked up, and there weren't no question it was Pop's work and not Mom's. The paints were thick and frantic, with none of the careful brush strokes of the beter half of the family's. Some of them canvases had to've used up whole tubes of paint, and they'd cracked in places where it'd been laid on too thick and the top had dried faster'n the bottom cause Pop hadn't been patient enough, hadn't taken his time and layered.

And every God damn one of 'em, had to be thirty-five or forty all told, was that God damn fucking sign of the Halloween man, that fucking brand, over and over all stylized and swirling, overlapping, receding, in yellow and black like bumblebees.

"Jesus Frank," Mickey said, "you gone pale as paper."

Frank nodded and told him the whole thing.

ooo000ooo

"Brother boy, you pardon my saying so, but it all sounds like a load of sound and fury to this fella," Mickey said, twisting the tab off each of the empty beer cans and dropping them in. "I mean, there's not a lot of, what do you call it."

"Sense?" Frank asked. Jessie had brought them down a six pack of Rio Grande beer, and they'd each just finished their third.

"That ain't what I mean. I mean even if -- no, I'm not saying I don't believe you, not on the facts, so let's say all the facts are true, right? You met that dude at Halloween and 'sold your soul' to him, some weird symbol showed up when Mom and Pop died, you saw it when the fam died, and you got a form says Ricky's not your son. All right. Those are the facts."

"And the paintings," Frank said, and Mickey just nodded. "Wait. You said it 'showed up' when Mom and Pop died, but I 'saw it' later. What're you getting at?"

Mickey shook his head, picked up a can like to drink and remembered it was empty. "Jess!" he called up the stairs. "We got another sixer?"

"I'm saying," he said, "maybe you associated the symbol with Mom and Pop dying, right, and so you saw it when Kriste and the kids died. I ain't saying that's anything out of the normal or nothing. It makes sense."

"All we got's the green chile!" Jessie called down, and Mickey made a face.

"That'll be fine! Love some limes too, babe! Thank ya and love ya!"

"Green chile beer?" Frank asked.

Mickey shrugged. "Jessie ain't over the novelty of New Mexico yet, she talks me into buying stuff like that sometimes. It don't taste like nothing you'd drink apurpose, but three beers in it won't be too bad."

"Yeah all right. So what you're saying is you don't think I'm crazy but you think I'm wrong."

Jessie brought the beer down with a little plate of chopped up limes and a bag of Fritos, and Mickey gave her a sitting-down side-hug before patting her ass. "Thanks a grand, Jess-dog."

"Much obliged, Jessica," Frank said, and she smiled and let them be without making a thing of it.

"I think you got the facts," Mickey said again. "Shit and shine, Frank, you're my brother, I'd know if you was crazy. You're still Frank, you ain't barking at the moon, and maybe you act a little peculiar sometimes but no more'n can be expected. What I'm saying is maybe your interpertation's off. You're taking as obvious a lotta stuff that don't seem necessary."

Frank snapped open one of the green chile beers, which smelled vaguely vegetal, and took a sip. Mickey was right, it wasn't too bad when they were three beers down anyway. But it tasted like a mistake, like you took a big sip of beer when you still had a spoonful of chile in your mouth, or someone'd knocked the hot sauce into the pitcher. "You ain't been there for it."

"Well, I'm here for it now." When Frank didn't say anything, Mickey went on, "Look, what's it mean anyway, you sold your soul? What you got to show for it? What you got missing cause of it? You think this guy's killing your family cause you sold him your soul? I think you ran into a nut on Halloween when you were half-drunk anyway, and maybe, yeah, maybe he's Ricky's biological father. Maybe that's why he was fucking with you, man."

"That don't explain the paintings," Frank said. "That don't explain Hank McCarty."

"Hank McCarty's an old man, a real old man, God knows how many cards he's got left in his deck. Damn, Frank, it seems to me you're just determined to blame things on something unreal like that, something you can't touch."

Frank flashed him a look, and Mickey grinned.

"There it is," he said quietly, leaning across the paint-spattered workbench. "There's that Frank. Look, you want to do something about this or you want to just wave your hands talking about selling your soul and all that? I mean, shit, you gonna blame the evil eye, you got no recourse. But if we're talking bout men, if we're talking about folks, if this Josh Marlowe guy's a problem ..."

79

"Yeah, he's a problem all right," Frank said, and found himself on beer five.

"Well there you go." Mickey stood up. "You know your problem, right? You're too much like Pop. He was only half-cowboy, the rest was artist. Too much thinking, too many ideas, too many abstracts. Me, I'm the oldest, right. I got the old blood, bro. I got the cowboy blood, like Grandpa, like Arthur Train motherfucking Senior."

"Uh huh." Frank was barely listening anymore. He felt down. Real down. Maybe it was the alcohol, maybe it was being surrounded by them paintings on all the walls, but all he wanted was to sit there drinking until he ran out of fuel and didn't have nothing left to think about.

"Frank!" Mickey said, and slapped the butt of a beer bottle down on the table. "Damn boy, let's go. Saddle up."

Frank stood up, a little unsteady, and nodded. "Where we going?"

"Well shit," Mickey said, grinning. "Thought you were on board. We're gonna go kick Josh Marlowe's ass, little brother."

CHAPTER ELEVEN

When they were kids, kicking someone's ass was a simpler proposition. They'd just go over to whatever hangout was the likeliest, kick something over, and go at it knuckles and shitkickers. But twenty-some years down the road, what was the first thing they did?

Checked the fucking phonebook.

Mickey shook his head to himself as they flipped through until they found MARLOWE J, residing at 108 Furthman Corner. "That's one of them new developments, ain't it," Mickey said.

"Yeah. Dinky Barela thought he could lure some of them Hollywood New York types up from Santa Fe or them artists down from Taos, built 'em a little community on a cul de sac."

"Did it work?"

Frank shook his head. "Not unless Josh Marlowe's a Hollywood New York type it didn't. I never heard a nobody else living out there. It's where Dinky's pop used to slop the hogs when he raised 'em."

The hogs had long since gone to bacon and chile, and the fields'd been churned up, squished around, mounded up and sodded to give the lawns some pretty curves, and paved over with an extra-wide street that'd have plenty of room for two of them SUVs to pass each other even if both of 'em had brand-new pimply teens at the wheel with their learning permits stuck in the visors.

Furthman wasn't far from Pond Drive, which made since seeing as how Frank'd run into Marlowe at the McGreavys. FOR SALE OR RENT signs dotted the street, and Frank and Mickey peered through the dark at the identical houses, looking for numbers. None of 'em was lit, and there weren't cars in any of the driveways neither.

"There we go," Mickey said finally, when the pickup had finished its crawl down Furthman to the last house on the left. "One oh eight."

"Don't look like nobody's home," Frank said, and Mickey got out of the passenger side, left the door open, jogged up to the front door and rapped his knuckles on the wood. When nobody answered, he waited and knocked again. Still nothing, and he came back to the truck.

"All right," he said. "So we wait."

"Ambush him?"

Mickey nodded, and lit a cigarette. "Man's gotta come home sometime."

They parked the truck behind 107, and waited in the back next to the coyote with the ragged ear, who huffled down half-slept with his head on Frank's leg and his paws X'ed together.

The adrenaline turned sour on Frank, made his sweat feel cold and his stomach twisted. It was one thing to follow an impulse and chase some beers with a rumble. It was another to wait in silence and the dark for the guy to get home, with nothing to do but keep still and quiet. Mickey seemed to feel the same. But now they were committed, they was on the train and they had to ride.

A pickup finally rambled up the road somewhere south of midnight, and Marlowe got out, his whistling of an old Jonathan King song audible just over the fade of the engine. Two other men followed him, a little wobbly like they'd all been to whiskers to whiskey, and Frank shot Mickey a look.

"That's him, right?" Mickey whispered. "Whistlin?"

Frank nodded, and his brother went charging across the lawns like a batter just got beaned by a pitch. Frank flinched. Didn't expect Mick to just leap into it like that. But fuck it, that was the way to roll, there was no point pussyfooting around with it.

So he ran after, and slammed one of Marlowe's pals in the jaw just as Mickey tackled Marlowe to the ground, the two of 'em landing in the gravel of the driveway with a crunch. Frank's hand hurt like a bitch, but he didn't take the time to worry on it or see who he was hitting, he just punched the other guy in the stomach, not soon enough to miss a clip to the shoulder.

Harder an' easier to fight more'n one fella at a time. On one hand, you had to keep movin'. On the other, you could keep moving, never really had to wait for an opening, you just went from one to the other and poked where you could, kicked what you had, and hoped you could take what you were gonna get in the process. Mosta the time when you're fighting two guys at once, it's not like you got a choice in it. You're making the best of the bad.

They'd been sitting long enough to sober up some, but Frank still felt sloppy, his hands winding up an inch east of where he'd aimed 'em, blows connecting with him that shouldn'ta, and when one of 'em got good hit in on his temple, he felt his teeth clatter and starbursts filled the sky as his head tilted back with the force of it.

"You like that?" Mickey was shouting at Marlowe, the two of them still down on the ground. Mickey was grinding the fucker's face into the gravel, a vicious move even for a Train. "You like fucking other men's wives there, Marlowe?"

Oh for Christ's sake, Mickey, Frank thought. You didn't have to fucking broadcast it.

And then he fell down, and one guy grabbed Mickey by the back of the shirt to try to pull him off Marlowe, while the other just kicked Frank in the ribs, the shins, the balls. Frank grabbed his foot with both hands, needing two tries, the first cracking a little finger and maybe breaking it, and twisted hard, yanking the guy off his balance.

They were all in the dirt 'fore long, punching and kneeing and kicking gravel aside like a buncha damn kids, until them flashing lights came up from behind and somebody shouted. Frank realized he couldn't hardly hear 'em, make 'em out, and when he held a hand to his ear, it touched hot wet flesh that made him recoil and grunt. He'd taken a mighty hit there, enough for blood to clog his ear.

Wasn't much he could do, when Lobo and the boys hauled the five of 'em off. All he wanted to do was sleep.

ooo000ooo

A paramedic tended him up, and he fell asleep in the cell while Mickey was on the phone with Jessie. They'd passed Ricky when they were being dragged in, but thank God the boy was asleep.

Neither Marlowe nor his boys had been charged with nothing on account of it being Marlowe's house and all, something Mickey bitched about soon as Frank woke up in the mornin'. They had to wait on the judge to wake up to set bail, which was Lobo's way of keeping 'em in the cell all night to cool off. For just fighting, chances were pretty good they'd be let off with a fine.

He woke up with Mickey looking at him from the bunk across the cell. Frank hated that. When they were kids, sometimes Mick'd come into his room and just sit there in a chair, watching him until he woke up. He'd never been able to explain why it bugged him so much, so Mickey'd never stopped doing it.

"Christ and the passion," Frank said, rubbing his temples. His head hurt like a hangover, and his hair felt greasy. He wasn't cleaned up too good, and a scab had crusted on his scalp, feeling brittle and dirty when his fingertips passed it. "What do you want, Mickey?"

"Bail'll be set pretty soon, and then Jessie'll have us outta here," Mickey said. "She brought Ricky to school."

"Fuck," Frank said, and untwisted the sheets from his feet, sat up in the cot. "I was hoping to be outta here in time to do that."

"So you wouldn't have to tell him, huh?"

"Yeah. Don't look too good spending the night in prison when I got him in here as punishment, right?"

Mickey shook his head. "Looks pretty shitty, you wanna know the truth."

"Goddammit, Mick. This was all your idea to begin with."

Mickey shrugged. "More the beer's idea. Look, we tussled, we got a night in the cooler, it happens. Ricky gotta figure shit like that out eventually. You don't want him growing up to be a pussy like Newt. Who the fuck names a kid Newt anyway?"

"Short for Newton," Frank mumbled. "And he's a math teacher, not a pussy."

"A pussy math teacher. And he used to do gymnastics."

"Jesus, whatever. We gonna get any coffee in here or what?"

"Hey BeckYYY!" Mickey shouted down the hall. "I'll make you my third wife if you could get us some coffee and donuts up in this bitch!"

"Hold your pecker!" Becky shouted back, but before long there she was, with a steaming thermos of coffee and the donut box, which still had a jelly and two lemons in it. "Y'all know I ain't supposed to give you no hot coffee, right?"

"What?" Frank asked.

"County law. You could, I don't know, throw it in my face or something. Like use it as a weapon."

"We ain't gone throw no coffee at you, Becky," Mickey said patiently. He'd always talked to her like she was a little dim, Frank thought. She was plain-faced, rough, but he doubted she was stupid too.

"Your call, Becky," Frank said. "I'd just like to widen my eyes a bit is all."

"Yeah, it's fine, Frank," she said, opening the door and handing the breakfast over. "I was just pointing it out, is all."

When she'd left and Frank had taken both the lemons in exchange for letting Mickey have the jelly, he asked, "'Up in this bitch'?"

"You know," Mickey said, wiping powdered sugar off his mouth. "Li'l Jon. Where the thugs at up in this bitch."

Frank shook his head and sipped at the hot coffee gingerly, the tip of his tongue taking the burn. "Only Little John I know's that cartoon bear."

"Anyway, I wanted to talk to you."

"Yeah," Frank said, sighing as he leaned back on the wall behind the cot awkwardly. It canted him at an awkward angle, lifting his feet off the ground without giving him the room to stretch his legs out. "I got that, with you steel-eyeing me in my sleep."

"What the fuck was with you last night, man?"

"What? It was your idea to go nail Marlowe."

"No, Frankie. I mean where _were_ you? Shit, nobody walks away from Frank Train in a fight unless they're limping or fresh off an apology. You know that. You _know_ that. You think I'd be stupid enough to say hey let's go kick his ass, if I thought you was gonna phone it in like that? You fought like a fucking housewife."

"Oh, for Christ's sake," Frank said, irritated. "And who was it gave you a hand the other week at the Harvey?"

"Well that's what I'm saying, Frankie. It ain't that you can't fight, it ain't that we're too old now. It's that you didn't last night. If you were a pussy, I wouldn't give you shit about it, cause you're my little brother, and if my little brother wants to be a pussy, that's his God damn given right and as far as I figure he's the best pussy on planet Earth. But you ain't a pussy. So when you act one, damn, I gotta squawk." Mickey fished for a bedraggled pack of cigarettes in his pocket, and flipped one to Frank after lighting his own.

Frank caught the lighter, pulled fire off it, and tossed it back. "Yeah, gee, I appreciate it."

They smoked in silence, until Mickey shook his head. "Naw man, we can't leave it there. This ain't a little thing. You ain't acting, I don't know, up to snuff. Like you've gone hollow. Like you ain't a hundred percent paying attention. The hell's on your mind? Where are you, little brother?"

Frank shrugged. "Told you. All this with Marlowe and all."

Mickey rubbed the filter of his cigarette with the ball of his thumb, thinking in frowns. "I dunno, man. I just, other than being pissed at a couple of things here and there, I ain't seen you passionate about much of anything in a long while?"

"We all get older, Mickadoo. We all get grey after enough washes."

"I guess having kids'll do that to you. Marrying down, having kids, getting a real job, then losing most of that? Yeah, I guess that'll wash anyone out."

"Uh huh," Frank said, and stamped his cigarette out on the stone floor. He could hear talking out in the hall, Becks on the phone with somebody or other.

"Goddammit, man!" Mickey said, and Frank realized he wasn't just making conversation, he was really upset, concerned. "It's like you're sleepwalkin'! Snap outta it!"

Before Frank could snap one way or the other, Becky came back with Jessie at her arm, and unlocked the door. "All right, Trains," she said. "You boys is all good now, your lady here paid the fine."

"No court appearance or nothing?" Mickey asked, scooting by everyone like he'd just farted up the cell and was anxious to get upwind.

"Naw, Lobo put a word in with Judge Stone. It's all good now."

"I appreciate it, Becky," Frank said, before giving Jessie a smile. "And Jessica, for taking Ricky to school today, too, that was handy of you."

"Yeah," Jessie said, looking tired. "Well, I'm nothing if not handy. Don't sweat it, Frank. I told him you'd explain it all to him when you picked him up this afternoon."

ooo000ooo

When Frank picked Ricky up, he took the long way home cause he remembered his own teen years well enough to know that when they got home, the boy would either leave or lock himself in his room, so any conversating to be done was gonna have to be in the pickup.

"So I guess you know I didn't have the best night of it," Frank said. He wanted a cigarette and hated that he was letting the habit develop. He wouldn't mind a drink, either, and a big greasy cheeseburger like the one he had at lunch, the Gutpuncher with a half-inch slab of pepperjack between two patties slathered in green chile mayo, bun gooey with nacho cheese. God damn God damn.

"Yeah," Ricky said. "I heard you got your ass whupped, is what I heard."

Frank eyed him. "Your Aunt Jessica tell you that?"

"Word around, is all."

"Around where?"

Ricky paused before saying, "School," and Frank wondered if the kid had actually skipped again, gone out the back when Jessie dropped him off. "Yeah, well, I fuc -- I screwed up, that's what I did. Your Uncle Mickey and I had too much to drink, got into a tussle. It happens. Men, it's what we do sometimes, we tussle."

"Yeah," Ricky said. "I know." His voice was flat but contemptuous, and maybe that was his age, maybe it wasn't.

"Well, I did my overnight for it and, you know, paid a fine. That's my beer money for a while." It was more than that. He'd be dipping into the savings if he wanted to pay Mickey and Jessie back. "So it's not like, it's not one of those things where you get in trouble and I get away with something."

Ricky rolled his eyes at him and crossed his arms belligerently. "I don't care about that. I'm embarrassed."

"What?" He forgot, before all this recent acting out, the boy had been quiet, sensitive. "Son, men fight sometimes, that's all, I'm sorry to --"

"You got your ass kicked by the art teacher. I mean God. That's so pathetic. It's not like he's a trucker or something, a tough guy."

"What're you talking about?"

"Mr Marlowe, Pop. The new art teacher?"

Frank took the next turn too sharply, didn't slow down enough. "The new art teacher? But --" But your grandparents were the art teachers, he was going to say. But of course they would have been replaced by now. Probably called in Mrs Wieringo to substitute until the Christmas break, while they found someone. "Well anyway, it wasn't him. It was his friends."

"Yeah?" Ricky said, mildly interested now. "More than one?"

"Uh huh. It was your Uncle Mickey got his ass handed to him by Mr Marlowe. I was going for his two buddies."

Ricky mulled this over for a moment and smiled just a little. "Well that's different, I guess. Poor Uncle Mick."

"Uh huh."

They were almost home, and both asked a question like it was just coming to them or they'd been waiting for the chance.

"Why were you fighting with Mr Marlowe, anyway?" Ricky asked, just as Frank asked, "Do you know Mr Marlowe, then?" What he really meant was <u>Did Marlowe visit you in the hospital,</u> but they never talked about Ricky's hospital stay, about his missing the funeral. The boy hadn't even been to his family's graves, as far as Frank knew.

"It was just grown-up stuff," Frank said after they'd both stopped to see who was going to talk first. "We got some issues to work out, me and him. And that's the thing about drinking, Ricky. Everything in your life that's giving you friction, it can rear up at you when you had too many."

Ricky's arms stayed folded, like that wasn't enough, and Frank repeated his question.

"Yeah," Ricky said. "Course I know him, he's the art teacher. He's not as good as Grandma, but I guess he's as good as Grandpa."

They pulled into the driveway, and like Frank'd predicted, Ricky headed straight to his room. "Hey," Frank called after him, "did Marlowe ever visit you in the hospital?"

He waited for an answer and didn't get one. Five, six minutes later, Ricky came back out in different clothes, ripped socks on his hands serving as fingerless gloves, chains around his wrists and dangling from the belt loops of expensive jeans Frank didn't remember anyone buying him. "Going out," he said.

"Back for dinner," Frank said, and when Ricky didn't answer, he said, "I mean it. Seven sharp, kiddo. You're on probation."

"Yeah all right," Ricky said, glancing at his watch like he wanted to make sure it fit his schedule. "Yeah, don't worry about it, serious. Like I'm gonna pass up a free meal?" He grinned, looking three years younger, and Frank smiled.

When the boy had left, Frank sat down at the table and opened a beer, knowing he'd have to pace them out, not to mention do his drinking at home where he wasn't paying bar markup. He thought about all the things he shoulda said to the kid, all the stuff he shoulda asked. Shoulda asked him how the fuck jail felt for three days, whether he'd learned his lesson, shoulda given him the whole "well, you've had your punishment, let's hash it out" speech like Pop would've given him. Shoulda asked him where the fuck he went these days and what the fuck was wrong with him.

Shoulda asked him again, asked him sooner, asked him louder, about Josh Marlowe.

But it all just went so quick. He'd had all those things in mind, but when he actually talked to the boy, none of it came out, and the next he knew, the kid was gone, like Frank didn't have no control over him at all.

Damn did the beer taste good.

CHAPTER TWELVE

Everything was quiet that afternoon for miles around the Train house at 1332 Borachon Creek Road, quiet enough that when the wind swushed one way, Frank could hear the Creek twitching through the scrub brush, and when it swushed the other, he could hear ESPN's broadcast on the Prescotts' teevee next door. Once a while he caught a dog barking or someone raising their voice in the MacKenzies' house next door th'other way.

It was a nice day, and the breeze brought the smells of wildflowers along the Creek, mesquite blooming who knows where, them cheeseburgers they cooked uproad and the greens the Prescott's visiting grandmother had brewing in that big mismatched kitchen, woodsmoke from somebody's house who had a chill on their bones, and a faint whiff of pot that was probably the MacKenzie kid and his friends out behind their chicken coop where Dirt Callister had used to grow arbor grapes.

It was spring, and on a day like that you felt like you could smell the whole state, the whole Southwest, not cause it stunk but cause it travelled, them mesquites, them cactuses and nobody said cacti unless they were just visiting, them creek fish and river trout caught by coy-otes with their bones left to rot in a copse of wild cotton. Out from the farms you could smell the corn shouldering up outta the soil and the shoots a garlic that were still green enough you could put 'em right onto your salad, not have to peel the bulbs or nothing. Maybe there were kids still smoked corn silk stuffed into pipes they found in attics or flea markets, or maybe they were all smoking pot rolled into cheap Mexican cigars now.

The world had moved on.

He had nothing to do and too much to do. He coulda gone out to lend a hand at the Wilatas, where they'd been having problems with javelinas that Old Man Wilata hinted darkly were the work of sorcerers hired on by the Rodriguezes, sorcerers an' maybe even skinwalkers like the old Jensen clan back when things were different. He coulda gone south of Borachon Creek and done his errands out there, but it seemed like too much driving to be back for dinner. He coulda mowed the few lawns on Church On Fire Road, and fixed that halogen night-light he'd promised to get to this week.

But he just plain didn't feel like leaving the house, and besides, he'd puttered through the day and skipped lunch while killing time until it was time to pick up Ricky.

So he puttered through the afternoon, working the garden on the roof. This was his first year handling it himself. Mickey had said he should just nevermind it, but Kriste'd kept the garden up every year, and it didn't seem sensible to let it die. He kept his ambitions slim so he had less to fuck up, but was planting multiple things, too, so if he fucked one up, there'd be eggs in another basket.

So as soon as the weather had turned its back on winter, he'd planted kale and onions in the soil on that roof, all rich from having dumped sheep shit and compost on it for months. Now that it was late enough any chance a frost had passed, it was time to plant the carrots and beets, getting em down good into the soil. The peanuts, chiles, and the two Crenshaw melon plants he'd decided on would have to wait a little longer, for a little warmer weather. Them peanuts excited him, even though he figured it wouldn't be many nuts. Growing his own peanuts, Kriste'd never thoughta that.

"Yeah," a voice said from below, "but they ain't gonna come up roasted."

From where Frank stood in the middle of the roof, weeding the kale and wondering if he shoulda weeded it before watering instead of the other way around, he couldn't see mucha the driveway. But he was pretty sure he knew the voice, and walking to the side and peering down sealed it.

"Marlowe. Mister Marlowe, I oughta say. Ricky says you're the new art teacher."

"Uh huh." Marlowe was wearing that Mexican suit of his again, tie-less with the collar and jacket unbuttoned, his hands in his pockets as the spring breeze mussed his hair. He looked like Harry Dean Stanton in Paris Texas.

"You're asking about my peanuts?"

"Yeah. They're best roasted, you know, especially with a little butter? That's why folks don't grow their own. Less you're looking at having 'em boiled."

"Didn't realize I'd been talking to myself."

"You weren't. I saw the shoots."

"Ain't no shoots." Frank paused, narrowed his eyes at the man on the ground. "Ain't been planted yet."

Marlowe shuffled his hands in his pockets like a shrug. "Guess I saw something else, then."

Neither man said nothing as Frank wondered if the Halloween man could read his mind, which wasn't no more unlikely than him causing car accidents and buying up souls, but somehow more disturbing since Marlowe didn't know he'd read his mind.

Yeah, that was an April chill on the old bones, right there.

"So how'd you get that gig, anyway?" Frank asked him, and after a moment added, "Being the art teacher."

"Well," Marlowe said stoically, "There was an opening." He paused too before adding, "I happened to be around. Ain't a bad line, teaching kids about perspective, vanishing points, shadows."

"Uh huh. That what you do, then?" Frank brushed soil off his gloved hands, shoved the trimmers into a loop on his belt. He hadn't seen his pistol since the tussle, figured either Lobo'd confiscated it or Jessie'd claimed it for him and hadn't given it back. Maybe by accident, maybe not. "You an art teacher, Mr Halloween Man?"

Marlowe cracked an eyebrow, then shrugged again. "Right now I am. You know how it is, I walk around. Sometimes I do one thing. Sometimes I do another. Ain't much different from you."

"So what kinda work you done before, then?"

"Worked oil," Marlowe said, thumbing a dry spot on his lip. "Wildcatting in East Texas. I been a fry cook, a long-haul trucker, caretook an amusement park. That ain't the least of it. Used to sell lightning rods to the Furies in Illinois. Used to train wolves in Carcosa. Used to be a rainmaker south of the Hyades. When I was hungry, I ate. When I was thirsty, I drank. When I was a stranger, I invited myself in. Where you want me to stop, Frank? How much you think you need to know?"

"More'n that," Frank said, and Marlowe drew a gun. Frank's Colt Defender.

"Catch, you untrusting son of a bitch." Marlowe tossed it up at him underhand, and the gun twirled in the sky as it made its hook into Frank's hands. He just nodded and stuck it in the back of his waistband. "You left that at my place last night," Marlowe said. "Were you planning on shooting me there, sport? Getcher big brother to soften me up and then bang one in the back of my head, was that the plan?"

"Wasn't no plan at all," Frank said, and he sounded petulant to himself. "Didn't plan nothing, is what I'm saying, just showed up. Wasn't gonna shoot you. No need to run off to Lobo again or nothing."

"Oh, you think I called Lobo?" Marlowe asked with a smile. "When? While your brother was kneeing my kidneys? What'd I do, draw my cell phone out and ring the old boy up, old pudgy Coby Davenant?"

"Hell of a coincidence him showing up just in time to save your ass."

"Yeah," Marlowe said. "I guess it would be." He shook his head to himself, pulled at the tip of his nose with his thumb and first two fingers, then scratched his neck under the shirt collar, like the suit was itching him, wincing like he was sore. He didn't look too beat up, though. "Came by to ask what the hell you were trying to do last night, old man."

Frank spat over the edge of the roof. "Whup your ass," he said. "Figured that was obvious."

"For <u>what</u>?" Marlowe asked. "Pick on the new guy in town?"

"You know for what."

"So this is about your wife still," Marlowe said. "I thought I caught something like that outta your brother before he started ringing my bell."

Frank shook his head slowly, then stopped, and sat down on the edge of the roof, feet dangling over the edge by the windows of Gina's bedroom. He had to take the clippers off his belt to sit, to keep 'em from poking him in the small of the back, and tapped them against his thigh as he watched Marlowe. "Why don't you tell me 'bout all that? Figure it's the least you owe me."

"You got a cigarette?" Marlowe asked. "You wanna come down from there?"

"Reckon I'm fine here, but I got smokes." He tossed down his pack, but hesitated to throw the lighter down.

"S'all right," Marlowe said. "I got my own fire." He flicked a girly-pink Bic fished from the breast pocket of the suit jacket, and got the smoke going. "Whaddaya wanna know, old pup? You want to know am I the one got Kriste pregnant? Without a blood test, I guess we'll never know for sure. But I'm eligible. Put it that way."

"How'd it happen?" Frank asked.

Marlowe rolled his eyes, an expression that made his ordinarily ageless face look old and weary. "Son, when a man and a woman love each other very much --"

"So you loved her?" he asked. He knew he was acting like a child, but it didn't make sense not to ask. Knowing these things couldn't hurt anyone.

"I always love them." Marlowe licked his lips. "Don't you? When you're inside someone, how can you not love them then? And however you feel about them later, or before, it's in the shadow of that."

"Did you love her before that? How long did you know her? How many times?"

Marlowe rubbed his lower lip with the butt of the cigarette. "You're getting agitated, old pup. You're not really being fair to her."

Frank tightened his grip on the clippers. "You're no one for telling me how to talk about my wife, Marlowe. Either you're answering my questions or you aren't, but I'm not playing picksies-choosies."

"Fine. Yes, I loved her before that, but I love easily, Frank. I didn't know her well, nor for long." Marlowe narrowed his eyes as he pulled a long drag off the cigarette, as though it were taking a real huff outta him. "Six, maybe seven times over the course of a week I guess. You oughta be able to do the math, figure out when that was."

He already had, months ago. He'd taken that job in Socorro, been gone a little over a week. Ricky was conceived either right before or right after the trip, he'd always figured, and Kriste'd never given him reason to think otherwise, never nurtured a glimpse of suspicion. "I guess I know."

"She loved you, Frank. Whatever else, that weren't a lie. If she didn't love you, there wouldna been no me an' her."

"I don't need you telling me how my wife felt about me, neither," Frank said, although he realized he'd all but asked it. "What brings you to say it?"

Marlowe looked around like he was expecting someone, or had to be somewhere. "Y'ever wonder why she married you, pup? I mean every man does. But you ever work it out? You were the bad boy. And the good boy."

"Yeah, that's what she used to say."

"You were the guy she woulda cheated with, if she hadn't married you. You know how it is. She wanted that excitement all the time, even when she didn't have the energy for it, didn't have the engine for it, she wanted a life where she woulda. Marrying the bad boy, that was as close as she could figure to get, cause she wanted kids, too, wanted a house and a fence."

"Ain't no need for a fence on Borachon Creek Road," Frank said, and Marlowe waved a hand.

"So she got a rooftop garden 'steada a fence, big fucking whoop. You gave her what she wanted, Frank, what she asked for, what she needed, and damn straight what she prayed for. Don't you do her wrong by thinking otherwise. Don't you make her somebody else. Me?" Marlowe stubbed the cigarette out with the toe of his boot. "Me and her fucked so she'd feel dirty enough to recharge her love for you, pal o' mine-o. Simple as sin. Ricky was just, you know, a reminder. A bonus. She loved you for loving him even though you didn't know you had any reason not to."

Frank didn't say anything for a long time, and when he was about to, when he'd worked up some fucking speech like back in the wayback when he woulda bid his time out in some cluster of teenage cars and then deliver a pronouncement from a haze of smoke, when he was gonna say Thanks for saving my marriage, then, Ricky showed up.

The boy was visible long before he was in earshot, so there was no worry of his having heard anything. Frank glanced at his watch and saw that it was just after seven, but not long after, and besides, he didn't have dinner ready, something Ricky'd be sure to comment on after Frank's insisting he be home in time. Frank stood up, making sure the pistol wasn't visible.

"You know where I live," Marlowe said quietly, his lips barely moving, "if you want to talk more. Just knock next time, old man."

"Hey," Ricky said as he got to the driveway, looking nonchalant. He'd had plenty of time to see who was at his house and cover up any reaction to it. "What, you here to beat up my dad now? Gonna need your friends for that, aren'tcha?"

"Ricky," Frank said warningly, but a thrill sank into him when he saw that Ricky had picked his side. If there were sides.

"Don't fuss at the boy," Marlowe said. "We're family, ain't we."

"Yeah," Ricky said, and tossed Frank a questioning look. "That's what he said when he stopped by the hospital, when I was, after I got hurt."

Frank didn't say anything, and both the boy and Marlowe were waiting for him to.

"I told him I was his godfather," Marlowe said to fill the silence. "Makes me half-responsible, I reckon, what with Kriste being gone."

Ricky nodded sullenly.

"Godfather," Frank repeated.

"Tends to be my way," Marlowe said with an easy toothy smile. "Always a godfather, never a --"

"Father?" Ricky asked.

"If you like," Marlowe said, and clacked his teeth together, pulling on his nose again. "Where you been, Ricky? Your pop know what you been up to yet?"

Ricky looked stricken, and glanced from Marlowe to Frank, maybe wondering, even assuming, in that teenage narcissistic way, if they'd been talking about him. "I've been out, I told him. He said be home for dinner, I'm home for dinner. Hey Pop, what's for dinner?"

"I thought we'd go out," Frank said. "That cool with you? You know, some guy time." It wasn't the best choice of phrases. "Guy time" had been this unofficial thing with the two of them in the last couple years, going out for a couple of burgers or pizza when the girls and Philip stayed home. But without anyone to stay home, well, it wasn't the same.

"I guess," Ricky said, and he hadn't really looked away from Marlowe yet, like he was weighing things out, vacillating between who he was acting for, his pop or his teacher. "You been fighting or anything?"

"Ricky," Frank said.

"Hey, I just wanna know, am I gonna have to have my dad go to jail again or anything, you know." The kid stood up a little straighter, pushed his shoulders back.

"More like we were straightening some things out," Marlowe said as he walked away from the house a little, putting Ricky between him and Frank. "There's a time for fighting, Rick. Don't tell your principal I said so, but there's no getting around it. There's a time for talking, too, though, and doing one --" He eyed Frank. "Doing one doesn't mean you gotta be done with the other. A time to reap, and a time to sow."

"Ecclesiastes said that," Ricky said. "A time to kill and a time to heal, a time to tear down and a time to build."

"It's a book in the Bible," Frank said. "And a song by the Byrds. But Ecclesiastes is the name of the book, not a guy. Not like some Greek philosopher or something, Socrates, Euripides, Ecclesiastes." He grinned but immediately saw he'd stressed the point too much and Ricky thought he was making fun of him.

"'I have seen the burden God has laid on men,'" Marlowe quoted, and patted Ricky on the shoulders from behind, looking up at Frank. "'He has made everything beautiful in its time. There is nothing better for men than to be happy and do good while they live. That everyone may eat and drink and find satisfaction, this is the gift of God.' Solomon wrote it, is what I heard."

"Yeah, I hearda Solomon," Ricky said. "He wrote the dirty part of the Bible, too."

"He was a wise man, Solomon. The son of David, Israel's greatest and most flawed king. Ain't that always the way of it? It's the great who have such deep shadows. But what salvation it musta been for David to look upon his son, this genius, this artist-philosopher who wrote some of the most beautiful words in the language. Some day you'll know what that's like, Rick -- it's a wonderful thing to be a father, to see what you've made and what it does once it's out of your control." He nodded to Frank. "Ain't that right, Mr Train?"

"Reckon so," Frank said. "It may have its trials, but they don't make it any less a thing."

"Venture to say they make it better," Marlowe said, and patted Ricky's shoulder again. "You got a lot of your father in you, Rick. A lot."

"More of his mother," Frank said. "He was always hers."

Ricky made a face at the first man and then the second, like he didn't know what was worse, being compared to Frank or having Frank deny the comparison. "I dunno, I guess I don't really want to be a handyman."

"Oh, Rick!" Marlowe said. "You don't think that's all there is to Frank Train, I hope. No, your father was a legend 'round these parts and still is in some, I'd reckon. A real terror to the menfolk and a pleasure for the ladies. They still talk about him, some of 'em."

The boy just shrugged. "Well, that don't sound like me either."

"I dunno," Marlowe said. "Seems to be you're working your way up to it."

Ricky turned around to look at him. "Hey, look, we don't need to --"

"You haven't told him, have you, boy?" Marlowe asked, and his voice sounded darker now, disapproving.

"Told me what?" Frank asked.

"Frank, our man Rick here has been spending his time down at the cockfights."

"What?"

"Aw damn it, Mr Marlowe," Ricky said.

"He missed a coupla my classes," Marlowe continued. "And when I found out why, I told him I'd give him some time to tell you, but I guess he's been dragging his feet on that one."

"Ricky," Frank said. "Goddammit, boy. You know how I feel about that shit. That's cruel shit they do down there, that ain't right. And the kinda people neither."

"It ain't like I'm killing them birds!" Ricky said. "I'm just watchin'. Making a little money. Mostly just hanging out. Damn, ain't like you're a stranger there, what I heard. What I heard, you used to be down there alla time."

"That was before," Frank said angrily. "That was before I met your mother, goddammit, and if she didn't want me down there she for damn sure wouldn't want you!"

"Well maybe she didn't want me," Ricky yelled, "but it doesn't matter now that she's dead!"

"Oh for fuck's sake," Frank said, but the boy was already storming inside, slamming the door behind him. Two more slams followed a moment later: his bedroom door, first open then closed.

Neither man spoke for a moment, and Marlowe broke the silence. "Leave him be for a few minutes, and then go in there and tell him it's time for dinner. Tell him where you're taking him, go, buy him dessert, and don't say anything about anything unless he talks first. He's caught between feeling ashamed over being caught and feeling confrontational cause he don't wanna recognize you got any right to make him feel that shame."

"Don't tell me how to father my boy," Frank said. "I think it's time for you to go."

Marlowe nodded, but didn't leave yet, and lit another cigarette. "Look, Frank. You want to know the truth, I'm good at pretty much everything for a little bit. It's just my interest goes away 'fore long and I wander off to do something else. But I still know my shit. We ain't too different in that respect."

"Yeah, how you figure that?"

"No matter what I do, no matter what I work at, art, language, sorcery, all my labors, it's destruction I'm best at. It's a killer I wind up. Reckon it's the same with you once you run outta rooftops."

"It's time for you to go home, Marlowe. Time for me to talk to my boy."

"Yep. I reckon." Marlowe walked backwards to the road, and stamped the cigarette out. "Ecclesiastes is my favorite book of the Bible, Frank, you want to know the truth. Ecclesiastes 12.

"Remember now thy Creator in the days of thy youth, while the evil days come not, nor the years draw nigh when thou shalt say, 'I have no pleasure in them.' While the sun or the light or the moon or the stars be not darkened, nor the clouds return after the rain. Then shall the dust return to the earth as it was: and the spirit shall return unto God who gave it.

"Let us hear the conclusion of the whole matter: Fear God, for this is the whole duty of man. For God shall bring every work into judgment, with every secret thing, whether it be good or it be evil."

"The whole duty of man, huh?" Frank asked, and had to raise his voice to more than casual to be sure Marlowe could hear him.

The Halloween man shook himself and pulled at his nose before smiling sadly. "That's it, old pup. That's how fucking easy the whole thing is."

Everything was quiet that night around the Train house at 1332 Borachon Creek. Frank took Ricky to a new pizza place in Lonely, a place opened by the son of a Santa Fe restaurant family. They sold green chile cheeseburger pizza that was a little too mild, and nuggets of fried smoked jack cheese, with a crunchy cornmeal batter like hushpuppies and a sweet chipotle sauce to dip 'em in. Frank passed on the beer and didn't offer Ricky any, although they both read the special drinks menu out loud, chuckling at the "prickly pear martini garnished with a fresh lychee" and the "rodeo margaritas," which were rimmed with tangy salt and served in novelty glasses shaped like upside-down sombreros. Another memory hit him, taking Gina out for her first drink when she turned 21. She got all dressed up like it was Christmas, and they drove to Santa Fe so she could get her drink at the nicest restaurant any of them could think of. Ricky and Philip put their little suits on, Philip tearing the tie off by the time they got to Santa Fe but Ricky suffering manfully through it. She ordered a "cowboy martini," which was just a margarita with a stuffed jalapeno, and put the cocktail napkin in her pocketbook as a keepsake. The memory was as vivid as his understanding that it hadn't happened, that Gina had died before she turned 21, that she'd never have that first legal drink. He knew that but could remember it anyway, the things they talked about, the tension because her boyfriend wasn't there and they were a few weeks out from a breakup.

Other than reading the menu, neither of 'em said a thing until midway through dessert, when Ricky looked up from the plate of churros he was dipping in pinon-chile fudge sauce and said, "These are better'n

Mom's."

"Yeah," Frank said. "I wasn't gonna say so, but damn, they're pretty good."

"It's the spiciness, right? It's not spicy spicy, but like the way ginger beer is spicy."

"Or cinnamon Red Hots. Yeah, spicy but still sweet. That's the main difference, that spice. Pizza was better'n hers, too."

Ricky rolled his eyes. "Mom never makes, never made pizza. She heats up Totino's."

"No shit, sherlock, that's why it's better here."

Ricky grinned. "'No shit, sherlock.' You're like a twelve year old."

"You're a twelve year old."

"You're a twelve year old girl."

It was a nice night out, and on the way home the breeze through the open car windows brought the smells of woodsmoke from somebody's house who had a chill on their bones, and the stench of skunky pot a few houses up from the MacKenzies', where that fool kid and his twice-pregnant fool wife lived off her mother's life insurance. They talked a bit about how all the candy bars and sodas came in more flavors now, and how many things were different since Ricky was a little kid, and maybe one of these days they'd have to get TiVo cause it was getting hard to keep track of which shows were on, and maybe they should check out Deadwood next time they were at Mickey and Jessie's.

The world moved on.

CHAPTER THIRTEEN

The cockfights were done at the fairgrounds these days, down past the Barela place towards the Cardenio Pueblo. Nothing else went on at the fairgrounds anymore 'cept two rodeos, the Fourth of July one and the April one coming up this weekend, and it was that rodeo that got Frank to head down right away to talk to folks about his boy. He'd put it off otherwise, and the weekend would roll on and he'd figure there was no doing it during the rodeo when he didn't know where to find folks, and then too much time woulda passed and he'd chalk it up to shrugs.

You wanted something done right, you hadda do it straight-on.

From the outside, you wouldna guessed there was anything going on at the fairgrounds, even with the rodeo coming up. Everyone parked in the back lot, which you couldn't see from the road, and the place was a mess. Old rusted-down beer cans littered the ground outside, and broken green glass that'd been heeled into grit by heavy boots. Any other barren but useful place like this, you'd reckon it'd be a hangout for kids smoking pot, but here the smells were of cheap warm beer, blood, and that fishy smell of frying oil that's due for a change. He was probably imagining the blood but it still made him grimace. You got used to it eventually, the way you did your own stink.

It was the warm-up arena where they did the cockfights, Frank'd guessed, and he judged the guess right when he saw the two guys hanging around the entrance smoking cigarettes. There were a buncha stubbed-out butts around their feet, and a few fresher bottles of beer. They'd been there longer'n hanging out. Nobody he knew, Mexicans from somewhere around.

"Hey," he said as he walked up. "What's the cover?"

"No cover on the weekdays," the guy on the left said. "Don't expect a lot of excitement today."

"All right," Frank said, and handed him a five anyway. "I can get by that."

"Hey man," guy on the right said. "You need pussy or anything, man?"

Frank palmed him a five too. "Not looking for it today, but I'll

99

remember you if I do."

"Cool man."

It always paid to be friendly with the door, and to show 'em respect.

And if I really wanted --

He shook his head in surprise at himself. Maybe he was technically single now -- it was the first time since Kriste's death that he'd thoughta himself as anything but married -- but the last thing he needed was cockfight pussy.

Inside were the betting booths, right next to the NO GAMBLIN NO MINORS NO CHAW hand-painted signs, and the vendors selling rodeo food. Chicken wings, pizza sitting under heat lamps, corn dogs and Frito pies, plenty of onion rings and French fries, but the smell of that broke-down oil made his stomach flop. Judging by the amount of food sitting there untouched, he wasn't the only one, although plenty a people had been at the beer that came in two kinds, medium and large. It slicked the concrete flooring, even though it was only just lunchtime.

Beyond the betting booths were the girls, some of em whores, some of em not, some of em open to possibility. At another booth, someone was selling gamecock paraphernalia for anyone raising their own: penicillin, vitamin feed, knives and gaffs, back issues of Grit & Steel magazine, cheap squarebound books about raising cocks, political polemics on civil rights and how they were being taken away in mosta the resta the country where cockfights were illegal. All this stuff was portable, set up and packed off faster'n a flea market table.

Mosta the bets, though, were just informal, nobody setting odds, nobody setting minimums, just "who'll take fifty on blue" and "I got two hundred says green wins." There were guys who worked these crowds for a living, just taking bets, getting a sense for when to pass and when to offer, and usually they had a hand in the drugs or women.

A fight'd just started, bringing the crowd into the hexagon of bleachers surrounding the makeshift pit. Just the one pit today, a fuller crowd woulda had three going, even five if the money was really flowin'. Frank scanned the faces, looking for somebody he recognized or who'd recognize him. Small crowd today, being as how it was a weekday, but there were still folks from Colorado, Texas, even a pair of Nebraska license plates in the parking lot that had probably come together. But there were locals too, even a few who were here on their lunch break, just long enough for a fight or two.

Gamecocks weren't like regular chickens. Hell, even a turkey wasn't much different from a big chicken. But a gamecock was built different. Its body was heavier, like an owl or something, and its tailfeathers were big and fluffy. It leaned forward a little more like it was always on the lunge, and its legs were thick and strong, with a bony spur that came outta the back of its leg by the foot. Normally the spurs were naturally sharp, like thorns. Cockers would blunt 'em down though and attach a weapon there instead mosta the time, a knife or gaff.

There was such a thing as naked heel fights, no knife or gaff, but they went on for hours and could end with one a the cocks dying a sheer exhaustion. Not the kinda thing for a midweek lunch.

These two were knife-fighters. Cockfights weren't like boxing, you just got matched up at random according to weight and weapon, and one a the cocks was "blue," the other "green." They were naturally aggressive, these birds, like genetically. The smell of another gamecock would just drive 'em batshit. The two cocks jumped at each other, wings flapping like dying bats, legs clawing like panicking cats. Feathers stained with blood covered the dirt, and flecks of it made it as far as the lowest bleachers, standing out against the peeling white paint and pale pine beneath.

Every minute or two, the referee blew his whistle, and the cock owners picked their birds up, pulled them away, blew on their backs or thwapped their beaks, and tossed 'em back at each other. Gave 'em a little rest, Frank guessed.

Not every fight went to the death. Sometimes they'd just get too tuckered to fight, too beat up, and the ref would have to call a decision. Today, the crowd was in luck. Green's knives kept landing in blue's chest, the blood coming thicker each time, and Frank coulda heard it if it weren't for the crowd cheering on. Finally blue just squawked, flapping his wings in a panic, and fell down twitchin'. Green pecked at his neck like to see if there was any fight left, and then backed off with what Frank woulda sworn was a sigh, before his cocker picked him up to tend to his wounds, see if he'd be up for another fight in a week or two.

Money changed hands, some threats were called over refusals to pay, but nothing got violent. It was the lunch crowd. Nobody was laying down the mortgage, nobody was pulling steel, and anybody who had trouble losing money to a Mexican or an Indian wasn't betting with 'em.

The fight over, Frank scanned the crowd again and saw himself recognized before he registered who it was looking him over. Agamemnon Chandler, who everybody called Aggie. They'd been friends, Frank and him, in high school and the days after. Hadn't seen much of each other since Frank got married. Ricky went to school with a girl Frank thought might be Aggie's bastard, she had the same forehead, the eyes. But it was hard to say.

He'd put on thirty pounds, Aggie, but he was broader too, like he worked out now at least once in a while instead of just relying on the natural strength of adolescence. "Well Frank Train," Aggie said as he came by and clapped him on the shoulder. "God damn, brother, I haven't talked to you in, what, three four years?"

"Robbie Bernard's funeral, I think," Frank said. "Or the wake?"

"Yeah, musta been. Fucking shame, that one. Fucking drunk drivers oughta be hanged, you ask me."

"Like you gotta tell me," Frank said, and Aggie nodded, gesturing over towards the beer counter. Frank followed.

"Heard about the fam damily," Aggie said. "Got no words, brother. And after your parents too, and now with your cousin."

"Bronco, yeah." Bronco'd been kicked in the head by a horse a month earlier, and still couldn't walk or talk right. Doctors said he was likely to die before the year was out.

"Forgot about Bronc. I meant Lisa, you know, with the cancer. Oh, and fuck me brother, I dunno if you know about Julie yet, who I been dating some over the years? She's kin to you too, come to think it."

Frank nodded. Julie and him had a cousin in common in Las Cruces, not the kind of thing you thought of as family per se, but enough to freak them out when they realized it after he'd felt her up at the movies and got a hand into her panties. "She's blood, yeah. What's doing with Jules?"

"Hit her head in a fall, now she's got this, this whaddaya call it, Superior Canal Dee-something Syndrome."

"The fuck's that?" They got their beers and went to sit down at one of the few tables.

Aggie pointed to his ear. "Her ear's fucked up. But I mean really fucked up, brother. Like she can hear everything, every motherfucking thing, loud as bombs. I was sitting in the room with her, right? Just sitting. She told me I had to leave or give her some Vicodin, because she could hear my eyeballs moving and it was making her sick."

"That's bullshit, Aggie. That's fucking comic book shit."

"Yeah, no, it's not. The doctor said it happens, something gets cracked inside the ear there. She's on the disability now, just lays in bed as still as she can. I got some of her Vicodin spares, you want to buy 'em?"

"Naw," Frank said, and then thought. "Eh, gimme five, I guess, how old are they?"

"Month, two months. She's mostly Percocet now, so you know."

"Sure." He fished in his wallet. "Ten bucks?"

"I dunno, man."

"Gimme a break, Medicare or somebody paid for 'em, right?"

"Yeah, okay, okay. And it wasn't Medicare, it was the prescription plan. I ain't a fucking Mexican."

Pills and bills traded hands, and Frank popped one of them, washing it down with the beer. Aggie eyed him for a moment, then said, "You oughta eat something with that if you didn't have lunch already."

"Didn't. Prolly oughta."

"I'm gonna get a couple dogs, you want something?" Aggie got up, and Frank nodded.

"Yeah all right, gemme two of the green chile cheese dogs if they still do 'em up like Maria Li did."

"'Like,' brother, she still does 'em her self. I'll be right back."

In between fights, the PA system that went unused otherwise played music. Used to be records, then tapes, now it was probably CDs or somebody's damn iPod. A Willie Nelson song'd been playing, and now it was the cover of "Black Betty" that Frank'd heard in the Dukes of Hazzard movie. He laid three bucks on the table for Aggie to collect when he got back, figuring the price had probably gone up from a buck since the last time he got those greasy spicy frankfurters, and then thought about it and added a buck more. Fuck it, it paid to have Aggie happy with him, too.

"So you seen my boy around here lately?" he asked when Aggie came back with the dogs. They were as greasy as he remembered them, buns buttered and toasted a golden-brown on three sides, crispy brown hot dog slid into it and bathed in half a can of Old El Paso diced green chiles and a squirt of nacho sauce.

"What, Ricky?"

"Man, these are fucking good. Yeah, Ricky, who else I gonna mean?"

"You send him here or what?"

Frank gave him a look and napkined yellow cheese sauce off the corner of his mouth. "It's a yes no question, Aggie."

"Yeah, I seen him around, talked to him, yeah. He's been here. A lot lately."

"How long now?"

Aggie shrugged. "I didn't know who he was till I'd been seeing him for a while, so I dunno, I didn't take notice right off. Somebody mentioned he was your kid, and I took a closer look, you know? He don't look a lot like you except for the attitude."

"How's that?"

"He throws off the vibe, brother, like you did back in the day. Not saying you don't now, no disrespect. But you know how it is."

"I went tame."

"Whatever it is. You got older, brother, same as me. Ain't like I'm whipping shit these days neither. We ain't fierce. Your boy Rick. He's coming up to fierce. He ain't there yet, maybe, but he's looking it in the chin."

Frank tapped a finger on the table as he ate the dog, thinking. Over Aggie's shoulder, cockers carried cages out from the locker area to show their gamecocks off to each other, and the ref made ticks on his clipboard, picking the next two fighters. "Fierce how? I mean, what's he done makes you say that?"

"Gets into fights sometimes, but not when he doesn't have to and not when he can't win. You know? You were the same way, except --"

"-- except I'd get into the ones I didn't have to."

"Yeah."

"That wasn't till I was older, though."

Aggie shrugged. "Hey brother, he's your kid, you know him better'n me. I'm just telling you he can take care of himself."

"He doing drugs?"

"Pot. Maybe coke, but I ain't saying he is."

"Uh huh, all right. You taking any bets off him?"

"See," Aggie said, and leveled his scarred index finger at Frank. "That's why I thought at first, maybe you sent him. Yeah, he's done all right. Had a few hard days, but never lost more scratch'n he could itch."

"Good to hear, I guess."

"So you had no idea, huh?"

"Nuh."

Aggie scratched his chin, and moved around to sit on the same side a the table as Frank so he could see the fight over the crowd's heads. The cockers picked up their cocks and heaved them underhand at each other once, twice, three times before letting go, getting 'em good and pissed at each other. "You ain't been around in a coon's, Frank."

"Uh huh. Ain't really my thing any more, tell you the truth. It's a vicious thing, all this."

Aggie snorted. "What, cockfights? Don't go fucking soft on us, brother."

Frank shrugged. "Ain't saying there's no sport to it. But it ain't like boxin'. Ain't really a fair thing, and it's fucking gruesome to boot. I saw a dogfight once, y'ever see a dogfight? An organized one?"

"Yeah," Aggie said. "That place outta Socorro?"

"That's the place. Fucking hard thing to watch."

"Yeah, I ain't arguing with that, that's true enough. Ain't saying it's wrong, but it ain't easy either."

"Sure."

"Cockfights're different, though. Man, they just chickens. They like it. A dog, you gotta make a dog mean. Fuck all they say about pit bulls, you know that ain't worth the dick they write it with."

"I know that, sure."

"Pit bull's a sweet fucking creature you don't go messing it up. But a gamecock? Like a jackal. Like a hornet. Fucking mean from hatching. I mean it."

"I ain't saying you're wrong, Aggie. But that don't make it sport, neither."

Aggie didn't say anything until the match was over. Green won, and money changed hands again, some of it coming to Aggie, some of it leaving him. "You sound all citified, you know. I mean, that's what it is.

Cockfights, even dogfights, all that stuff, everything but, what, fox hunts, they still do those?"

"I dunno, probably."

"Anyway, cockfightin's country. You know? You gotta raise the chickens. It's not, it's not fucking Pokeymon. You gotta raise actual cocks, you gotta know what you're doing, there's science to it, there's farming, it's work. Country work."

"It is that."

"Fucking cityfolk, it's just one more thing for them to smack down as primitive, right, as redneck. Man, NASCAR ain't country. You know anybody drives a car around in a circle?"

"Other than kids in empty lots?"

"Yeah, I don't mean four-wheeling and shit, you know what I mean."

"I catch you. I dunno that NASCAR ain't a little country, but I know what you're sayin'."

"Wrestlin'? Fucking wrestling ain't country, it's a buncha dipshits in tights trying to act. It's fuckin theater. Baseball's country, but do they talk about it like it is? Buncha Mexicans these days, and that's fine, but man, it was ours first. It was farm kids out in Kansas and Nebraska made them bats sing."

"Fucking right, you know I always said that. New York Yankees, Boston Red Sox, San Franfuckincisco Giants, the fuck's a city boy know about baseball? They got basketball, a parking lot game."

"Right on. And we got cockfights. It's, you know, like basketball, making use a what you have? A ball and a hoop, that's all you need, everybody's got space to play it. Cockfightin's the same thing, man, it's making use a your resources. If it was a city thing, no way they'd be cracking down on it. It was fucking Boston outlawed it first, you know."

"Yeah, I didn't know that."

"I been reading a lot of <u>Grit & Steel</u>. A lot of it's shit, it's the <u>High Times</u> of cockers, but your basic facts are your basic facts. And when you come down to it, the whole anti-cockfight thing is all Disney's fault."

"What? The cartoon guys?"

Aggie thumped his fist on the table, and took cash from somebody turning it in. The first was well-scarred, and that went a long way explaining why the money came to him without him having to go get it. "The cartoon <u>guy</u>. I mean, he's the one got people thinking a animals as people with fur. Right? I ain't saying he did nothing wrong, he made some good cartoons, I love Donald Duck and them chipmunks."

"Sport Goofy."

"Right!" Aggie grinned. "I forgot about Sport Goofy, you remember they used to show that on the Wonderful World of Disney?"

"Course I remember, man. When our TV was on the fritz, we'd go over to Bobby's, you were there sometimes too."

"Yeah, we had trouble with them VHF stations sometimes, so all we could get was 32 outta Cabredo. You'd think it'd be the other way around, but no."

"You had your antenna set up wrong, sounds like. Thirty-two, the one with that old cowboy on the morning show, the kids' show, right? And that puppet, what was it, a puppet dog?"

"Big ol' sheepdog, yeah. But what I'm saying about Disney. You know? Think about it." Aggie pointed to his own temple, then Frank's. "Think about it. All this PETA shit. Hey, I ain't saying we should be torturing animals for fun or making mice wear makeup. Shit, I don't even eat veal, brother. I figure, I ain't missing that much, what's the harm in leaving it alone? I do a little good that way."

"Sure."

"But cockfights?" He waved a hand at the gamecocks, the locker rooms. "Man, none of these birds, <u>none</u> of these birds, would even exist if it weren't for cockfightin'. They ain't reg'lar chickens, and they ain't tiny little people with feathers. They ain't Foghorn Leghorns, and yeah I know that wasn't Disney."

Frank nodded. Neither of 'em said much more for a bit. When Frank had finished his second dog and his beer, the Vicodin had given him a hell of a buzz, like the back of his head was melting away, and he smiled a warm smile. "Thing is, Aggie, it's still pretty fucking primitive, the whole thing. You're making chickens fight. That ain't right. That's a buncha shit right there. They're killing each other. They gonna do it on their own, let 'em do it on their own. Hey, kids fight too, that don't mean I'm gonna give 'em knives and toss 'em in a cage for five bucks on the winner."

"Man, you don't know what you're talking about."

"Maybe not," Frank admitted. "I ain't given it much thought at all, is the honest truth. It just ain't my thing. But here's what is my thing: my boy. I don't want Ricky around here. He owes you money, I'll cover it. He owes anyone else money, I'll cover it. That's as of right now. I ain't running a tab. You see him here, it's a favor to me if you send him off. Don't gotta send him home, I just don't want him here."

"Christ, Frank, don't be a faggot --"

"Hey." Frank flexed his hand open and closed. "Hey. Aggie. Look at the girls there. When we were kids, we didn't have AIDS to worry about, all right? We worried about whether our <u>parents</u> would find out. Whether our <u>priest</u> would find out."

"And crabs."

"Man, crabs ain't shit, who's faggot now?"

"All right, all right."

"You remember what that was like? How young we were? Kids ain't that young anymore. I don't want my boy around here. He's too young, too stupid, and that's a pure fact. When he's grown, he can set his mind on the matter however he likes. But he's mine for now, and I'm telling you it'd be a personal favor to me if you give me a hand on this."

Aggie stared at him for a long silent time, then nodded once. "Dad of the year now, aren'tcha. I'll do it, but lemme tell you why."

Another fight was starting. Shorter knives this time, so it was bound to last longer. The cocks themselves were heavy, thick-bodied, and looked pissed-off before they were even tossed together. "Yeah, tell me why."

"Arthur Train Junior, that's why. Your Pop used to take you here sometimes, same as mine. Well, not here here, but to the fights."

"Yeah," Frank said. "That's true, he did. Cockfights weren't nothing to him. They had a couple Mexicans at the ranch used to put 'em together when he was cowboyin'."

"Well now, if some church ladies had said it wasn't right for a man to bring his son to a legal event, I woulda said back off and let a father be a father. I'm seeing the same thing here."

Frank grunted. "You know, Aggie, I don't give you enough credit. I kinda thought I might have to bribe you."

Aggie rolled his eyes. "It's them at the door you want to talk to. I ain't here all the time and I can't kick the boy out."

"Yeah," Frank said. "I'm gonna do that. How many boys on the door am I gonna have to talk to?"

"There's five all told, but they ain't all here right now, of course. Maybe I could talk to 'em for you."

Frank paused, then took his wallet back out and started counting bills.

"Might be six," Aggie added. "I lose track sometimes."

"Uh huh." Frank handed him six hundred dollars, then made a point of adding another two fifties. "Make sure they're all taken care of." He thought for a sec. He'd brought more money, just in case. "And how about three hundred on blue there."

Aggie raised an eyebrow, then eyed the cocks. It was still an even-looking match, both of them blooded but neither of them losing any of their spunk. "Three hundred on blue. You got it."

Frank got up to toss his trash, and bought another hot dog on the anticipation that he wouldn't be back to the fairgrounds any time soon, except during the rodeos when Maria Li wouldn't be workin'. He didn't watch the rest of the fight, which would be turning his stomach if it weren't for the soothing fuzziness of the Vicodin. He stood by the trash can at Maria Li's cart, eating his hot dog in slow bites. They didn't just fall apart like Oscar Mayers. You had to bite down on these for real, and they snapped, skin splitting and juice squirting hot into your mouth.

When he was done, he wiped his mouth, opened a Handi-Wipe and cleaned his fingers with it, and turned back to the table where Aggie was exchanging money with a gaggle of Mexicans and a few Indians who were probably late for work. Aggie gave him a look, and held up six hundreds between his fingers. "You got an eye, Frank. You still got that luck a yours, that Train luck."

Frank nodded, looking at the dirt floor stained dark, where one of the cocks was being rolled into a bag and the other looked like he wasn't gonna last much longer either. "Yeah. Dad of the year."

CHAPTER FOURTEEN

Saturday wasn't an ordinary day for anyone.

It was the weekend of the April rodeo, a brisk crisp day that snapped like a peapod under a sky blue as a little girl's eyes. Ricky spent the night at the house, and Mickey and Jessie were planning on taking him over to the rodeo early. Frank would join 'em later after he'd got his usual chores and so on done, which were even more important now, with the money he'd spent on bribes at the cockfights. He was up a bit before dawn, making rounds and repairs, and then broke his fast in town at the Rockinghorse Diner.

Like mosta the singletons, he sat himself at the counter, but at the short end of it by the March of Dimes jar and the corn muffin display. Alyse got to him when she could and he ordered the Number Four, chilaquiles verde with a side a bacon and a corn muffin, coffee and cranberry juice, $3.75. He ate methodically, using pieces of muffin to push the food onto his fork and wipe up the traces of egg yolk and avocado-green chile sauce. It was plain food and simple, not very spicy, the cheese salty and dry.

"Cranberry juice, huh Frank," Alyse said with a smirk when she refilled his coffee and he asked for another juice. "Getting old, watching out for the bladder?"

"Sour and dry like me is all," he said, and took a big sip of coffee while it was hot enough to burn his tongue. "Sour and dry. Ain't got much a sweet tooth no more, and grapefruit juice gives me heartburn."

"Uh huh, cause you're getting old," Alyse repeated. "Happens to all you men eventually."

"Women too."

She shook her head. "Women just get more mysterious," she said. "We don't get old."

Frank reckoned it was the other way around. The least mysterious women he'd known had been his grandmothers, and the most was his daughter. But maybe family was another somethin'. So he smiled and grinned for Alyse and drank his coffee, unwrapping a couple chalky

Tums from their Chevy-blue roll and chewing them until the touch of burn from the coffee had gone away, then sipped at the cranberry juice and nibbled on the extra side of bacon Alyse had brought him. She was always doing little things for the regulars like that, usually consolatin'ly. The fella who'd lost his wife to a carpet salesman'd get a few more eggs in his migas, the girl just lost her baby'd get a few sopaipillas on the side of whatever she'd ordered, the couple too broke to order more'n a special to split would find a piece a melon too big to be just garnish and two glasses a milk that didn't make it to the bill.

The Rockinghorse was the kinda joint that worked that way, reg'lars showing up every morning for a muffin and coffee or a big farmer's plate, families coming in on Sundays maybe for the blue corncakes with chocolate chips and pinon nuts, and once in a while somebody with a hangover needing some protein and caffeine to put 'em right with the world again. The counter was L-shaped, three stools for the short end put closer together than the ten for the long, and there were six tables to boot, two two-seaters and the others four-seater booths that could fit six if you needed to squeeze.

The wall clock was Coca-Cola, the colors of the restaurant Montana blue and Tulane green, agave blossoms long faded by mud and Pinesol in the tile floor and overtaken by the echo of sharktooth bootprints that trailed behind feet like Mighty Mouse's cape, the 1988 NCR cash register bisecting the long part of the counter behind a small and neatly organized plate of homemade choc. chip brownies (w/ or w/o pecans) you could buy for $1.25 that used to be 40 cents. Most of the menus were paper printouts, although there were four or five laminated jobbies that were stacked at the register for whoever wanted to look through 'em.

The register made a typewriter-like sound when it was used, the keys heavier and more reluctant than the soft plastic-and-dimple things they made today. Frank'd repaired it a couple times, but like Alyse and her old man pointed out: if it ain't broke, why buy a new one? They had a separate doodad for taking Mastercard and didn't take Visa cause a some dispute Alyse's sister had had with 'em over some charges God knows how long ago.

Alyse herself was in her fifties, and hadn't grown up in Cardenio but'd moved from the big city a Denver for one reason or another when she was in her twenties but still looked pretty young, pretty fresh. Least that's how Frank remembered her having looked when he was himself barely a teen. She'd caught the eye of Lou who ran the Rockinghorse, where she had a job as a waitress, and 'fore you knew it they were married in the church. She'd never had no kids, and no one knew who was more disappointed by that, Alyse or her old man.

Saturday morning, most of the regulars either weren't coming or already'd left, gone to the rodeo, to get good seats or a look at things or just to be around everyone. "Going to the rodeo later?" he asked. The two of them sitting so proximate with everyone else further away, it was like they were at the same table and he felt he had to make conversation.

"Like every year, I guess," she said. "Not as much fun as when I was young and wild."

"Not much is."

She smiled. "How are, I mean, how is Ricky, anyway?"

"You know, he's a teenager."

"Uh huh." She got his food for him and let him eat, not exactly hovering but not far away either. "How's Ricky really?" she asked gently, her voice low although nobody was near enough to 'em to overhear by accident. "It's not an easy age, 'specially for boys like him."

"Yeah?" he asked, and he felt his feathers ruffle back. "Boys like what?"

"I'm sorry, it's just, well, Ricky's never been just any old boy, has he? Always a little smarter, a little more charming, a little stronger. That's not easy, Frank. Not in a town like Cardenio especially, and not at that age. It means no matter what he does, he stands out, you know?"

Frank thought about the kind of music Ricky listened to, the way he was dressing lately, and didn't think Ricky cared much about whether he stood out. Or at least didn't have a problem with it. "I was the same way," he said, which wasn't really true. Stronger than most, sure 'nough. Charming in a certain way, but only to people who liked the cut of his jib. But smart? Frank'd never been stupid, but he hadn't made much time to be smart, neither.

"You wanna see my coyote?" he asked to change the subject.

oooOOOooo

The coyote with the ragged ear was looking downright domestic these days, curled up on an old Indian throw rug Frank'd tossed into the bed of the pickup, where it'd got all covered in fur pretty quick. Who knew even coyotes shed when the weather got warmer?

"Well, that's a cuter devil than I would've thought," Alyse said. At the moment, that about nailed it. The coyote was laying in the sun, a chewed-up stuffed animal at his paws, a rabbit Frank'd given him cause he thought it was funny and that the old boy needed something to chaw on that wasn't food or bones. "He looks happy to have someone taking care of him."

"Careful now," Frank said. "Cute maybe, but coyote for sure, you know? There's a reason I don't take him inside with me except at my own home."

"Does he bite?" she asked him with wide eyes.

"I ain't saying he won't."

She grinned like they were both twenty years younger, and he went on his way after paying the bill.

It was passing the road to Marlowe's house that reminded him to call Newt. Not sure if his cousin was gonna be going to the rodeo or not, he'd wanted to wait, it being a Saturday morning when Newt might be sleeping in. Newt was a Mondragon, Isaac Newton Mondragon, the youngest son of Uncle Rafe, a few years older than Frank. There were pictures of him as the ringbearer in Mom and Pop's wedding, the photos looking impossibly old like something out of some documentary on PBS, wearing a bone-white cowboy hat at the reception, which Rafe'd said was "as much a hoot-n-holler as anything else."

These days Newt taught math at Cardenio Public, pretty much the brainiest job of anybody in the family Frank could think of, although there was the librarian girl and the court clerk, and those were brainy in their own ways too. More importantly, though, Newt was now a co-worker with one Joshua Marlowe.

"Morning," came Newt's laconic voice at the other end. He was always like that, saying morning insteada hello, sounding like he knew who you were and was just saying howdy.

"Hey there Newt, it's Frank," he said.

"Uh huh," Newt said. "Saw the caller ID. What's up?"

"Well listen," Frank said. "I wanted to ask you about this Josh Marlowe, this new art teacher. You talked to him much yet?"

Newt seemed to think it over, and a spoon clanked against ceramic somewheres in the background. "Little, not much. I'm coaching boys' lacrosse this year."

"Oh yeah, I didn't know that."

"Yeah, so I don't have as much time in the teachers lounge as I would otherwise. It's a few extra thousand a year, not bad, and it's actually pretty fun. Looks like a crazy sport, right? We got the weirdest mix of jocks and stoners on the team, you wouldn't believe it."

"Uh huh. I'll come out see a game with Ricky some time."

"Yeah, that'd be good, that'd be good. I'm gonna get Ricky in class next year, I think."

"Well, that'll be good too. But what can you tell me 'bout this Marlowe guy?"

"Hey, you got in a fight with him, didn't you? Huh. He does look kinda a rough customer, I guess. Reminds me of your Pop, you know."

"What way?"

"Like he could kick your ass, right, but he'd rather read Proust."

Frank grunted to himself. He hadn't heard his father described like that before, and it was on the money but he didn't like the comparison to Marlowe. "You seen him talking to Ricky or anything?"

"Like I said, I really haven't seen much of either of 'em. Hey wait, is

112

that what this is about, the fight with you an' him? Did he touch Ricky?"

"No! Shit, not that I know. Why you ask that, you think he would? He seem like a pervert?"

"I don't know! Frank, I'm just trying to figure out what you're asking about, what you're looking for." Frank thought about it long enough that Newt had to ask, "You still there?"

"I'm here, I'm here."

"I said --"

"Yeah, I know. He ain't a good guy, Newton."

"Ricky?"

"<u>Marlowe</u>. There's a lot to it, a lot to him. He ain't a good guy, and he's dangerous."

Now it was Newt not saying anything, though Frank could hear something at the other end, maybe the TV. "I heard some rumors 'bout him and your Kriste, I guess."

"You guess or you heard?"

"Well, overheard. You know."

Uh huh. "Might be they're true, depending on the rumor."

"Hell, Frank. You can't hold it against the man all this later, even if it is weird a him coming back to the town where he done the, well, the deed. Don't make him any worse'n most."

"Newt," Frank said heavily. "One of these days maybe I'll try to convince you. Right now I gotta tell you my give-a-shit's broke. Just keep an eye on Marlowe, is all."

"Yeah, all right, all right. Listen, while I gotcha and we're all talking family, though, you aware of the doin's with Mickey?"

"How so?"

"Well, he's in for a penny at cards. Owes big to your cousin Lincoln, I hear, and maybe somebody else too."

"Somebody else too? Linc's family, I ain't worried there."

"Somebody else, is all. I hear what I hear, Frank. And me, I'd worry on Lincoln Train. But then he ain't my blood."

"Reckon he ain't," thinking <u>no Train would ever be a pot-smoking math teacher, that's for sure, coaching fucking lacrosse</u>. "Thanks for the heads up, though."

"See you at the rodeo later on, then."

"Uh huh."

ooo000ooo

It was unnerving how different things looked at the fairgrounds during a rodeo than it had during the week when he went to the lunchhour cockfight. Looked cleaner, for one, even though there was more litter around, like it was fresher litter, litter you expected'd be picked up insteada litter you knew'd been there for a long while. Kids and locals everywhere, coupla clowns, horses, ponies. Driving in, you could smell horseshit and cotton candy, straw and beer. That was rodeo all right.

He lit a cigarette in the parking lot, smoked it on the way over, and lit another one. Didn't want Ricky to see him smoking, didn't want to set a bad example. God damn God damn.

"What was it Grandpa'd been so good at?" Mickey asked him without so much as a howdy, when Frank found them and sat down in the seat Jessie'd thrown a jacket over for savin'.

Frank ruffled Ricky's hair, which was tacky with some kinda styling product and left his fingers feeling like he'd just gripped a pine-tarred baseball bat. "Calf roping and bareback," Frank said. "That's what Pop always said. Old Arthur Train Senior was a hell of a rider in his day, a real rough dude. He didn't like the rodeo, thought it was frivolous, but he'd compete when he was courting or cajoled into it."

"And he won every time," Mickey said.

Frank nodded. "So the story goes."

"Pop wasn't one to tall tale, Frankie."

"But if he was of a mind, reckon his Pa would be where he'd start."

Mickey shrugged at that, and passed Frank a beer, which he took without comment only because he didn't want to have a conversation about pre-lunch drinking in front of the boy. It was just beer anyway, and watered-down no doubt.

This morning was barrel racing, which was more or less your figure-skating of the rodeo world, being as it was a women's competition. There were no judges in barrel racin'. Fastest time won, with each woman riding her horse in a cloverleaf around three barrels. Sounded easy, which was the whole thing: you had to be fast, and winning times could be less than a second over the closest losers. Had to make them turns tight, have a horse smart enough not to knock over the barrels, one good at sprinting and precision.

That made it as much about the horse as anything else, so just like with straight-out track races, what people watched was the animals, marvelling over the breeding and ability of this'un or that'un.

"What'd he die of, anyway?" Ricky asked.

"Who, Grandpa? Your great-grandfather?"

"Uh huh."

"Heart attack," Mickey said. "Just wound too tight, Uncle Butch always said."

Frank grunted. "Uncle Butch is a mean old son of a bitch. I reckon Grandpa had, you know, a congenital condition. Kinda thing they'd spot now. His clock just ran out."

Everyone was looking at him.

"What?"

Jessie touched his shoulder. "Sugar, we figured somebody called you, but Butch died last night."

"What?"

"Yeah," Mickey said. "What, you think we're drinking the barrel racers' health? We're in mourning here, little brother boy."

"Got kicked in the head by a bull," Ricky said, watching the girls ride their horses around and around them barrels. The one who seemed to have him fixed was a looker all right, a Norman Rockwell painting with sex appeal: red checkered shirt tied in a knot below her breasts, red hair in pigtails. "Died 'fore they even got him to the hospital."

"Christ the bastard," Frank said. "He was too fucking old and too fucking mean to die, and too mucha either to be unpacking the rodeo, too."

"Ayeah," Mickey said. "But he did and he was, bro. It's a real fucker, ain't it."

"Don't swear in front of Ricky," Jessie said.

"Christ," Frank said again, thinking about mean old Uncle Butch, Pop's older brother, Lincoln's father who'd been drunk most of their childhood and used to throw firecrackers in the fire pond, sitting on the tailgate of his truck and just lighting em, tossing em in, lighting em, tossing em in, making a little game of it, trying to get that balance where they'd blow up in the air, or even better right on the surface of the water, without holding em so long he blew his hand up or letting go too soon and sinking em unexploded.

"Christ the son of a bitch," Frank said, and drank down the luke-cool beer Mickey'd handed him.

"It's like everybody in my family keeps dying," Ricky said, and Frank saw it'd been something he'd been worrying over all mornin'.

"Don't worry about that," Frank said before he could think not to, "God knows you're safe."

"It's a God damn cuckoo-clock world," Mickey said as he pulled a flash outta his boot and splashed it around his plastic cup a beer. "It's all just piss drying under the sun."

Frank tried to think of something to say to Ricky, who'd given him a fisheye after the "you're safe" comment and then turned away, but nothing came to mind. The boy pulled a wad of cash out of his pocket, as the hot dog guy came near, and bought three dogs, a pretzel, and a Coke. The cash worried Frank for a minute, but it was just ones, thirty, maybe forty of 'em, dirty and bunched up together. The kinda money a kid accumulated from change back here, scrimped something there.

"God damn cuckoo-clock world," Mickey said again, and he was scoping out the money too, and Jessie was watching him watch the cash with this sad-as-droopy look on her face.

115

None of 'em was talky much the resta the day, and they split up and regrouped several times, Ricky watching more'n a few of the women's competitions, sometimes backing out and changing his mind if Jessie offered to go with him. Mickey meandered here'n'there, and Frank did what he usually did: watching the roping and wrestling, and in between settled for whatever meant the least running around.

Sometimes that meant watching women, just watching for the sake of seeing them. He didn't know whether to feel guilty about it, and flirted with a few until it made him feel good, too good. He'd always liked that. That old Frank Train, back in the day, that bad Frank Train. He'd liked making people <u>feel</u> things. Liked making em laugh. Liked making em back down off a fight. Liked making em feel stupid when it came to that. He'd liked it when girls liked him, more than liking <u>them</u>, he'd liked <u>being</u> liked, although he wasn't no son of a bitch and he'd never had sex with a girl he didn't either like or pay.

But what he'd liked was finding out how they felt, how they thought, and moving it over. Shoving it around. All she wanted was a Saturday night fuck when she was feeling horny? He'd make her fall for him. Didn't have to lie, just had to shine the right light, the way you'd change the shape of a shadow with nothing but a twist a the lamp. Had to get her to see a different side of him, was all, but still him, still real. Once she fell hard, once she started talking 'bout all them feelin's she was having, well, sometimes they'd date a while, sometimes they wouldn't, and a coupla times it'd gone bad when the girl in question had already been dating somebody else.

The ones that went better, they were the ones who didn't wanna fuck. They just liked him. Oh, but I don't wanna go all the way, Frank. Oh, but I'm saving myself, Frank. Oh, but my last relationship was just sexual, Frank, I want to take it slow from now on, not rush into anything. I wanna do it right this time.

Oh baby we'll do it right, he'd say. We'll take it slow.

That was the game <u>every</u> guy played, every guy in Cardenio and every guy in the world. He'd actually paged through the Bible one time thinking even it had to have a guy talking a girl into the sack, what with all the other kindsa stories in there, but the closest he found were Reuben and the concubine, and the thing where Isaac put in seven years work for the wrong sister.

Everybody played it, so it was like a contest. Not like a race or anything, not like the rodeo. More like how you'd compare high scores in Defender, at the arcade. Or how many times you could hit the mailbox with a baseball chucked from your porch. There was a little bit where what Frank'd liked was getting girls in the sack who had a reputation for being frigid, not virgins necessarily, cause he didn't like the drama of some of them church girls, but girls who'd <u>had</u> sex and acted like now that they'd had it once, they were done with it forever thank you very much.

Some of them, oh boy how he'd changed their minds. And some of 'em, well, he hadn't.

He'd been the same way with guys, although not the <u>same</u> way. Just th emind-changing thing. Getting one guy talked into marriage, another one talked outta the Army. This'un broke up with his girl cause he was going to Mexico for three weeks and why worry about what she might get up to? That'un got back together with his ex cause there must be a mighty good reason it'd hurt so much to break up.

He never told nobody to do anything he didn't think they should. He wasn't a son of a bitch about it. It'd just been, you know, kinda his way of helping along. Moving the show.

Till Kriste came along, anyway, the finest thing under the sun, taking up so much of his attention and devotion he just wasn't interested in any a that, and parenting, well, it was kinda the same game, only harder and you didn't get a break from it. Marriage, family, that'd opened a whole new world to explore, a deep one he hadn't had a chance to get tired of yet.

But Kriste was gone now. All them frontiers was closed.

CHAPTER FIFTEEN

"Boy, we gotta talk," Frank said.

A few mornings after the April rodeo ended, he'd piled Ricky and the coyote with the ragged ear into the truck to drive to Santa Fe, on the chance the verdict in the Hanion case would be made that day. It was raining pretty fierce, so the coyote hunkered down in the cab on the floor between 'em.

"Whatta we gonna do if they don't make up their minds today?" Ricky asked. "It'd just be a waste of time."

"Then we go back tomorrow," Frank said. "And the day after. And all next week if that's how it takes 'em to decide if the man killed your grandfolks."

"Gonna miss a lot of school if they do," Ricky said, folding his arms like he gave a damn. He'd given himself a haircut Sunday night, and his shiny black hair hung in his face now, uneven.

"Fuck missing school. Some things are more important. What, you worried about art class?"

"Man, fuck a buncha art class."

Frank grunted. "Don't say fuck."

"Christ!" Ricky said, with that indignant tone he'd worked so much on lately. "You just said it yourself!"

"I ain't a boy, Ricky. And you ain't a man yet, which is what we gotta talk about."

"Don't act much like it," Ricky mumbled, and Frank let that pass.

"You wanna tell me what you been acting like, then? This business with the cockfights, and what I hear about you and the Davenant girl?"

Ricky shifted in his seat and studied the glovebox, obviously uncomfortable. "Figure that's my business."

"Well damn, boy, you figure wrong. You got another ten years at least before you get to keep things like this to yourself, and I ain't promise you'll ever be old enough that I ain't gonna ask. What's going on with you two? You datin'?"

"Naw."

"She's a bit old for you, Ricky."

"We ain't 'dating,' Pop."

"Bit old for you to just be sleeping with, too."

At that, Ricky didn't answer, and just shuffled his feet, pulling his Gameboy out of his pocket and popping a cartridge into it. Frank waited a moment, then reached over and gently took it out of his hands.

"I said we gotta talk, Ricky," he repeated.

Ricky kicked the underside of the glovebox. "It's Rick now. I like Rick."

"I know," Frank said, and sighed himself. "I forget. I'm sorry."

"Word I heard is you ain't my father," Ricky said, and the world seemed to tighten, him just coming out with it like that. "It's going around that Mom had an affair with Mr Marlowe." Frank'd swear the truck got more crowded, that the road felt slimmer like he was gonna careen off it any moment, and his peripheral vision just plain went dark, nothing in front of him by the windshield needing a wash and that yella double Morse-coding by saying it's all right, it's all right, passing is allowed.

ooo000ooo

They got to Santa Fe before saying any more about it. Wasn't intended that way, but every time Frank thought about responding, he let a little more time go by and the more time went by the more it seemed like what he said oughta mean more, and next thing he knew, there was the courthouse. He took the ticket from the attendant at the fronta the lot, stuffing it into his breast pocket so he'd remember to get it stamped inside.

"This is stupid being all dressed up," Ricky said, buttoning the jacket he'd had folded in his lap. There were traces of coyote fur on one side, and when Frank reached over to brush them off, Ricky flinched at the touch. Under his jacket, his shirt was rumpled where he'd crossed his arms. "It's not like we're going to church."

"It's court, for God's sake," Frank said. "You don't go in a T-shirt and cut-offs like some God damn Okie."

"Whatever," Ricky said. "Who'm I impressing?"

Frank didn't answer, and they went through the metal detector, Ricky dumping a bundle of stuff in a tub and getting a dogeared laminated ticket in return. A guard directed them to the appropriate courtroom, where another told them that the jury was in deliberations.

Ricky looked at his watch as they sat down on a bench. "It's like not even ten o'clock. Did they finish the trial yesterday and just wait until today to start the jury?"

Frank shrugged. "I dunno, I don't think they can do that. The jury's not supposed to talk to anyone or anything."

"That's only if they're sequestered."

"They had the closing arguments to do today, I think. Guess they wrapped them up quick."

Ricky rolled his eyes. He was sitting in the bench leaned way forward with his elbows on his thighs, like he was trying to fold himself in half with irritation at the world and all its stupidities.

"Well, I don't think it's like on TV, kid," Frank said. "It ain't gonna be this big dramatic speech every time. You want a snack or anything? I bet they have a cafeteria."

Another eyeroll. "Why would they have a cafeteria? There's like a million restaurants across the street. There's a Burritoville and a Krispy Kreme right next to the parking lot. Don't be stupid."

Frank sighed, folded his arms across his stomach, and leaned against the hard wooden bench that his dress slacks wanted to slide right off of, trying not to rumple himself. "Well, they had a cafeteria on <u>Night Court</u>, anyway."

"It ain't like on TV, kid," Ricky echoed, nasal and sarcastic practically to the point of incoherence.

Frank cracked his knuckles, one by one, knowing the kid hated it. Kriste had too. "Tell you what, why don't we go on a trip sometime soon."

"Oh Christ," Ricky said, and Frank thwapped his elbow.

"Your Mom'd freak, she heard you taking the Lord's name in vain. What's wrong with a vacation?"

"You mean a re<u>treat</u>, don't you. One of those father-n-son camp things, right? Bang the drum around the fire and cry?"

Frank sighed. Ricky sounded so angry, so fucking pissed off, like every word he was forcing out with bellows through some crack in this shaking steam-pot of rage. Like he was holding back tears, every God God damned minute. "No. You oughta know I think those things are stupid too. I mean a damn vacation. We're going to see the game in the fall, but we could do something before that. Something cool."

"Not a damn road trip, seeing the world's biggest balla wax and the place Sam Houston had lunch one day."

"No no, geez, calm down. Like Mexico, maybe. Mexico City or something. Or New Orleans, we could find out when Mardi Gras is."

"It's before Easter," Ricky said. "We missed it this year. But I dunno, maybe we could find something cool."

"Well, if you get ideas, you let me know, all right? That's what I'm sayin'. It's just you and me, so it ain't gonna be me picking a place and telling you where we're goin'. If it's somewhere we can afford then I'll call your cousin the travel agent, and we'll see what's a good time."

Ricky took out a pack of cigarettes, not lighting one but just playing with the pack. "Yeah, that could be cool, maybe. I'll ask around."

"All right." Frank waited a minute then asked casually, "Who you gonna ask?"

"I got friends ain't so poor as us, they been places."

That stung. They weren't poor, God damn it, they were solidly middle class. They paid the cable every month, owned the truck, and did it without letting the health insurance slide or anything like that, like some a the guys Frank knew who drove expensive cars and bought hundred dollar shirts but never had a bank balance bigger'n their last deposit. "Well," he said. "Lisa Davenant's well set, I guess."

"Uh huh," Ricky said. "She been to Disney World a few times when she was a kid, you know. Disneyland, too."

"What's the difference?"

"One in California, one in Florida."

"Huh, yeah."

"Her pop took her to see the New York Yankees in the Yankees Stadium, too, last year."

"Fucking New York Yankees." They both spit on the floor, and Frank covered it up with his foot.

"Well, I'm just saying, you know, she's been a lot of places. She said New York's got everything, got more fucking spics than Santa Fe does."

"Watch your mouth, dammit, your Mom was a fucking spic and you know it. God damn, you're one too, you and me both. The Mondragons been in Mexico long as there's been one."

"That ain't Mexican," Ricky said. "That's Spaniard. Ain't you ever heard Great-Grandmother going on about it, her family being in the Crusades and the conquistadors and shit? Not that it matters. Ain't my family. That's your family."

"I thought I was gonna be the one to have to bring that back up." It'd be just like a God damned movie, Frank thought, like a God damned drama, if the bailiff were to say the jury's back now. He actually turned to look, but nothing was doin'.

"It's true, right? Mr Marlowe, Mr God Damn Art Teacher Marlowe, he's my real father."

"Your biological father. Yeah, I think he is."

"Think?"

"Your Mom and him had an affair. She had a test done to see if I was your Pop, and I'm not. That's the whole a what I know, son."

Ricky kicked his heels against the bench a few times, the echoes thudding down that hardfloor hallway. "How long you known?"

Frank wasn't sure he should tell him but couldn't come up with a good reason not to, neither. "Christmas," he said. "After the accident, going through your Mom's papers."

"So she kept the test? All this time?"

"Uh huh."

"Guess she musta wanted me to know," Ricky said, and he said it like it was something he'd been wonderin'. "Musta wanted one of us to know."

"Well, I reckon." Frank hadn't thoughta that, hadn't wondered why Kriste'd kept the test results around. Maybe she expected to divorce him at some point. Maybe she'd wanted Marlowe to have some kinda role in the boy's life, in, well, in just such a case as this. Maybe she'd wanted to tell the boy when he got older. "Thing is, Rick," Frank said. "This isn't when she wanted you to know, or she woulda told you. And this ain't how. How you find out?"

The boy's face colored dark. "Lisa's Pop mentioned it to her, she told me, I asked Mr Marlowe."

"Lobo?" Frank'd just assumed Marlowe'd told him direct. "How the hell'd Lobo know?"

Ricky shrugged, and then the bailiff <u>did</u> come to tell 'em the jury was back. People filed into the courtroom, and Frank didn't hear nothing of what was going on, nothing of what was being said, he just fixed his eyes on the back of David Lucas Hanion's head. He'd shaved his head and got a tattoo there, the damn Marlowe brand, yellow outlined in black all stylized. It looked like a prison tat all right, looked like the kinda thing you'd see on the thick arms of them boys worked the fields in the north, 'cept for the yellow which hardly didn't show up anyway.

"Your Honor," the forewoman said, as Frank watched the tendons in Hanion's neck work, the skin on the back of his head move like something was under it, crawling, "on the first count, murder in the first degree, we the jury find the defendant, David Lucas Hanion, guilty. On the second count of murder in the first degree, we find the defendant, David Lucas Hanion, guilty."

She kept reading, and Frank didn't hear. He'd been afraid that the son of a bitch was gonna get away with it, get off on some loophole or other. He felt Ricky relax next to him, too, like the boy'd been tensed.

The rest a the formalities got went through, and the guards led Hanion back out to whatever holding cell they put folks in before sending 'em off to prison. The sentencing wouldn't be till the next day, and Frank didn't reckon they had any real need to be there for that.

Hanion smiled at Frank as he walked past him, the moment queering down to slow motion just like you'd figure it would, his teeth gleamed in the fluorescence of the overheads, and his eyes looked wrong like one was a little bigger'n the other, and then them rows of teeth was going up an' down, up an' down, and it took Frank a sec to realize the guy was talkin'.

Ricky'd pressed against him, was leaning over him to yell at Hanion, "Why'd you do it, you son of a bitch, why'd you kill my grandma and grandpa?", and the guards were looking at Frank like he was supposed to yank the boy back, but he'd just been off in his daze thinking bout nothing at all.

"I had to!" Hanion was gabbling back, and his mouth looked all outta proportion to his words. "I had to do it for him! I had to give back what I owed!" He looked pained, but Frank got the feeling it wasn't 'cause of what he'd done but why he'd done it.

"All right, boy," he said, pulling Ricky back by the belt loops. "All right now, that's enough."

"Let's settle down some," one of the guards said, and Frank locked him down with a look.

"Let's suck my crank," he said. "Go on and get the fucker outta here, for Christ's sake, you taking the scenic route?" He patted the boy on the back, and told himself the kid was getting back to normal, reacting like you'd expect.

ooo000ooo

They got lunch at Buck Burgers, a sort of fast food dollar store: green chile cheeseburgers you could eat in a coupla bites, styrofoam cups of queso and Fritos, two bags of tiny glazed doughnut holes the size of Tater Tots. "Well that's that," Frank said, washing down one of the burgers with orange soda. He couldn't remember ever drinking orange soda anywhere but a burger joint, and wondered if that's what kept the orange soda folks in business. "Do you want to come back for the sentencing?"

Ricky shook his head. "I guess all that matters is they said he's guilty. He ain't gonna stay in for as long as they sentence him, and he ain't gonna get the death penalty, right?"

Frank crumpled up his burger wrappers. "I dunno. I guess not. The DA ain't asking for the death penalty, and I dunno if they ever get it without the DA asking for it. How long he's gonna stay in ... well, hopefully we won't know. You know? I don't think it's healthy for us to be, like, watching him, waiting to see when he gets out."

"I guess."

They didn't say nothing, picking at the fries, and something caught Frank's eye across the street, something that took him a minute to reco'nize why he was so fixed on it.

Terry.

The homeless guy with the mark of Marlowe on him, the one who'd disappeared after Frank had chased him down, the only man Frank knew other than Old Man McCarty who'd made a deal with the Halloween man.

"I gotta go," Frank said, mouthful of fries. "Stay here. Be right back."

"The fuck --"

"Stay here, God damn it."

Frank pushed the Buck Burger door open hard enough it bounced back and caught his elbow in stars, and ran to the truck, where the coyote howled to see his master in such a fuss. No time for it, and this time 'round Frank was gonna get some God damned answers outta Terry. He grabbed the gun outta the glove box and took another look. There was Terry, in his Army jacket and too many shirts, just now looking around.

When he saw Frank, he jumped and then ran, just like fucking last time when Frank tried to get him to talk about the tattoo. Frank thought about following him in the truck, but there was no use to that, the guy would just leave the road soon as he could. Fuck it, then.

Frank raced after him, fast as his legs would go, God damned grateful that work kept him more or less in shape compared to most fellas his age. He jumped onto the hoods of parked cars and off the other side, steada running around 'em, took running leaps over those short stone walls that surrounded some a the nicer lawns like hedges, doubling as benches, step-ran up a picnic table in the park and jumped off it to tackle Terry, and rolled him over, jamming the pistol at his throat.

"Why you running, Terry?" he shouted, or meant to, but his lungs were brushfired and his throat dry, and it came out quiet and raspy and ragged. "What you running for, you son of a bitch?"

"Easy Frank," Terry said, scared like a mouse, holding his hands up. Frank had him pinned down with his knees, but knew it wouldn't be long 'fore he'd have to let up or some good Samaritan was gonna cause a ruckus or call a cop. "Easy, we ain't enemies!"

"Fucking shit we're not," Frank growled, and twisted the gun so that it's barrel left a cold red mark on the homeless man's neck. "You ain't getting away this time. You leave me hanging, you're killing my family, you understand? You're killing my family."

"All right! All right! What you wanna know, then?"

Frank looked around. Yeah, people were looking, but holding back like waiting to see if anyone was gonna get hurt. Maybe they thought he was a cop. Maybe they didn't give a shit. "What'd he give you, the Halloween man? What'd you give him?"

"Eyes," Terry whispered, and reached up to touch his eyelids with his fingertips, gently. "I once was blind, but now I see, and he made me tell him all of it. Everything I see. For Christ's sake, Frank, someone coming, you better let me up you want me to tell you."

Frank paused, nodded, put the gun in the pocket of his jacket. "I still got it on you," he said as he stood up.

Terry nodded. "May as well," he said. "You wanna buy me a cheeseburger?" The man looked withered with hunger, and Frank grunted.

"Jesus," he said. "Fine." He waved a hand at one of the vendors in the park, brought Terry over there and laid down the cash for three large green chile cheeseburgers with bacon and beans, an extra large orange soda, and a bag of Fritos. They sat down at a green-painted picnic table greasy with pollen, and Frank put the gun on the table, cradling it with the barrel facing Terry. "Talk while you eat. Start at the beginning and stop when you're done."

Terry stuffed greasy hunks of meat in his mouth, wiping away the residue with bundles of napkins. "I had a twin sister," he said. "We were both Terry, see Frank? Terry and Terry. Sit tibi terra levis. Neither of us was good people, but shit, that don't surprise you none, there ain't no good people, is there? Terry became a ghost town whore, and me I was a preacher who hated her for it."

"Guess I might feel the same," Frank said, watching the milky wet of Terry's eyes and keeping his patience in hand to get the old man to keep talkin'.

"Guess you might, cause we ain't neither of us any damn good, huh. Well, one of them other whores give me a call one night cause she thought Terry was in trouble. I came out, reluctant, dragging my heels, you know, and heard the ruckus when I got there, forced the door open, and some asshole son of a bitch cocksucker john was beating Terry to death. I saw her bloody and naked, and that was the last thing I saw. My eyes just sewed themselves right the fuck up."

"The john get away?"

"Oh no," Terry breathed. "No, I killed him something awful. They kicked me outta the church for that, but I didn't go to jail. Justifiable homicide, you know, and I was a respected man a the cloth. Wrote books about Wisdom literature. They went easy on this Terry, thankyouJesus oh yes, oh moon."

"All right," Frank said, recognizing that singsong tone. "Stay with me here, Terry. You ain't got to the Halloween man yet." He tapped the barrel of the gun against the picnic table, and Terry nodded faintly.

"Worst thing wasn't being blind," Terry said. "Oh no. 'Cause my eyes worked fine, you know, it was the brain that didn't. Like it stopped listenin'. They couldn't fix that, the doctors. Told me I just had to get over it. But I couldn't. All I could see was Terry, naked and cut open and blood all over."

"But the Halloween man gave you your sight back."

"Not at first," Terry whispered, working his fingers together in worry. "First time I met him was on the solstice, an' he offered. Just flat out straight up, Terry my man, he said, I can give you your eyes back. All you gots to do is tell me what you see."

"You didn't believe him?"

"I believed him. I was afraid. But I went back, that Halloween, I went back to them crossroads at Sparkwood and Twenty-One, under that traffic light, and I waited, and round about midnight he came up and we shook on it. Blood on blood, palm to palm, and everything came back, all the world before me again and visible. And that's what I give him. He sees everything I do, all I see, past, present, future. He opened my eyes all the way, Frank. All the fucking way."

Frank shuddered but didn't know why. "You disappeared last time. You keep running away. Why? You know I need to know. You know I need to stop him."

"We're not ourselves anymore, Frank," he said. "We're not good men, not our own men. I told you that before. This is a ghost story, my love, and only ghosts will understand it."

Frank murmured that to himself, looking around, making sure cops weren't on their way or nothin'. "You ain't saying we're dead."

"I ain't saying we're alive."

Frank grunted. "How do I stop him? How do I make it go away?"

"What'd you ask him for?"

"I ... didn't." And here Frank felt a fool. "I told him, uh. I left it up to him."

"Oh, Frank. Oh, sparrow." And that singsong again.

"Goddamn it, don't go nowhere!"

"I can't help it, Frank. It's part of how I am now, throbbing between two lives. Ain't neither of 'em mine. But I'll tell you why I run, if it'll put you at ease any. I told you my eyes got opened all the way, and I see it all. You're the one kills me, Frankie boy. You're the one who makes it stop. Much as I want it, I'm scared to piss of it."

Frank eyed the gun, and Terry shook his head.

"Oh, not today." He closed his eyes. "No, today your boy's in far, far too much trouble for you to worry on me." He smiled a sweet smile that was almost seductive, and licked his lips. "Hurry, Frank. Ricky's got the knife. Snicker-snack!"

And he was gone.

There was no rounding a corner this time, no fog, he just stopped being there. Frank looked around to see if anyone'd noticed, then stuffed the gun in the back of his jeans and untucked his shirt so it'd hang down concealing it.

Whatever he had to chew on, that crazy fuck said Ricky was in trouble, so the rest could wait.

Frank's legs hurt from having run after Terry to begin with, so he jogged back, seeing right away Ricky wasn't in the burger joint. He looked around, saw the coyote still in the truck, the door still a little open 'cause he hadn't slammed it hard enough after he got the gun. He did a little up-and-down the side streets, peering whenever a building got outta the way so he could have a look, and a block or two away heard his boy's voice around the corner:

"Gimme a dollar."

Frank rounded the corner into an alleyway behind a coffee shop, where Ricky was walking quickly away from some pierced-face teenager, stuffing a dollar into his back pocket. The teenager had a sickly fascinated look on his face, the kind of look Frank associated with being a kid himself and poking roadkill with sticks. "Oh man," the teenager murmured, to a pink-haired girl next to him. They were both wearing thriftstore leather and studded belts. "This is fucking unreal, I'm so fucking hard right now."

Someone was coming outta the back entrance of the coffee shop, an employee in their green smock, looking for a smoke break or some damn thing. Quick as the dollar had disappeared into his ass pocket, Ricky pulled a knife outta somewhere, a butterfly knife like Frank used to be so fascinated with.

Snicker-snack.

Just walking right by, Ricky jabbed the knife at the guy, slicing through the apron and poking in, coming back wet and dark. He kept walking, never moving any faster, wiping the blood off on a napkin he dropped on the ground and putting the knife back wherever he'd had it.

"Fuck!" the kid yelled who'd been stabbed, and the two teenagers whooped, hugging each other like, well, like Frank didn't know what. But Ricky was gone.

Frank met him at the truck, engine idling, coyote sitting on the floor like he knew he had to leave room for the boy. Ricky got in the passenger side, looking pissed off and just plain teenage, and said, "What the hell was that all about?"

"Yeah," Frank asked. He felt sick, his stomach clenched, his head light. "What the hell _was_ that all about?"

"You fucking bolted! You even got your gun outta the glove box, didn't you? What the fuck for?"

"Enough with the swearing already, and nevermind me. The hell were you doing behind the coffee shop?"

Ricky paled at that, and Frank pulled outta the parking lot, headed for the High Road. "What do you mean?"

"Ricky. The dollar, the knife, that poor guy? You could've really hurt him! What'd he do to you?"

"Nothing," Ricky mumbled, and then looked up, and his face was aglow with _something_. Aflame. "He didn't do _nothing_, that's the whole thing. It's just random. No one ever gets really hurt, I'm good. It just looks bad. Band-aid and he'll be fine."

"You fucking stabbed him, Rick!"

"I know." Ricky grinned, and brought his feet up on the front of the seat, rocking back and forth as he held his knees to his chest. "I didn't pick him, he was just the one who was there. It's like, art. You just don't understand anything I do."

"Christ Almighty --" But he left it there. For the rest of the ride home, he'd start to say something, and they'd just go over the same ground. Finally he dropped it, and said, "You know, boy, I never learned how to be a good person. That's the long and short of it, you wanna know the truth. I had your Mom making me a good person, but it was like having training wheels, you don't always ride straight when you take 'em off, 'specially if it's too soon."

"Uh huh." The boy was barely listening, if at all. He had that sick happy look on his face.

"So I think I ain't taught you right how to be good yourself."

"Oh, this," Ricky said with a disgusted frown. "This is where you're gonna talk about saving me, right? Like Mom's preacher? I don't need Jesus in my life."

"Fuck Jesus," Frank said, and had a little thrill that Ricky gasped a bit at that. "I'm talking about lithium, kiddo. Or Prozac. Or ... fucking Pepcid, I don't know what they give kids like you these days --"

"'Kids like me,'" and oh did that sarcasm drip.

"Troubled fucking kids who don't know it ain't right to hurt people. You got troubles, Rick. You got problems, and maybe it ain't just you miss your Mom and brother and sister, maybe you just ain't right in there. I don't know, but I know I ain't the man to make it right. Now I don't know that I like all them fucking pharmaceuticals, but I know I'd rather have you doped up and not stabbing nobody than in prison somewhere 'feeling free to express yourself.'"

Ricky just shook his head like Frank was the dumbest son of a bitch on the planet, and when they got home, Frank cracked open a beer he drank in what tasted like a single sip and waited for the boy to go take a shower. When he had, Frank went into his room straight off, opening drawers, moving clothes aside but carefully so it didn't look like he'd been rummagin'. If he got caught, fuck it, he'd own up. But he'd as soon not deal with it.

The kid would be jacking off in there, so Frank didn't have to rush it completely. But his cell phone rang after he'd done the desk and under the bed, and he picked it up so Ricky wouldn't jump out to see if it was for him, or hear where the ringing was coming from.

"Yeah," Frank said. "Make it quick."

"Frank!" Took him a sec, but it was Jessie's voice. "Frank, Mickey's in trouble! We're out at the fairgrounds -- oh Christ, Frank, hurry!"

"Jess? What's up, what's --"

"Bring your gun -- oh Jesus! --"

She hung up or the connection got lost and Frank pocketed the phone absently while looking at what he'd found under the stack of Hustlers in Ricky's sock drawer.

Crumpled up, rolled up, folded into squares, one after another, the drawer was filled with what had to be hundreds of one-dollar bills.

CHAPTER SIXTEEN

God knew what the hell kinda trouble Mickey'd got himself into, but Jessie didn't strike Frank as the kinda girl to panic easy. No way he could bring Ricky along, but after having just threatened him with psychiatry and the like, and seeing him stab somebody, not to mention all them singles in the drawer, well, he couldn't just leave him to his own devices.

When the boy got out of the bathroom, Frank was waiting with lengths of duct tape already measured out. He said simply, "I wish I didn't have to do this, and I'll be back soon," and the rest was like roping a calf. It made him sick again, 'cause he could tell Ricky was pretty panicky too, but Christ, what choice did he have? He didn't hurt him none, taped him to the easy chair that was too big to fit through the door even if Ricky'd been strong enough to scoot around the room with it, too big without angling it like an L, which he couldna done either.

This was gonna wind up feeding a fucked-up first day of therapy, that was for sure.

The tape left Ricky's fingers free so Frank put the remote in his hand and turned the TV on. "I swear to shit, boy, this might be the crappiest thing I ever done as a father, but it's only cause I think it'd be even worse not to. This ain't punishment, we'll have cheeseburgers and pizza for a month to make up for it."

Ricky hadn't said nothing of import, just a lot of fuck you this, fuck you that, cocksucker motherfucker, and Frank hurried to the truck, the coyote leaping over his lap to the passenger seat. He hadn't filled the tank since the trip back, and he'd have to kiss knives and blow dice to eke out the last drop to make it 'cross town.

Without thinking about it, like it was just natural, he unlocked the drawer in his workbench and took Pop Train's old pistol outta it, the Series 70 Frank had used up till recent when he'd come by the Colt Defender he still wasn't used to yet.

He tried Mickey's phone on the way over, with no luck, and then thought to call the sheriff's office before trying Jessie. The evening dispatch took his report down, and he made sure to give his name a coupla times so it wouldn't get ignored despite his having no idea what was going on. Finally he called Jessie, who picked up after a couple rings. The connection was staticky, and there was a lotta noise in the background.

"Jess, it's Frank, I'm on my way. What's going on, girl?"

"It's Linc--," she said, and then someone shouted something before the phone clattered on the ground. More muffled shouts and the connection snapped shut.

Mickey owed a lot of money to Lincoln Train, and they mighta been family, but it wasn't hard to imagine Linc busting up the car, putting the fear a God into him to get his point across. He'd been that kinda kid and no reason he shouldn't be that kinda man. Frank hadn't run across him much since they were kids, and when Frank had been what an old TV Guide summary woulda called a local tough, a hard case, Linc had been living in Denver.

Colorado, Mickey and Jessie's red Trans Am, was sitting parked a couple buildin's away from the cockfights, sticking out like a fox in a box fulla rabbits. Jessie wasn't in it, and the car looked fine, that bumper sticker peeling at the corner, mud on the bumper, pollen residue all over the back winda. Frank parked next to it, got out, and listened.

Around the corner was where the commotion was coming from. He slid the Series 70 into the back of his jeans, and it felt comfortable right away, the weight just right, like an old beat-in leather jacket. He rounded the corner without running, didn't wanna surprise nobody. There was a bad smell to all this. A damn awful bad smell.

Mickey was on the ground, both lips split open and bloody, nose busted, looking like he'd took more'n a few kicks and bruises too. It was Lincoln the deliverer of 'em no doubt, and four of his buddies around, Jessie sitting uncomfortably 'gainst the back a the wall, holding her chest. Bastard'd knocked the tits outta her, and there was mud all over her red blouse.

They were in a kinda circle made by the backs of all the buildin's, moonlight and the pale glow of the automated parking lot lights forming the bulk of the illumination, with a little extra bleeding around the sides whenever someone opened the door to go in or outta the cockfights. Nobody over there was looking twice over here, and that wasn't accidental. Lincoln was in more puddin's than Frank'd realized, and you could read it on the body language of his so-called buddies. They didn't mind him kicking the shit outta Mickey cause it meant he wasn't kicking the shit outta them. That scar on Will's neck, the busted hand Jake had took that time that he said was from a tractor accident, how mucha that stuff was Lincoln's temper?

It was Will, Jake, Buck, and Tom Boy who were with Lincoln, the kindsa tough guys who didn't know how to be tough without being around somebody, tough guys only cut out for bit parts. Buck and Tom Boy'd been part of Frank's circle before he got himself married, and he didn't know how he felt about them being with Lincoln these days, kinda betrayed, and kinda bemused that they saw in Linc what they'd seen in him. He never woulda described himself as cut from the same cloth as Lincoln.

Jake would be carrying a knife, and Buck would have two or three. Always liked knives, that boy, the kinda guy who had fifty of 'em at home from flea markets and magazine ads, a fucking Klingon sword on his living room wall that he spent good milk money on. Buck'd been the first and last kid to take karate lessons after Chuck Norris became a big deal, and used to have a stack of Master of Kung Fu comics bigger'n his porn collection.

Frank shook his head. He had to stop thinking a these guys like they were in their teens, their twenties. They were men grown now, and maybe dangerous. He wasn't the strongest boy on the block no more, wasn't a boy at all, and his bones would creak sometimes, his back get sore till he put an Icy Hot patch on it. He wasn't a fucking kid and had to stop sinking into the mud of the world like one.

Tom Boy, now, Tom Boy would have a gun cause he was a nervous sumbitch who didn't trust no man, and he figured himself for a tougher guy than he really was. Packing heat made him feel bigger, heavier. Chances were good he'd never pull it. Chances were good he'd forget he could. But it was a thing to watch.

"I can get the money!" Mickey croaked at Lincoln, and oh shit he didn't sound good. That was a wet fucking voice coming outta that mouth, one Frank never woulda recognized, like a strangled fucking fish. Mick's lips were red with blood that mighta been local and mighta been coughed up, and every breath ended in a gurgle that was sick to hear.

"I know you can," Lincoln said, voice smooth as snake oil in comparison. Buck cringed just before Lincoln moved, like he knew what was coming, and Linc's boot connected hard with Mickey's chest, up high, knocking his head back too.

"Frank!" Jessie shouted, seeing him just then when she looked away from her man. She jumped up and he could see she was hurt too, hurt bad but not real bad, and making that distinction brought it all home that this was a "real bad" kinda night.

He wished she hadn't said nothing cause he hadn't decided how to play this and now he didn't have much choice. "Get the fuck off my brother, Lincoln," he said, and he didn't reach for the gun or make any other kinda move at all. "And you other boys, get the fuck outta here. Will. Tom Boy. Buck. Jake." He made sure to name 'em, made sure they knew he knew 'em. "Get on the fuck out. Cops'll be here soon."

Buck was the one to laugh at that, and even poor boy Jake chuckled.

That wasn't a thing Frank liked none at all.

"Well damn, son," Lincoln said, turning around from Mickey, and oh fuck, that look on his face was a chill all right. This man weren't right in the head. He looked all too damn happy about the evenin's proceedings. "We all practically deputies here. I guess the cops don't need to bother."

"If it's about money, Lincoln, we can settle it. Money ain't ever worth blood. There's always more of it around. You shoulda come to me."

"I mighta," Lincoln said, "but Mickey told me not to."

"Well I'm telling you otherwise." Frank took two steps forward, eyed Jessie. "Girl, go on to the car."

"Oh no," Lincoln said. "She's staying and watchin'."

Frank eyed him up and down real slow, and then licked his thumb. "Go on, Jessie."

She skaddled, looking guilty for doing it.

"Ain't no good thing making her watch this," Frank said, and looked at Jake, whose mother had pulled him out of a fight that coulda gone real bad once. "Ain't no good thing at all and all you boys should be ashamed of it."

"Well now," Lincoln said with a grin that coulda split your head open. "If it ain't the voice a moral authority. Boys, we in church?"

"We ain't in church, Lincoln," Tom Boy said.

"Shut the fuck up, Tom Boy, you meth addict shit," Lincoln said, that voice still never wavering, never showing no emotion but distanced amusement.

"Let's settle this, Lincoln," Frank said. "Mickey's piled on gambling debts before, we can deal with that ledger like men. Like Trains, fella."

Jake laughed, and Lincoln joined him. "Gambling debts ain't even half of it, son, less you getting poetical, and don't pull that fucking Train family bullshit on me. You think anyone but family would get this deep in hock to me? You think I'd fucking let that happen? Ain't but love got me being so fucking goddamn generous to this cocksucking piece a shit brother a yours, ain't but sweet filial love. This man here owes me for heroin, Frank. How you feel about that? How you feel about your ever-loving older brother being a fucking no-good smack junkie?"

Mickey started to stand up, like everything was settled now, and Lincoln back-handed him hard enough that the sky itself snapped, the sound echoing across them empty buildin's. Inside somebody yelled and whooped as one chicken killed another.

Frank rushed Lincoln, and Jake stepped in his way but got knocked down for it, Frank's arm right across his fucking neck the son of a bitch, and the next thing his hands were on Lincoln's shirt, grabbing him away and tossing him down. 'Cept the son of a bitch didn't go down, he just stumbled and pulled himself away.

"Boys," Lincoln said. "Leave young Mr Train be. I ain't fond a the notion a beating the shit outta two cousins in one night, but I reckon if the kiddie table wants a tussle it can get a tussle. Jake, put the knife away or I'll kill your fucking dog."

Frank glanced at Jake, who'd turned pale in the blue parking lot lights like he took the threat for serious before stuffing the butterfly knife back into his pocket. Snickersnack, Frank thought, and oh, oh fuck, he was sure he was gonna puke. Ricky still taped to the God damn chair in the God damn living room.

"I think I need a ambulance," Mickey gurgled from the ground, and Frank glanced at him but Lincoln didn't. Blood was pooling on his neck and the ground, his mouth full of it, and he lay in a weird position like he couldn't straighten his neck out. "I think I need a ambulance, Pop."

And suddenly everything felt red and cold.

Lincoln was still grinning that little grin, waiting to see what Frank was gonna do, so Frank rewarded his patience. He plowed his fist into that stupid fucking grin, first once, then twice, the second time splitting his middle knuckle open on Lincoln's porcelain crown. Linc put his hands up to grab him, but Frank got a fistful of his collar and twisted it, bunched it up, then pushed his cousin down to the ground and jumped on him, slamming his knee into his crotch as hard as he fucking could. The high-pitched yelp, like a God damn kicked dog, was a relief. That grin, that voice, had Frank thinking Lincoln had gone untouchable.

Lincoln clawed at him, kicked at him, fought vicious right from the start, which felt good, God damn it. There was no pussyfooting around here, no putting on a show for some barfly. Buck obviously panicked cause he lunged at Frank and grabbed him around the midsection, pulling him off his boss. Frank yanked the gun outta his jeans, having to use his left hand, but at this range it'd be just fine, and pointed it at Buck, who backed off immediately.

"Get outta here!" Lincoln shouted at the boys. "Get the fuck outta here, damn it! I told you this is family business."

When they didn't run right away, Frank fired a shot in the air and they scattered. He put the gun down on the ground behind him, making sure Lincoln knew he wasn't gonna use it and then crouched. "You done it now, Linc," he said. "You woke the bad man. That's my fucking brother you been messing with. You don't know no better than to fuck with my fucking brother?"

"You ain't the only bad man in town, Frankie boy. You're not ready for me yet."

Frank grunted. "Let's see it."

They went at each other like animals, like the cockfight a walk and a wall away. Linc scratched his face, kicked him in the thigh, grabbed a sharp rock from the ground and hit him in the face with it, tearing his cheek. The wound felt cold and exposed, like when a peppermint candy's so strong it takes your breath away.

Frank pushed him against the wall, kneed him in the crotch again and again until those yelps went hoarse, then brought his hands down on the back of Lincoln's neck in a double fist. Kicked the man in the face as he crumpled and tried to get up, slammed a boot down on his hand. Lincoln got hold of his leg, though, pulled him down and twisted it, kept twisting like he was trying to snap a turkey drumstick off a bird ain't been cooked enough.

God, it felt good to fight.

He had to be grinning as he turned over and tangled his hands in Lincoln's hair, twisting it before pulling him down hard and leaning to the side so his cousin's head collided with the hard rocky ground insteada his shoulder. "Rotten son of a bitch," he said. "Fucking heroin, fucking gambling, who the fuck you think you are. Who the fuck you think you are."

He kicked Lincoln in the balls again square on, and when he saw him reaching for the gun, picked it up and tossed it away, hard. It clattered on the rocks somewheres, and Frank jumped on Lincoln's back, trying to get all his weight to land on the small of his back, to drive that fucker into the rocks, smash him against the ground, and he punched the back of the fucker's neck.

Frank kinda zoned out a bit. He was focused on what he was doing but thinking about Mickey at the same time. <u>Heroin</u> for fuck's sake. They'd both done coke before, but not in a long time. Heroin was for God damn burn-out rockstars and the city. The fuck was Mickey doing on heroin? It was New Mexico, for Christ's sake. Was it worse than meth? He didn't have a damn clue, come to think of it, but it <u>sounded</u> worse than meth. Frank knew twenty, thirty people did meth, and most of 'em were trash who woulda drunk themselves to death if they'd been born thirty years earlier, but didn't know nobody who did heroin.

Nobody except his no-good brother.

He tried to imagine Mickey shooting up in their parents' house, <u>in their parents' house!</u>, tying up his arm so a vein bulged out and putting the needle in, sinking back into his chair. This was Marlowe's fault. No way Mickey would do something like this. No God damn way.

The devil made him do it.

Frank pounded Lincoln's skull into the ground, and Lincoln reached back, got hold on him, twisted him over. The man was strong, give him that. Stronger'n Frank, you come down to it. Maybe smarter too, as far as book smarts and shit like that went. And hell, Frank would admit it, smarter for "street smarts" too, Lincoln being in the game and being connected with things these days, where Frank had gone domestic and tame for twenty years.

But Frank ...

Frank was more <u>vicious</u>. Frank could out-vicious fucking anybody. That was who he'd been. That was what he'd done. He was the bad man. He was the bad man.

Lincoln grappled with him and they rolled in the dirt, rocks tearing a huge gap in Frank's jeans, and when Lincoln grabbed his balls and squeezed so hard he was sure they were gonna pop, he bit down on the son of a bitch's neck, hard as he could, blood everywhere, skin torn, and Lincoln screamed a deep, dark scream and let go. Frank could barely see, his eyes all stars, blood all over his face and wet on his mouth, bruises already covering half Lincoln's face. Frank was pretty sure he had a few busted ribs and maybe a broke foot, maybe a sprained wrist, and he tossed all that shit aside.

He tossed that shit right to the curb, as they both struggled to their feet.

"Son of a bitch," he said, and his mouth tasted like mud and sour coffee grounds. "My fucking brother." He couldn't stand up straight without fire lancing his guts.

Lincoln grunted and spat out a tooth. One of his eyes wouldn't open. A deep gash had swole up across his eyebrow and sagged down, forcing the lid shut. "I fucked your wife, Frankie. I fucked her before you married her and I fucked her again after."

"Fuck you, Lincoln."

"She wasn't any good. No fucking good at all. You got no standards, boy."

Frank lunged at him, awkward, slow, sludgy. Lincoln got outta the way but only just. "Fuck you, Lincoln."

"S'where she got the taste for it, boy. S'why she liked the bad boy, the bad man. She just wanted more a my dick, and had to settle for you." Lincoln grinned and his mouth was pure red. He took a swing, and Frank caught it, a lucky catch but he'd take it, and pushed back, pushed hard, knocked Lincoln down to the ground and got his arm in an awkward angle, snapping the wrist.

It was a sickly, wet sound, the kinda sound made you expect something to spurt you in the eye, but Frank's hands were completely dry.

"Frank!" Jessie yelled. The stupid bitch had come back from the car, hysterical about this that n' the other. "Frank, we've got to get Mickey to a hospital! Stop it, Frank!"

He kept hitting Lincoln, kept slamming his fists down into that face, into his collarbone, into his chest, punching his throat, slamming his head back into the ground. Everything sounded wrong, tinny, blood in his ears, blood streaming like sweat from a bad cut under his hair. Jessie sounded a thousand miles away, too far for him to get to, she'd have to help Mickey to the car herself, call an ambulance, couldn't she see Frank was busy?

His balls ached, and he knew Lincoln was lying about Kriste, he knew it, but it pissed him off more that Lincoln would lie about something like that. The man had no fucking decency, no God damn morals, no spiritual bone.

His hands felt greasy and stupid, like nothing in his body would work the way it was sposed to, and his mouth felt like somebody'd bit his lips off. He kinda blacked out for a while, swimming somewhere, and came to still pounding on Lincoln, all wet and wild, coming up with handfuls of nothin'. There weren't anything recognizable to Lincoln's face anymore, Frank'd been pounding the butt an' barrel a the gun into it over and over until it was just raw sausage, nose gone broke and soft, cheeks bruises on rags, forehead all tore up.

Lincoln wasn't breathing no more, and down in the hollow of his chest, Frank realized he hadn't been for a while, that Jessie was weeping a thousand miles away, and he just kept hitting him. Just kept hitting him. "I'm the bad man," he kept telling that no-good son of a bitch, "I'm the hard case." He only stopped to lean over and puke on the ground, and it came up cold and rancid on his numb lips.

Michael Gabriel Mondragon Train was admitted to the County General trauma ward and pronounced dead from respiratory failure at 8:47 p.m. Lincoln Forrest Train predeceased him by an unknown duration, dead on the scene when the ambulance arrived.

Frank Train was treated for severe abrasions, blood loss, and multiple fractures, after which he spent the night in the Intensive Care Unit under armed police guard on loan from Santa Fe.

CHAPTER SEVENTEEN

Mickey's funeral was on a Thursday. Jessie sold the Trans Am to bail Frank outta jail, hire a Santa Fe lawyer, and cover the funeral costs Mickey's life insurance wasn't enough for. That left her with not a whole lot, Mickey's bank accounts being empty an' overdrawn and her own not in the finest state a health. Frank knew she'd want to talk 'bout selling the folks' house and he knew she'd be right about it.

But first they hadda bury Mick, that son of a bitch son of a gun.

"I know it's customary to read something from the Bible or a good poem," Jessie said, staring straight down at the yellow college-ruled paper in her hands and not out at anybody in the crowd. "And Mickey respected the Bible as much as any man, but I don't know that any one passage of it stood out for him. So I hope y'all will forgive me if I read something else instead, something I know he enjoyed."

Some folks chuckled at that, 'cause especially with the way Mickey died, it wasn't no secret he wasn't a churchgoing man. God-fearing maybe. But not much a one for church or the Bible neither. Frank just felt thankful that the business about heroin had been kept outta the public ear and, far as he could tell, the grapevine too.

"This is from The Reivers," Jessie said. "That was Mickey's favorite book, he kept a copy in the glovebox of Colorado -- that's our car, was our car -- to read if he got bored when I was shopping or what have you. It's by William Faulkner. Okay.

"'Sometimes you have to say goodbye,' Boon Hoggenbeck said. 'Sometimes you have to say goodbye to the things you know and hello to the things you don't.' There's another place where it says --" Jessie grinned nervously. "Well, this isn't really appropriate, I know, but it's Mickey all right. This part, this was underlined, in his book? It says, Boon knew something I didn't, that the rewards of virtue are cold, and odorless, and tasteless, and not to be compared with the bright and exciting pleasures of sin and wrong-doing."

She paused like for breath and said, "I didn't want to say anything bad about Mickey and if I only said the good it wouldn't be honest. So I figured Mr Faulkner could do the talking for me, and I hope you understand."

One of Jessie's brothers who'd flown down put a hand gently on Frank's shoulder by way of condolence. The gentleness wasn't meant to be tender so much as cautious. Frank knew he looked half like Frankenstein, and it'd taken some talk just to get outta the hospital, pointing out he couldn't damn afford to stay there a week racking up bills just for laying in bed with a pan for pissing in.

He had one wrist in a thick cast heavy enough that his arm wore out quick just walking around, and he pictured himself with a Popeye-huge forearm in the future from all that extra work. His ribs were bandaged up, and there weren't much else they could do but keep that wrapped up all tight, but he had a brace to put on to keep from moving around too much, if need be. He was covered with bruises places he didn't even remember getting hit and they were yellowing like stained sheets, all over his face and chest.

There were stitches on his left cheek, right temple, forehead, right leg, and chest, in addition to the ones under the cast: a hundred and sixty-eight all told. Two kindsa antibiotics for infections, an anti-inflammatory to keep the swelling down, codeine for the little pain and Percocet for the big, Valium to sleep at night or get through the day. He'd spent a couple hundred dollars on fucking pills, and that was after what the insurance covered.

Him being all banged up, it was an easy thing for people to talk about. It was like talking about the elephant in the room insteada everything that mattered. He just kept telling 'em, "Pain don't hurt." When folks looked at him funny he didn't know if it was 'cause a how he looked or 'cause he was the only survivor of so much, so damn much. Like there'd been a train wreck none of 'em knew about.

He laughed at that, covering it with a cough into his fist so he wouldn't interrupt Jessie. Train wreck.

He stood near the front of the huddle, facing Jessie and the casket an' all. Ricky was nearby but making it clear he wasn't standing with Frank, and didn't veer too close to the Mondragons, either. There weren't as many of 'em as there'd been six months earlier. Cancer'd got the ones who'd been dealing with that, hearts went on them old enough to have used 'em up, a farming accident here, a carjacking there. The herd had thinned, and people knew it. Frank kept catching peoples' eyes wandering over the Tom Mix Circle Cemetery, seeing how there were a few less faces than there'd been at the last funeral or the one before that. Nobody joked about it no more.

And there Frank was, last of the Trains by blood. Jessie was married in, Ricky wasn't his, if you wanted to climb anything else on that family tree you had to crawl out to the other branches -- the Archuletas, who had a great-something-or-else in common with Arthur Train Junior, the

Playforths one a whose somethings had married Arthur Train Senior's little sister before she died in childbirth, the Lancasters who'd moved away to Castle Rock and the long-outta-touch Trains of Ponchatoula, Tucson, Cali-Fucking-Fornia, alla whom mighta been dead too for all Frank knew.

The grass was greener over Kriste, Gina, and Philip's graves than some a the others. One a the worse things about the funeral was being by them graves, so soon, too soon. Mosta the other Trains weren't buried that near, but Uncle Butch wasn't far away and Lincoln's plot was dug and good to go later in the day.

Father Michael said it'd be inappropriate to bury a man and his killer at the same time, but he couldn't stop 'em from being in the same cemetery. Couldn't stop Frank from standing right there in view of the man he killed neither.

The same fucking day.

Here'n there were flowers on graves, mostly roses that died too quick and carnations that lived too cheap, bundles of local yucca flowers and Mexican hats brought by folks who'd grown 'em themselves, and at the edge of where the dead were buried, clumps of wild-growing nodding onion, which drooped with little lampshade-shaped pale purple flowers. It was a nice day, latest of a bunch of 'em, with a little bit of a breeze that was kinda damp, kinda cool, but not unpleasant. The air felt good on the backa his neck where the brace pinched his bruises every time he had to wear it, and made him feel more alert despite the pills. They'd given him Prozac an' Risperdal too, but he'd been making the boy take those. Wasn't like Frank'd been going around stabbing people for money.

There hadn't been a wake, that was one blessin'. Frank didn't figure Jessie woulda been up to it, but the reasoning was that Mickey hadn't lived in town in so long that mosta his friends weren't gonna be able to make it, cause they weren't the kindsa guys who showed up to funerals to begin with, and even if they would've, they weren't easy to find on short notice. Poker buddies, business partners of one kind or another, drinking partners, that sorta thing.

Wake or no wake, the food had come anyway. Jessie'd been asking Frank what some of it was, not being from the area, and he'd pointed out tamale casserole and posole and just how many of them Tupperware containers were filled with green chile. Some folks just brought wine, even a case a beer. Now, for a widower a case a beer made sense enough, but a widow woman not even 35 yet? Frank'd already heard whispers he hadn't meant to hear, "at least she's young enough to remarry," "someday, someday."

The Mix was where things looked most like spring, green green grass far as you could look, unlike the thirsty stuff most folks had if they even bothered planting grass at all. The soil was soft and loamy, so when the breeze took hold of wildflower seeds, they took root here quicker'n anywhere else. It was like Easter Sunday here in some technicolor movie from a generation ago, like everybody should be in white suits and pastel dresses, top hats and parasols.

Across the way, some a them wildflowers swayed towards the breeze steada away from it, little bluebells dangling and ringing back and forth, and Frank remembered the stories of the ghost girls who'd been buried in the wrong cemetery, Mexican girls whose spirits were restless 'cause they hadn't been buried in Catholic ground. Would Mickey give a shit?

The coyote with the ragged ear perked his head up towards the wildflowers and trotted over there, to the visible relief of a lotta the folks around him. That white crow Frank'd seen at Kriste's funeral musta had a nest nearby, 'cause it fluttered outta the trees when the coyote got near, and the coyote of course felt compelled to chase.

The coyote chased the crow down Tom Mix Circle through the lines of cars parked alongside the street for the funeral, and past the traffic light onto Church On Fire Lane, where a coupla old men were drinking cheap whiskey from Mason jars on the stoop a the house that'd been built on the lot where the church'd burned. There was a little plaque on a stick at the enda the yard by the mailbox, giving the date and name a the church and all, and they got a little bit a money from the New Mexico Historical Society for being a historical spot an' all. The yard was pockmarked with rocks that were the only thing kept the weeds from taking over, an' a roadrunner pecked at the little groundbugs that crawled around their edges or clung to the scalloped leaves of the weeds.

When the coyote passed by, that white ol' crow flapping its wings, the old timers just watched it, one of 'em saying something about the Train family to the other, and how them poor folks had fell on hard times all right, hard times like in the old days when a drought might do your farm in an' leave you hauling sacks at the mercantile if you were lucky, while your cheeks shriveled into your face 'cause you gave your food to your kids. They'd both of 'em seen it happen, and nothing much surprised 'em anymore, not even a coyote passing by or a roadrunner who never left their yard.

"Well you see there," one of 'em said to the other, "ain't all crows black."

The other one didn't say nothing at all and might not've been convinced.

Church On Fire crossed Burns, something everybody loved even though there weren't anything at the corner a Burns an' Church On Fire, hadn't been since Garrison's relocated to the proper center a town, where it was still, the coyote and the crow running an' flying past it and across the parking lot for the Loan Gunmen check-cashin'. The crow lit down onto the rooftop of the Taco Casita, ruffling its feathers and grooming itself as it perched on the orange vinyl adobe.

The coyote rummaged 'round the dumpster, fulla wilted lettuce and mealy tomato ends, orange grease an' glops a sour cream an' guacamole spin dip sogging up corn chips. Pawing through deep-fried tamale pies and tater tots, the coyote finally sniffed up a Muchisimo Sancho Burrito stuffed with certified 100% Angus beef seasoned with an authentic blend of herbs and spices, rolled in a Fresh-Maid(tm) flour tortilla with Maxi-Mexi rice, red <u>and</u> green salsa sauces, fiesta queso, crispy corn chips, and our famous guacamole spin dip, along with an unadvertised helping a las cucarachas.

Yazzie & Son Funeral Home was next to the parking lot, and the coyote sat in the shadow of it as he wolfed down the burrito. The crow mighta figured it'd been unnoticed and took flight again, but the coyote followed straight off, breaking into a full gallop down Center Street, past the washateria with the Royal Crown machine in front that still gave up glass bottles, which you could get for free if you dropped the right size slug in insteada your quarters. But you hadda have two of 'em and some kids hoarded their slugs 'cause there was that rumor that somewhere in town was the nudie machine, the little kinematoscope that showed flipbook-type pictures of a lady taking her clothes off and turning around so you could see everything. You dropped in your quarter or slug, turned the crank, and the pictures would flip by like a little movie. When Frank was a kid, the rumor was the lady was old Mrs Hadderly, the ancient math teacher, but he realized now odds were the photos had come with the machine, probably bought at a bank sale for some old nickelodeon arcade.

The crow's path carried the coyote past the bank where Chelsea Loker handled one deposit after another. It was Thursday, after all, when the Rodriguezes and the Meeres both handed out paychecks and the early morning workers were getting off for the day and getting their deposits in so they'd clear for the weekend, wasn't nothing worse than waiting for a Monday morning go-through so's you could pick up them eggs and beer you were out of. She was thinking to herself about the Trains and Mondragons, about how everybody'd seen Mickey's end coming the moment he rolled into town in that cherry red Trans Am that rode smooth as oiled leather.

There was a sale on chuck roast at the meat market, which meant a lotta folks'd be making green chile with beef this weekend insteada the traditional pork. There were tamales, too, three for a dollar still warm in little brown paper bags, not as good as the tamale ladies had at the holidays but you made do with what you could get. Next door at Tuck's grocery, the handwritten signs in red marker on white butcher paper advertised early season chiles -- milder by far than the ones'd be grown in high summer, but some of 'em still with a bite an' sold like they did in Hungary, with one superhot pepper mixed in for every nine milds so you never knew whatcha were gonna get. They had Bounty paper towels on sale, too, and them new Coca-Cola flavors six for a dollar.

The baggers were understaffed at Tuck's, two of 'em been Mondragons and both dead now, bless 'em both, the other a Garcia by way of his mother and over at the funeral to pay his respects to his departed cousin-once-removed-in-law, or however you'd go about phrasing that. Mid-day shoppers waited a mite impatiently for their pinto beans an' frozen macaroni to be piled into paper or plastic, two baggers covering four checkouts and one of 'em grousing that he wasn't supposed to come to work till six o'clock anyhow and when was he gonna get dinner? The manager was engaged to a Mondragon cousin but didn't feel obligated to go to the funeral for that distant a relation, given how many she'd gone to lately anyhow.

Way things were going, she just didn't see the sense in spending a sick day on this funeral when for all she knew she'd just be going back to the Mix to bury her father-in-law-to-be in another week. Cynical, superstitious, downright cold maybe to see it that way, but sometimes the world was like that.

The Navajo Bar & Grill had four customers who'd called in sick to work to go to the funeral and decided they'd rather be drinking, being as how the Navajo was more bar and not much grill. The coyote chased the crow through the back lot and across the old stone property marker, undeterred by the smells of microwaved nachos and spatula-pressed cheeseburgers, the sourness of beer and plastic-jug tequila vastly overpowering 'em.

Wasn't long 'fore the crow'd led the chase to the old County Road that ran from Oak to March, where a lot of the old small farms, family farms, were. These farms had been founded when you didn't need much that you couldn't grow yourself. You sold this and that to pay for equipment that'd last for years, household items you could pass down to your children, who wouldn't complain that they wanted internet and cable television and compact discs. These days mosta these farmers either part-timed it or had spouses who worked. Some of 'em just retired there, after a long life a insurance adjusting, office management, and the like.

The coyote with the ragged ear trotted across careful rows of tomato plants and the thin wooden stakes they were tied to, stumpy stalks a corn, early vine growth a squash and long, low-built arbors for grapes, the crow still in his sights and flapping across the green fields. A coop a chickens went squawking when he passed, scenting the predator smell on the wind, and he took up short for a minute as if wondering if he wanted to eat a chicken, or at least kill it. But the crow kept flying and he kept the chase, through the cul-de-sacs and checkerboard avenues of housing developments that'd been built in the 40s and 50s for soldiers' families, which is why the Veterans of Foreign Wars monument was here instead of the center a town, which hadn't been quite so bustling back then.

Out here the housing developments gave way to hills soon enough, the picturesque kind that made good backdrops in real estate pamphlets, green for now, though they'd yellow as the weather got hotter and the refreshment of spring thaw further away, but still bulbous and hearty in a pleasant kinda way, as abrupt in their curvature from the earth as young breasts. The spring air carried the smell of the sheep ranches, woolly and gamey, but they were far enough away that they didn't deter the coyote.

Borachon Creek wound through the land here, wilder and easier to track outside the confines of Cardenio. The Rodriguez farm's workers tilled the fields irrigated by the Borachon, planting flintcorn an' the chocolate-colored chiles that hadda be planted late cause they were so finicky when they were young. The crow darted at bugs on the surface of the water while the coyote with the ragged ear followed along the bank, scaring field mice an' prairie dogs outta the way. At the shallower bends, it splashed across, zig-zagging back an' forth and slipping on the rocks that broke the current, cooling itself off as it kept up the chase.

On the other side a the High Road, halfway to Chimayo, the Borachon fed from a tributary of the Rio Grande, and the crow and coyote followed that as it grew wider, passing fishing cormorants and javelinas. As the tributary gave way to the Grande itself, the river with two names, light as a feather and broad as the interstate, the shore became dappled with palo verde, puffy green bushes taller'n a man with needles fine as filigree sticking out like Einstein's hair.

It was in one a them bushes that the coyote finally lost track a the crow, who mighta changed course to follow some upwards draft the coyote couldn't scent, or maybe settled down in the branches of a mesquite tree back a ways. The coyote with the ragged ear darted one way then the other, panting like a hound dog, before finally giving up with a whine and settling down at the side of the river, lapping at the water as the current splashed it up.

All that seems Earth, Frank thought. Is Heaven or Hell.

The funeral cleared out bit by bit, people mumbling condolences to Jessie or Frank or both or sometimes not knowing who to say sorry to. He an' her exchanged a number a looks throughout the course of it, not so much commiserating, not really any meaning at all beyond "yeah, I know." Just that and nothing more. "Yeah, I know."

The Garcias had come, Kriste's family, and Frank wasn't sure he felt all right about that, but decided that feeling they were intruding was only 'cause he knew this wasn't about them. No matter how many a his kin died, it wasn't on them, 'cause they were Kriste's family and no blood a his. So it seemed like they didn't belong, but that wasn't none a their doing, and they didn't belong any less than mosta the folks there.

But he shook hands with the men, hugged the women, hugged the children, said thanks for this and yes for that, and that's all right, he said, we'll manage. Some a the younger cousins was giving him weird looks, and it wasn't just cause a how banged up he was.

From now on, he'd always be Frank Train, who killed a man. Frank Train, who killed his cousin. Frank Train, beat a man to death to avenge his brother. Thing like that, it didn't leave you. Followed you like a stink. People might be intimidated by it, but it didn't win you any a the right kinda points.

Some of them Garcias, though, they lingered. And so Frank had to linger. And so Jessie had to linger. And so before long, Father Michael was kinda waiting for everybody to leave, and Jessie clearly figured she had to be the last what with being the widow, and ... well, it went like that. Finally Frank saw that the Garcias were hoping Jessie would leave so they could talk to him in private. His heart sank stupidly in his chest, the way it woulda when he was a damn kid, like he was afraid he was gonna be dressed down by his girlfriend's pop.

"Say, Jessica," he said, then realized he wasn't sure at all what he was gonna suggest she do in order to give them the space, but she knew what he was going for and nodded and just left, taking Father Michael by the arm to talk about this that or th'other.

"Bruno," Frank said, shaking his father-in-law's hand again. "Like I said, glad y'all could be here for this, seeing as Mickey weren't your own family and all."

"He was Ricky's family, though," Inez said, and her husband nodded, like that was the point that mattered. Frank wondered yet again if they knew their daughter'd cheated on him, and if it would ever dawn on 'em that was why Ricky was alive. He wondered for the umpteenth time what it woulda took for him to piece that together if it hadn't been for Marlowe's hints, if it was something he ever woulda believed just cold, with no proddin'.

"How you feeling, son?" Bruno asked. "You still look like a mule kicked the shit outta you."

Frank nodded, which hurt the back of his neck. "Still feel like it. I'll be all right. Gonna sleep solid tonight after I take them pills, I tell you."

"Uh huh. Like I said, you have any trouble getting a refill, I got that brother-in-law owns a pharmacy."

"I appreciate that. I think I'll be all right. Don't wanna risk getting hooked, you know, like them damn Hollywood celebrities."

Bruno grinned and nodded silently, and Inez said, "Sure, sure. You gotta take care of yourself, Frank. You gotta take care of yourself."

No one else seemed anxious to say anything, and Frank rubbed his hands together gingerly. "Well speaking a which, I'm really feeling pretty cat-drug, you know, so I oughta get home and lay down, the hospital was talking about how they had this fund, they could send a nurse for a couple days."

"Yeah," Bruno said. "Ain't that somethin'. Frank, listen, we're gonna have to take the boy."

The silence was great enough that Jessie looked over like she'd heard somethin'. Funny how that could go.

"What?" Frank asked, but it made sense he guessed.

"Frank," Inez said. "You're just not ... in a position to take care of Ricky right now."

"You're gonna have a trial and all," Bruno said. "And well, son, you killed a man. Look at you. I'm sorry, I can't have my grandson around that. Not without Kriste."

"If Kriste were alive, it'd be different," Inez said.

"Sure," Bruno said. "And it ain't like you can't see him! Just come on by. And when you're feeling better, well, we'll see about weekends or something."

"Bruno, look," Frank said. "You want Ricky to come visit you, we'll set something up. But right now I think what he needs is some stability, and --"

"Frank, let's not upset the boy with any arguing, all right? We talked to a lawyer. We can sue for custody, and if we do, the judge might rule you can't see him unsupervised -- not ever. Even if we want you to."

Frank grunted. "Don't make out like you're looking out for me."

"Frank," Inez said, putting a hand on his arm.

He jerked it away and it hurt like hell. "You're right," he said. "About upsetting Ricky. Do me a favor. I'd like to tell him he's going to stay with you for a while. While I'm recoverin'. All right? We'll take it from there as we take it."

"No," Inez said, "We're not lying to --"

"You can't fucking spring this on me at my brother's funeral and expect me to be okay with it," Frank said in a low voice near a growl, "and I'd rather upset the boy than give him away."

"Bruno --" Inez started to say, and her husband shook his head.

"No, the man's right. This wasn't the time or place if we wanted things that way, dear. We'll tell him it's a vacation, Frank, and we'll hash things out later."

"All right," Frank said.

"But we will hash them out," Bruno added. "Soon."

Frank nodded, out of words, and looked around for Ricky. He found him at the opposite end of the cemetery from Jessie and Father Michael, taking a dollar from Josh Marlowe, who turned and left before Frank got there. He decided not to comment on the art teacher, and just told Ricky he'd be visiting his grandparents for a while.

The boy nodded, like he'd seen it coming, his eyes bright and unreadable.

CHAPTER EIGHTEEN

"Yes, damn it, for the last time, I know I duct-taped him to the chair. It was a stupid thing to do, but I <u>still</u> don't know what else I coulda done." Frank shifted in his chair. It was hard to stay comfortable for long, and the shrink made him more nervous than the lawyers did. He had two now, Tensen handling the criminal end a things what with the murder second degree charge they were trying to get bumped down to justifiable homicide, and Seria working family law to try to keep the custody thing outta court. He said that was key. At worst, they had to delay any court involvement pertaining to Ricky until Frank had been declared innocent in the criminal matter.

Neither of 'em talked about the fact that if Frank <u>wasn't</u> found innocent, it was gonna be moot 'cause he'd be in prison till well after Ricky turned 18.

But the shrink was Seria's idea and Tensen thought it might help them too, show that Frank was an upstanding citizen concerned with his well-being and the well-being of his only living son who depended on him and so on and what-all. Ricky and Frank saw him separately once a week and then Fridays they had a double feature.

"Frank," Dr Mack said. "You know that's not true." He tapped his pencil on his desk, and Ricky kicked at something from his slump in the couch. "Stop that, Rick, let your father answer."

"All right," Frank said, scratching at the edge of his cast where it itched to Hell and back. "I could've called a neighbor or a friend to come watch him. I could've trusted him. If I was really that worried, I could've called family services and tole 'em it was an emergency."

"You could have stayed with him, too," Dr Mack said quietly.

"My brother was dyin'!"

"You didn't know that!" Ricky said, almost shoutin'. "And now you're gonna go to jail the resta your life and Uncle Mickey died anyway, so what the fuck good did you do?"

"Stop it, Rick," Dr Mack said. "We've talked about your anger problems. Remember your calm place?"

Ricky grunted just as Frank did, and neither of 'em looked at each other.

"Look," Frank said, and all this made him so tired. "I just, I think we keep getting away from the core thing here, the thing that made me tape him to --"

"Nothing makes you do anything, Frank," Dr Mack said. "We make our choices."

"All right, the thing that made me choose to tape the little fuck -- oh, God damn it." He clenched and unclenched his fists and wanted to reach for the flask tucked into his jacket, no matter how foolish he knew that'd be. "Ricky, I'm sorry. I'm awful fucking stressed out, and it ain't your fault. I ain't angry at you, I'm just angry."

"Do you understand that difference, Rick?"

"Course I understand it," Ricky said, taking a lighter out and flipping it open, flipping it shut, flipping it open, flipping it shut. "I'm not a retard like some a your patients."

"Frank, go on."

"I'm just saying, I ain't -- I ain't trying to getcha to ignore the fact I taped him up, but --" Frank struggled with the kindsa phrases he knew he had to use in this damn office, which was chillier, draftier, and sparser than television had made him think shrinks' offices were. Wasn't nothing like Dr Melfi's, that was for sure. "I feel we're glossing over what Ricky done in Santa Fe and what I think he has done many times, which is to stab someone unprovoked. I was bothered very much by that, and reacted out of panic and desperation."

"I think that's a fair assessment of your motivation," Dr Mack said. "Next week we'll talk more about whether you feel you have a tendency towards rash behavior -- given your actions later that evening. Ricky, is there anything else you'd like your father to discuss with me at his next meeting?"

"Ask him what it's like to kill a man," Ricky said, looking at his fingernails. "What it's like to beat him to death, to pound on him till he just up and dies on you."

Dr Mack took a breath and didn't reply to that, just asked Frank, "Is there anything you would like me to discuss at Ricky's next meeting?"

Frank spread out his hands helplessly. "Ask him why he fucking stabs people!"

The doc made a note and nodded. "Well, I think this went just fine, we're making progress. See you both next week."

ooo000ooo

They had the rest of the day in Taos to themselves, before Frank had to bring Ricky back to the Garcias. No later than 8:00, Inez reminded him every time, unless they ran late at dinner and he called to let them know. Christ it was like having a high school girl out on a date.

Inez wouldn't say a damn word to him about how Ricky was doing, how he was getting on in the Taos school, if he liked his room, anything like that. Bruno would answer practical type questions. Whether they'd made an appointment for his next physical, if the school had gotten Ricky's transcripts from Cardenio all right. The clear sense Frank got from both his in-laws was they wished he'd just dry up and go away, that he'd up and died when their daughter had. Bad enough for the boy to lose his mother, but better he'd lost both his parents. Oh, they'd never put it in those words --

Well come to think of it, Inez might. Her distaste for him seemed to be growing into hate, and Frank wondered what Ricky said about him, how he was talked about behind his back. He knew he'd become one a those fellas, the fellas who's walking into the Rockinghorse Diner stopped some a the conversations cold. For some folks he was Poor Ol' Frank, Country Song Frank, lost his woman and his family, lost his kids and raised another man's bastard, killed his cousin for killing his brother, and all he had left was his pickup and a ragged coyote. For other folks he was Dangerous Frank, Vicious Frank, who'd gone unhinged after losing too much and lost his mind last, beat a man to death with nothing but his fists and a whole lotta bloodlust.

What Bruno did let him know was that Ricky was getting in trouble in school, and wasn't allowed to take the bus no more. There'd been talk of police, apparently, but Bruno an' Dr Mack had both explained that Ricky had gone through a tough time and blah blah blah, and he'd got off with a warning. And then another. Frank got the impression Bruno'd had to pull some strings, but his father-in-law wouldn't elaborate on what'd happened, and went pale when Frank asked if the boy had a lot of singles lying around.

Only reason Bruno even told him that much was he wanted Frank to feel guilty, wanted to blame it on him. Easier to distance the boy's problems from Kriste that way, like Ricky was a true Garcia who'd been tainted by Frank, contaminated by him. After all, Bruno'd all but said, Ricky might've assaulted someone, but he never killed nobody.

"So how you liking Taos?" Frank asked. He asked it every week but never felt like he got an answer.

Ricky shrugged. He'd been even less talkative since Frank an' the Garcias sat him down and told him that he'd be staying with 'em "for the time being," not just as a break. "I dunno, I might be moving to Dallas," he said casually.

"Oh yeah?" Frank checked the odometer and sighed to himself. Long drive left. The four hours to Taos and back every week made his back and leg hurt like fuck and today it'd be longer with bringing Ricky down to Cardenio. "Who you gonna live with?"

150

"I got some friends," Ricky said. "We're talking about moving there and getting an apartment. You know, splitting rent an' the bills an' all. I can cook a little, so we won't have to eat out."

"Yeah, that's a good way to save," Frank said. "Didn't know you were cooking now. Your grandma getcha on that?"

The boy shrugged again. "Whatever. I make noodles and enchiladas and stuff. It ain't hard."

"What do your grandparents figure about Dallas?"

"They don't care. They're totally okay with it."

Frank was sure Ricky'd never brought it up to them, but kids would be kids. They always had plans. "Well, you hungry? We can hit a drive-thru."

"What, we're not sitting down for lunch today?" Ricky looked out the window suspiciously. "Where we goin'?"

"Down to Cardenio for a bit. We got some stuff to do."

Ricky snorted. "We gotta be back by eight or else. That's a lotta drivin'."

"It's barely noon, keep your damn pants on. We'll be back in time."

The boy fiddled with the radio but wasn't much coming in. "You didn't bring that stupid coyote, huh."

"Must be taking classes on observation skills up in Taos, I guess." The pain and discomfort made him cranky, he couldn't help it.

Ricky looked hurt, though. "My real father wouldn't be such a dick to me."

"Son, your real father don't give a shit about the difference between you an' a wad a Kleenex he tossed in the trash."

Neither of 'em said nothing till they were nearly to Cardenio. Every time Frank looked at the boy, his heart sank down to his stomach, just made him feel sick. His chest tightened up like he had to remind himself to let out a deep breath every once in a while, and by the end a the drive, his neck and hands were sore from being clenched.

"I'm selling the house, by the way," he said finally.

Ricky jerked. "Grandm-- you mean your parents' house? I thought you already did, you an' Aunt Jess."

"Yeah, no, I mean our house."

Ricky scratched his ear and kicked at the glovebox. "Why the fuck you doing that?"

"I need the money, kiddo. We need the money. I can't hardly work at all right now, and with the lawyers and this fucking shrink --"

"So stop going to the shrink. I don't fucking need Dr Mack."

"Stop swearing, for Christ's sake. I can't stop going to Dr Mack and neither can you. I don't like it neither, but that don't mean it ain't doing any good."

"Thought you had insurance."

"Not for this I don't, and it didn't cover alla the hospital either. I had to pay Jessie a lot back when we sold the old house, and I ain't saying that's all spent, I'm just saying ... son, I got no choice. That's all she wrote."

"Where you gonna live?"

"Well," Frank said. "I just don't know. I reckon I'll move closer to Taos to be near you and your grandparents, you know. Till I find a place, I'll make do." His folks' paintings were up for auction, and he an' Jessie'd split that, but he didn't have any inkling how much it'd be or when. Who knew what a painting cost? He'd paid fifty bucks for one once, but he knew Ma and Pop Train charged a hell of a lot more'n that and probably deserved it.

"So that's what this is about?" Ricky asked. "Me saying goodbye to the old home an' all that shit?"

Frank kicked at the gas pedal in frustration, and the pickup shook as it hit eighty miles an hour. "No, God damn it," he said. "This is about burning off some a that stupid God damn teenage energy you got. This is about getting you laid."

oooOOOooo

They had lunch out southa Borachon Creek in the middle of nowheres, at the Cinco y Dime that stood perfectly square and white surrounded by a handful a nothin'. Two green chile cheeseburgers each, greasy an' wet with slick pink juice that mixed Christmasy with the chopped roasted chiles that slipped off the burger as the Velveeta melted. They sat in the bed a the pickup cause there weren't nowhere else to sit, crumpled burger wrappers accumulating in fronta their Indian-crossed knees, an' when Frank saw Ricky mighta still been hungry after the second, he hopped down, went in, bought two more an' some warm sopaipillas wrapped around Rolos, so that the chocolate melted from the heat a the sweet tortilla an' the caramel got all soft an' gooey.

"You know," Ricky said, and for just a sec he sounded like the old Ricky, not Rick but <u>Ricky</u>, quiet an' shy an' reading a lotta books, "these are damn good cheeseburgers. These might be the best cheeseburgers I ever had, no kiddin'."

Frank nodded with a mouthful. "Best thing about working out here, you come down to it. How else'd they do any business in the middle of nothing, right?"

"True that," Ricky said, and reached for a sopaipilla.

"I don't reckon they have green chile cheeseburgers in Dallas, though," Frank said casually, and Ricky gave him a look.

"Why the fuck wouldn't they have 'em?"

The boy'd barely ever been outta the state, and mostly when he was younger. Frank grinned a little. "Kid, you got no idea what the resta the world's like. You don't gotta leave the country for everything to change. Most folks make their chile red an' use kidney beans, can't make tacos worth a damn, never hearda no sopaipilla, and wouldn't know a green chile cheeseburger if it bit 'em on the ass."

"That's fucked up," Ricky said, looking uncertain, like he wasn't sure whether to believe it. "They got hot dogs in Dallas?"

"They got hot dogs. Mac n cheese too, but not with chile. Tamale pie probably, but come to think of it I ain't for certain on that one."

The boy looked glum now, licking grease off his thumb and wiping his hands with napkins folded up to catch the bits a melted chocolate that'd squidged outta the sopaipilla. Frank pulled out his flash and handed it over. "Go on and have some."

"What is it?" Ricky took a long drink before answering, and made a face that made it clear he was trying not to spit it out or gag.

"Whiskey. Go easy, it's the cheap stuff. Can't afford tequila these days."

Ricky grunted and drank more of it. "Thought you always said it wasn't worth drinking if you were stuck with cheap shit."

"Said a lot of stuff that didn't add up, didn't I."

The boy handed the flask back, empty, his hand shaking a little. Frank figured he needed the courage -- and when they got back in the cab of the pickup, tossing their trash in the rusting can outside the Cinco y Dime, he drove 'em to the Widow's.

ooo000ooo

Once at the Widow's, Frank parked around back like he did when he was fixing stuff for them girls. The huge garden was flourishing despite the recent chill, the tomatoes still green an' small but looking firm, some a the chiles already a bright an' enticing shade a orange. There were rolls a plastic bungeed up to the side a the garden in case a worser cold front came through, to protect from frost, an' sprinklers spraying a fine mist a water over everything.

Ricky'd never been here before, and his mom woulda thrown a fit, picked it up, dusted it off, and thrown it again twice as far, had she been alive. He barely said a thing as Ricky brought him in, introduced him to the girls downstairs and the fella tending bar, and shook hands with the Widow.

"Well well," she said, hands on her hips and eyes on the boy. "And who is this fine gentleman?"

"This here's my son," Frank said. "Rick Train. And, well, I reckoned I'd treat him to a ..."

"... to a treat?" the Widow asked, grinnin'. Frank nodded, and could see that upside a that grin there was some concern in her eyes, like she knew a year ago this never woulda happened like this, he never woulda brought his son here no matter how nice he was to the girls and the Widow herself. "You bet. Honey?" she asked Ricky. "I don't want to put you on the spot or anything, but do you have a special preference? A redhead, someone closer to your age, someone older, anything like that?"

"Uh," Ricky said, and Frank could picture how he <u>would</u> have reacted, when things were different and more a the world was alive: he woulda looked at his shoes, woulda shuffled, woulda blushed. But not this Ricky. Not this strange young wild thing. This one made eye contact after that leftover pause, and shrugged. "Just as long as she's tight," he said. "I can ride whatever filly you see fit to set me up with."

The Widow's smile never faltered. She'd heard worse, and Frank knew just as well as she did that when men talked like that in the downstairs of a whorehouse it was cause they were self-conscious. One a the johns at a couch in the bar area didn't feel the same, though, and got up from his seat, putting down his wine glass. "Now hang on there, young fella, you watch your mouth --"

"It's all right," the Widow said. "If I couldn't stand a little rough talk, I'd be a bank teller. Abby?" she asked, gesturing to a woman who'd been speaking to a man who, Frank suspected, had already finished his business and was just getting a drink. "Could you take our young gentleman upstairs and introduce him around?"

"Why sure," Abby said, smilin'. She couldna been more'n twenty-three, twenty-four, just right for Ricky. Frank and the Widow watched them ascend the stairs, and then Frank turned to her.

"Can you keep him busy long enough to wear him out?"

The Widow smiled. "Why Mr Train, I'll have you know I and the girls can keep him busy enough he'll be twenty pounds lighter when you pick him up. Now is there someone I can find for you?"

"No," Frank said. "No, ma'am, I'm a married man."

The Widow looked at him blankly and then tilted her head to the side with the faintest smile. "Let me buy you a drink? Business is slow this time of day."

"Oh, I'll take a tequila if you're buying," he said. "No salt, just a piece a lemon an' I'm all right." They left the foyer by the stairs, heading into the bar area and sitting by the long mahogany bar that'd been around since Custer wore knee socks. She poured three shots herself, doing one of 'em before sitting down next to him.

They sipped insteada shooting the rest, and the Widow just sat there like she was waiting for him to say somethin'. Finally she asked, "He a little young, you think?"

Frank grunted. "He's having a time."

"All men do."

"It's been a rough patch for us. With him acting out an' all, I thought ... shit, I dunno. Burn off some steam."

"Do something nice for him, buy some affection."

He dunked the rest of the booze down his throat. "Fuck yes, if I thought it'd work."

She smiled and shrugged a half-shrug. Lord, she was pretty, even in the day. "We'll treat him right."

He shook his head. "I feel a mite weird sitting down here in the parlor while my boy, well, you know."

She nodded. "Your father wouldna felt weird, you know."

"Well," Frank said heavily. "One thing I ain't is my father."

The Widow kissed his cheek with some affection and squeezed his hand. "No man is, don't worry."

Slow day or not, she had to get up to deal with a customer, an' one a the girls came by, brushing the backs a her fingers along the side of his neck. "Help you out with anything, sugar?"

He didn't recognize her and wondered if he knew her family, or hell, knew her father. "No miss, I reckon I'm fine with just the tequila."

She pouted at him till she realized it wasn't a rejection a her with him preferring some other woman, an' then it was like alla sudden he was neutered for her. She flounced off, lounging on a couch and leaning back, breasts showing off under her low-cut top, flirting with one a the johns.

When the Widow came back, the bartender'd already refilled Frank's tequila and he'd had to ask for a club soda just to slow himself down. "You ever met Josh Marlowe?"

She looked at him closely, and her eyes reminded him what a sharp girl she was. "No, I never did," she said. "He never has been in."

"All right," he said. "I guess you know the name, though."

"Rumor," she said. "That's all."

"Yeah, well." He shifted in his seat. The tequila was numbing the pain a his ribs and back some, but not enough. "They're true. Some of 'em, anyway. Kriste an' Marlowe -- well."

She took a silver cigarette case engraved with fancy Western designs from behind the bar and lit what looked to him like one a them British cigarettes you could get in Santa Fe. "An' all that time," she said. "You were saying no to everything I offered you, and the girls offered you, when she was off betraying you."

Harsher words than he liked hearing from somebody else's mouth. "Thing is," he said. "Kriste went ahead and got one a them parenty tests?"

"Paternity."

"Paternity tests, an' I ain't the father, so probably Marlowe is. Of Ricky. The boy ain't mine."

She sighed, exhaling a line of smoke across the spout-topped bottles

155

of simple syrup and lime juice. "The kids you had you lost, the kid you didn't lose you didn't have."

"I reckon."

The Widow tapped the cigarette on a nice glass ashtray. "You gotta love him all the more for it, Frank. He needs you that much more'n he would if he were your own natural-born son. You know that, don't you?"

"I dunno, last thing he seems to want is anything from me. I dunno if you know, but he's living with his grandparents these days after, you know, Lincoln and Mickey."

"I heard," she said. "Lobo mentioned it."

Frank shook his head. "God damn it ain't nothing Lobo won't tell somebody, and what's he doing here anyway?"

She rolled her eyes. "What do you think? Besides which, this isn't exactly a legal operation. Keeping Lobo happy keeps my house in business."

There was no denying the sense a that. Frank looked at his watch and was trying to calculate how many shots a tequila he'd had when there was a scream from upstairs. He jerked so suddenly his neck spit pain at him just as much as if he'd clamped a red hot poker down on it.

"Ned," the Widow said, and the bartender-cum-bouncer nodded, grabbing a thick wooden stick from behind the bar. Frank caught the lines a the bulge under his jacket as he moved.

Ricky was up there, so God damn, Frank had to follow and quickly. This had been one stupid-ass fucking idea.

"He bit me!" a girl was yelling, indignation coming through hysteria an' getting all stained by it. "The little fucker bit me, look what he did!"

Frank got up to the room just behind Ned, where a naked as you ever saw girl was crying an' screaming by the bed, blood all over her tits an' neck. The one side a her neck had purpley bruises on it, just overexuberant hickeys, but the other? Teeth had sunk in deep there, awful fucking deep, and the upstairs bouncer had the same thought Frank had, 'cause back in he rushed with some Ace bandage to staunch the bleeding, which was something fierce. Not just a little blood-letting, but a real fucking wound.

Her tit took it worse. Just above her nipple, the skin was ragged, a little flap a dimpled aureola visible above the shiny dark red that'd sheeted down her breast and dripped onto the floor, the sheets, her legs.

"Go get him," the upstairs bouncer said to Ned. "I tossed the sick little fuck out the window."

And it had to be Ricky. Frank knew it, and when he turned around, he was ashamed to see that the Widow knew it too, even though neither of 'em had known which girl Ricky'd end up with. "I'll get him," Frank said. "Is he runnin'?"

"Uh huh," Ned said, glancin'. "Over towards the Cinco. That's miles away."

Frank glanced at the Widow, who gave him a hug. She was shaking like a leaf, but kept it in tight. You couldn't see it, not even on her face, but you could feel it all right. "Don't bring him back, Frank," she said quietly. "Not ever. Not when he's 21. Not when he's forty. But since he's yours, I'll leave it at that."

"I won't," Frank said. "Let me know the girl's all right, and bill me for whatever needs payin'. You know I'm good for anything I tell you I'm good for."

"I do indeed," the Widow said. "Now go get your boy." She took another look at the girl, who was sobbing silently now, clutching a towel to her breast, the blood turning that off-white over-laundered thing pink. "I don't reckon I want any outsiders around just now."

Frank near fell down the stairs as he went down, the tequila shaking through his head like warm jelly, his drunkenness not yet peaked. Fuck it, wasn't nothing he could do about it. He'd pop some greenies for the trip to Taos if he needed to.

He hopped in the pickup, wishing he'd brought the coyote after all, and high-tailed it down the road towards the Cinco and then veered off into the empty land at a diagonal, cutting Ricky off. The boy flailed his arms at the truck, breathless, pantsless, nothing on but his shirt and his underwear.

Frank slammed the door open hard enough it bounced back against him as he got out, and it took a lot more strength than he thought he had to keep from pounding the shit outta the boy. He didn't touch him. Didn't even grab his collar. Just looked at him. "No more running, son," he said, not soft but fierce, like he felt. "Get in the truck."

Ricky wiped his mouth with the back of his hand, which came away coppery. The blood was all over his mouth, on his chin, staining the collar of his shirt in little grapefruit-squirt droplets. The boy smiled, red all over his teeth and gums like when you get hit real bad, only the teeth were fine, even them two baby teeth he hadn't lost yet. It wasn't a gloating smile, not a look-what-I-done smile, not any kinda teenage smile. There wasn't no resentment to it, no complication. It was a child's smile, the kind you saw on a little kid who just had a piece a chocolate cake for his birthday and got a new bike.

It was a smile of contentment that held them bloodstained baby teeth.

He didn't say a God damn word the whole way back to Taos, and after an hour, Frank stopped trying to make him.

CHAPTER NINETEEN

Frank sat at the kitchen table surrounded by boxes he'd already packed, going through photo albums. He hadn't meant to, but he'd been going through everything to make sure he had all the family stuff, the stuff to keep, put aside separate from the stuff he was selling or giving to Goodwill. He'd send it to Jessie. She was the only Train left, really, the only family left, and prob'ly should get some a these photos, too, 'specially the ones from when Frank an' Mickey were kids, snot-nosed an' stupid insteada just stupid. There were a few Mondragons left, but they were dying like flies and he knew damn well they'd all be gone soon enough.

He could live pretty light, and figured he'd camp out in the pickup for a while, see how the trial went. No point using up his money renting a place he wasn't gonna keep for long. He might need that money later. But a lotta this stuff couldn't be got rid of. It needed to be kept, needed to be with someone who'd give a shit, someone who'd know what it all was. That wasn't Ricky just yet, but Frank still hoped someday it would be.

Bud was gonna take a lotta Frank's work stuff, his equipment and whatnot, an' put it in storage. Be another two months before his hand was outta the hard cast, an' then he'd still prob'ly be in a soft cast or splint for mosta the summer, with all the breaks he took. Ribs weren't feeling too good neither. Healing maybe, but by damn and cats he wasn't a young man no more. When things healed, they didn't heal back the same. He couldn't do the work he used to do, and by the time he could he'd be older, wouldn't he. And somebody else woulda been doing that work, somebody who might not wanna hand the reins back. At least he didn't have to wear the brace no more, and he'd come down to milder doses on the pills he still took.

He washed a kava kava down with a swaller a whiskey from the grubby glass he'd been drinking Jack Daniels from. The kava kava, Jessie'd recommended. Some kinda herbal thing to keep you calm, didn't fuck you up like Valium. When he couldn't sleep he'd take four of 'em and they did the trick, an' during the day they just kept him even. As for the whiskey, he'd gone to the liquor store after cashing the deposit on the sale a the house, an' asked for two bottles a their best American whiskey, so the fella set him up with some limited edition extra-aged Jack from back before they changed the formula an' made it sweeter. Still cost less'n the foreign stuff. Them expensive Scotches were way too expensive, and shit, he wasn't gonna know the difference. It was one thing realizing how different thirty dollar booze was from twelve dollar shit came in the plastic jug. It was another tasting the difference between fifty bucks and three hundred, and Frank wasn't about to complain that his tongue couldn't do the math.

He'd cashed in savin's bonds too, not that he'd had a whole lot, but there was some stuff'd been in Gina's name and Philip's, christening gifts an' the like. Every li'l bit helped, an' he spread it out some. Most of everything went into his savings account, but he kept a couple hundreds folded up in his sock, another few hundred in twenties in his wallet, and three thousand dollars in his glovebox. Looked like a lotta money when you put it in your hand. But if the pickup broke down, if Ricky didn't get better soon, if some non-Train kin a Lincoln's fucking sued him for killing him ... well, the biggest bottle a water dried up pretty quick on a hot day, that's what Frank had found.

The kava kava worked pretty good. These days he got jitterbug nerves a lot, hard to sit still, hard to think still. Couldn't focus on nothing, an' maybe some of that was the pills, sure, an' the bennies he took to keep from feeling too sleepy when he popped a couple Vicodin if he turned too quick and his ribs cried out at him. Every little thing felt like the last straw, like the freezer breaking four days before the move-out date so he had no reason to fix it or replace it and a buncha food going bad, stuff he was too embarrassed to give away 'cause it was things like pinon fruitcake from eleven years ago, green chile casseroles from Kriste's funeral, one Swanson Hungry Man after another. He ate the ice cream an' the fruitcake, gave the TV dinners an' frozen burritos to the neighbors, threw everything else out in thick black garbage bags, an' hauled the freezer to the junkyard. Somebody'd dissect it for some a the parts, and power to 'em.

Still, when the freezer'd busted and he'd sat there with his tools an' his cast hand gone stupid, he just about cried, and felt black as could be when he was eating that ice cream an' fruitcake for no reason other than that he didn't wanna throw it out. He was putting on weight an' he knew it, weight he didn't have the build to hide. He cared enough to hate it, not enough to do nothing about it.

It was pretty good whiskey, this expensive Jack Daniel's. Smoother than the regular, nevermind the cheap shit Frank'd been drinking the last coupla months. Like vanilla an' caramel without being sweet, hard an' strong without being bitter or harsh. This was exactly why he always said you should drink the best stuff you could afford, an' drink less so you could drink better. But he'd said a lotta shit that seemed to hold in a world that was dead now, a world that'd moved away from him. What'd he have now? He had some work contracts that were technically his even though he'd had to farm 'em out -- at a loss in a coupla cases 'cause it wasn't easy getting the skilled labor on short notice -- an' he had the pickup.

That was it. That was fucking it.

It's you an' me forever, Jack, an' forever's gonna stop at the enda the bottle.

He hadn't seen the coyote since Mickey's funeral, and hadn't told nobody neither, like he was embarrassed by that too, like the last thing he wanted to see on anybody's face was more fucking pity, more fucking oh sorry to hear that Frank, more sorry for your loss Frank. He was a hard case, God damn it. He was a <u>bad man</u>. Pity was his God damn kryptonite.

One thing he liked about this whiskey was that it made him mean. Gave him that same buzz he'd got back in the day when he was young and fulla vinegar an' guys were scared of him. Girls too, but when they were scared they just got wet. The fellas respected him back then, and woulda known if he got in a scrape like this it wouldn't be nothing he couldn't kick the ass of.

But what was the point now?

Ricky wasn't his boy to begin with, an' he knew it. Worse, the kid was --

No, he hadn't had enough whiskey to give that one the floor yet.

All the Train artwork'd been sold or given away, maybe a dozen pieces each from Mom and Pop had been sent to their alma mater for an exhibit, the school paying for the shipping and so on. Everything else except a few pieces Frank kept for himself and considerable more Jessie kept for her.

There was this thing on the computer, on the web, where you could put addresses in and it would show you a map. It was for families and alumni and things like that, to show where folks ended up, how they spread out. Frank'd sat there at Gina's computer, cryptic and catty and often smutty emails still sitting undeleted in the folders that popped up automatically when he turned the thing on, and plugged in the addresses for all the folks who bought his folks' stuff, or at least the town an' state when he didn't have a full address. The map ended up looking all weird, which he guessed it always did. There was Train art in California now, lots of it up in New England 'round Boston and Connecticut, in Chicago an' other partsa Illinois, in Seattle an' Vegas an' all over New York state.

The freaky bits were where one piece, sometimes a cheap one but sometimes one a the more expensive ones that the art consultant they'd commissioned had priced at something Frank thought was pretty God damn crazy, wound up in some middle a nowhere town. Hollis, New Hampshire. Rome, Texas. Sugar Church, Florida, although Frank reckoned that was more the ass end a nowhere than the middle of it. Three pieces in Matchhead Bay, South Carolina. One fourteen thousand dollar sculpture in Fairbanks, Alaska.

You could click a button and make the map resample, which took forever and the website said it worked better for alumni things where you had a whole lotta people, but it redid the map so that the physical scale was based on population density. If you had five cousins in Texas but fifteen in Nebraska, Nebraska would end up drawn three times as big. When Frank'd clicked it an' waited for it to reload, the result was this crazy lopsided world where California an' the northeast bulged out like squeezed balloons, those little one-sale towns rose up like stalactites, an' New Mexico, well, New Mexico just disappeared all together, squoze to nothing between the west coast an' Texas.

He kept thinking about that now, how the Trains had got squoze outta New Mexico, and wondered what was the fate of them Trains who were elsewhere, them cousins and uncles' uncles and such like who'd moved away long enough ago that ain't nobody in touch with nobody even for weddin's an' Christmas cards. Were they dying too? Would they come next? An' what about the Mondragons in Mexico an' Louisiana? Them ones in Spain? What about them folks he shared blood with through his grandmothers, his great-aunts? What was happening with them Loves, them Lincolns, them Martinezes and Gilchrists, them Lassas an' Zeplers? Titty Zepler got shot in the head by his cheating wife day before Valentine's. Was that Frank's fault? The farming accident took Tom Lassa, his mother's cousin's grandkid, the leukemia that finally did ol' Artemus Love in, his great-grandmother's second cousin's son, Dap Martinez, Sienna Borachon whose mama was a Gilchrist, Trace Jacquet the grandson of a Zepler bastard, were all them deaths Frank's fault?

And when would it stop? It'd go right up the tree to Adam an' Eve eventually --

"No," Frank mumbled to himself. "Noah. Don't matter 'bout Adam an' Eve, cause a Noah's kids."

He opened the next photo album at random, winding up at a picture of Kriste late in her pregnancy with Ricky, and he sighed and poured another glug a whiskey. At least it was good whiskey. Good whiskey was kinder to you in the morning after.

It'd been a different pregnancy for her, he remembered. Gina'd been a hell an' a half to deliver, one a them labors mothers still bitched about eighteen years later. Kriste'd been more scared with Ricky than she'd been with Gina, cause she thought it'd be like that all over, the baby twisting and turning and taking forever to get his self in gear, all that pain, all that panting and exhaustion. And that's how it was with Philip, later, which took her by surprise, cause Ricky'd been easy as kites, slick and clever and all but painless from what she said.

Being pregnant, though, hadn't been so easy on her. She'd been hungry all the time with the damnedest cravin's, all them stereotypical things, pickles and donuts in the middle a the night, donuts that had to be piping hot. That was the hardest damn one for him to help her with, and twice it'd meant driving her forty minutes to an all-night coffee-n-donuts place an' waiting for their next batch, cause they weren't gonna stay hot on the trip back. God, he could remember the place just thinking about it, remember that surreal feeling of driving practically an hour at four in the morning with Gina whining then sleeping then whining again in the back seat, then struggling just to stay awake at the donut shop while waiting for the five o'clock batch to be done. Kriste sat at the front the whole time with her jar of Vlasic pickles, looking both contrite an' relieved. She didn't usually insist on that kinda thing, but if she woke him up with it at that kinda hour, he knew better'n to figure it wasn't a big deal.

A lotta pork and cheese she'd wanted, too, hot dogs and cheese, pork chops an' cheese, cheese on green chile, cheese an' sausage sandwiches, pretty much every lunch was some kinda pork and some slices a cheese cut from a big block she kept next to the buttermilk in the fridge. They still got home delivery back then. When'd that stop? Frank couldn't remember now, and wondered if Javier the milkman had retired or died.

The next few pages were Ricky Ricky Ricky. Lord they'd taken a lotta pictures of that boy when he was too much a baby to look like anything at all yet. You get pictures of 'em when they look like every other baby, an' the more they grow up an' start to get more recognizable, more standoutish, the less you keep the habit up. There were four pages a pictures when he was still little enough to be all bundled up all the time, and shit, those were just the ones they kept. Ricky and Mom, Ricky and Grandma, Ricky and Grandpa, Ricky and Big Sister, an' on an' on.

There was a pretty nice one a Frank holding Ricky, in that old chrome an' vinyl Laz-E-Boy they'd thrown away four or five years later. The boy was holding on to Frank's finger like a bottle, and looking up at him with -- well. With love. Much as a baby could have it, anyway, much as a baby could know what it was. It wasn't the same look he had looking at his grandparents. In none a them pictures did he look at anybody but Kriste and Frank with quite that look. Wasn't whiskey saying that, cause these days Frank weren't sure he even wanted it to be true.

Ricky's first haircut, that dark hair snip snipped onto the floor, so fine. You could tell it was baby hair just to look at it, the way you could tell a boy's beard from one that'd been through a lifetime a shaving an' Aqua Velva. Kriste'd taped a lock of it into the photo album, an' some of it'd come outta the tape over the years, some strands'd gone missing, but Frank ran his fingertips over what was left. So fine an' soft like first growth in a forest. So young. Kriste had a lot more Mexican in her than Frank did, more a the dark an' the glossy hair, an' it showed in Ricky of course. Was there anything a Marlowe in him?

Had he ever seen the shadow of another man in the boy he thought was his?

Ricky's first day a school, with that dark green Incredible Hulk backpack he'd carried till fucking fifth grade, the straps needing to be patched and stitched twice not 'cause they was too poor to buy him a new one but 'cause they did buy him one an' he kept using the Hulk anyway. The back flap was a dark purple patch like the Hulk's pants an' had a picture a the guy on there, big an' mean looking but still silly in them ripped pants an' green Lou Ferrigno moptop. Ricky'd always liked comics, but especially the Hulk an' Batman.

Frank'd read both when he was a kid, an' gave the boy what comics he had left, them old Steve Englehart Batmans with Silver St Cloud, them Hulks when Bruce Banner stayed smart even when he became the Hulk, but General Thunderbolt Ross still wanted to take him down. The big coup, the big score, was getting this Hulk versus Batman comic where the two met an' tussled even though they were published by different companies. It was like getting holda James Bond Meets Indiana Jones or some damn thing. They'd both read that, pointing out it was kinda cheesy but it was still -- it's cool, Dad, was what Ricky said -- cool. And it was. Something could be cool even when it was cheesy, even when it wasn't good. Cause cool was its own damn thing.

That was prob'ly the height of their friendship, their relationship, whatever -- Ricky'd been in that perfect place for a son to be, old enough he didn't get in little kid trouble, young enough he didn't get in teenage trouble or fucking stab people. Gina hadn't been so easy at that age, if anything had been harder, 'cause it was when she started to turn most female. An eight year old girl ain't much different from an eight year old boy, but a twelve year old -- hoo boy. Another story, another fucking author.

Come to think of it, Frank and Gina'd been gone through some tough times when Frank an' Ricky were closest. Not one causing the other or nothing, just a function a age an' maybe Gina being the oldest. She'd been in high school, way too old to want to do anything with her father unless it was him driving her somewhere she needed to be an' picking her up with the grace to not make a big thing out of it. Not that he'd minded that. He had buddies who bitched, you know, and Kriste even tried to be more of a hen about it, tried to be that annoying parent yelling don't take any drugs, be home by ten, call if you need us. Frank, he remembered being a teenager better'n his wife had.

Frank an' Ricky'd gone to a lot of movies, not going outta their way for father-n-son time or anything but because they were "the boys" in the family, Philip still "the baby" especially back then three, four years ago, and they wanted to see the same thing which more often'n not "the girls" didn't. They saw <u>Fight Club</u> on DVD, which pissed Kriste off but it seemed to Frank like it was a good movie for a boy to watch with his father, one he'd understand better when he got older. <u>Spider-Man</u>, that'd been a big 'un. <u>X-Men</u> too, but it wasn't as good. <u>The Matrix</u>, <u>The Lord of the Rings</u>, The Transporter, those were Frank-n-Ricky movies. Frank'd rented <u>Army of Darkness</u> for Halloween, <u>First Blood</u> for some night they'd sat on the couch with a sausage-n-chiles pizza for who knew what the fuck reason, <u>Young Frankenstein</u> where Ricky laughed at all the wrong jokes but that was all right, and <u>Cool Hand Luke</u> which the boy'd just been bored by. Frank figured he was too young, and wondered now, would he ever like it?

At the "youth facility" where Ricky was now, they saw movies on Friday nights, nothing R unless it'd been edited, even though some a the boys in there was seventeen. They sat at tables that, when Frank'd been given the four-minute tour, looked like grey picnic tables, an' they had to keep their hands on top a the tables where the counselors could see them, at all times. "We've had problems in the past," the touring counselor had whispered to him, "with boys <u>masturbating</u>."

It'd finally been too much for the Garcias. Maybe Bruno'd pulled his last string. Maybe Inez had woke up an' seen that either Frank Train hadn't been the problem in her grandson's life or his taint had been too dark an' permanent. They couldn't fix him, an' they gave up tryin'. "We just can't do it anymore, Frank," Bruno'd said to him, all fucking apologetically. "We just don't have the strength. I never had to deal with anything like this with my kids." Faint emphasis on the <u>my</u>, like again, wasn't the <u>Garcia</u> genes at fault here. Well, he was right about that, but wasn't no Train acted like this neither, biting girls' tits practically off, stabbing people for art, practically raping that girl in the hallway of his school. He'd pierced his ears again, an' his nipples too, shaved his head and got a fucking huge tattoo on it, a map of the moon.

Last straw, though, had been when Ricky put photos of people he'd stabbed up on a website, taken with a digital camera he'd paid for in singles. Somebody from his school'd seen it, seen his real name there, and boom: welcome to the circus, Ricky. Quicker'n you could say Columbine he was behind bars. They didn't call it that. It was a center for troubled boys. It was a youth facility. Man, there were so many things you could call prison without calling it prison.

Tensen the lawyer'd explained some a the upshot to Frank. If Frank got found guilty of murdering Lincoln, chances were Ricky would be declared a ward a the court, an' if <u>that</u> were the case, there was a higher probability he'd be found insane an' incompetent, an' when he turned eighteen he'd be transferred to a state mental health facility until they deemed him cured, or let him go for budget reasons. "All depends on how violent he is," Tensen said. "When you come down to it, how sane you are isn't the determining issue. It's how likely you are to hurt somebody."

Well, Frank had to admit he was pretty fucking likely, but who wasn't? Everybody hurt <u>somebody</u>. Everybody did.

He drank the next glug, two glugs, three glugs a whiskey straight from the bottle an' tossed the glass aside, letting it break on the floor, liking the sound of it an' wanting to kick something over, wanting to hit something, but he didn't have the energy to deal with the guilt he'd feel afterward. Everything he did these days left him feeling guilty or helpless, cause it was all his fault, wasn't it. It was all his fucking fault, everything came from that Halloween at the midnight crossroads. Maybe Ricky had always been Marlowe's son, but he hadn't <u>acted</u> like it.

And where was God in all this? Maybe he had left the grace a God, like Father Michael said. But Ricky hadn't. Ricky hadn't done a God damn thing until Frank had. Where was God to protect him? To protect the ones he hurt?

Frank leaned back in his chair, almost balancing an' almost fallin'. "Anybody there?" he called out to the darkness. Weren't no lights on in the house 'cept the overhead in the kitchen that he'd been looking at photos by. Nothing more unreal than a Polaroid under fluorescents.

"Hey, Old Man, you home tonight? Can you spare a fucking minute? It's about time we had a talk." Frank pushed the Colt aside cause he was sloshing the whiskey a little, and gestured with the bottle knowing he looked a drunken fool.

He stood up, kicked the other chairs over, picked one up an' broke the side window with it, staggering too much to do it clean, had to jab at the glass with the chair till it was finally gone, then let the chair hang there in the frame, legs out an' back gazing at the ceilin'. Some a the glass had landed on the counter, some on the floor, most of it outside. He punched the pantry, felt the cheap wood door crack but not break, and why would it, it was his left hand he had to hit with these days, his sinister.

"You made me like I am!" Frank shouted hoarsely, and he wasn't sure it was God he was shouting at, or Marlowe, or Arthur Train Jr, or the world, or just that thing you call Father. "God damn it, I didn't come out the womb this way! I started out pretty strong an' fast, Old Man, but I gotta tell you, I'm wearing out. When you gonna end this? What you got in mind for old Frank Train?"

He waited like there was something to wait for, an' tossed the empty bottle a Jack at the bathroom, where it bounced off the open door and shattered on the tile floor that needed regroutin'. "Yeah," Frank said, "that's what I thought. I guess you're a hard case too."

Frank picked up the Colt Series 70 an' shoved the barrel in his mouth till he gagged on it, the nose of it poking that soft spot in the back a his throat. The angle was all awkward cause he was pitching southpaw, an' as he closed his eyes, all he could imagine was the bullet shredding his throat but leaving him alive an' having to explain this pathetic state he'd let himself come to, let himself get pushed to. Shit, when he gagged again an' drew back outta reflex, the nose ended up rubbing against the inside a his cheek. Wouldn't that be a sight. Wouldn't it just. Old Frank Train with his cheek shot out, old scarfaced Frank Train no worse for the wear 'cept where they stitched up his stupid like an extra grin.

The pistol tasted like the oil he cleaned it with, but not like the oil smelled. It was bitter an' metallic an' chemical, this sharp poison tang that was still somehow pleasant like the smell a gasoline. It clacked against his teeth as his hand shook, an' the sight at the enda the barrel jabbed the roof a his mouth as he pulled it back out.

He was breathing hard an' felt wet all over, like sweat alla sudden had just leapt outta him making a series a concentric Franks. He was hunched over like he was gonna fall down, an' he sat back down again, his shirt sticking to his back, sweat crawling oily from his armpits.

He tried again with his thumb on the trigger, eyes open this time, looking at the grips just past the enda his nose. The taste made his tongue recoil, like it kept trying to force itself against the floor of his mouth, and he pulled the Colt back out, thinking about his father carrying this gun in his cowboying days alongside Rafe Mondragon his mother's brother. Them boys riding the range, practically living on horseback, drinking tequila in the sunset an' cooking brick chile in old cast iron pots. Them boys with their cheroots an' their Stetsons, skin getting tougher by the day, sleeping in earshot a the cattle and looking out for rustlers -- still a real problem even these days, an' Arthur Train Jr had shot a man more'n once an' had to file police reports over it an' everything.

A cowboy's like the land, stomped on, kicked down, rained over, shit on, stormed on. Don't matter what kind of shape he's in when it's all over. Whatever happened, he's there.

"Not no more," Frank whispered, and put the gun in upside-down this time, easy peasy just flip your hand up an' there you were. Any other shot, this'd be even worse'n them young toughs who held their guns sidewise 'cause they saw some rapper do it. Gun held like that wasn't accurate at all past point blank, the bullet went all wrong. But at this range...

Well, this range wasn't even far enough to call it range, now was it. Wasn't a long way from a fella's mouth through the back a his skull. An' this angle, with the gun upside-down it was easy to hold it so it was pointing up, up through the roof of his mouth to all that meaty grey. No throat-tearing an' hospital-going this way, no sir. Not with that trusty Colt aimed right up in there. No gagging on this one.

Wasn't no sense left to anythin'. Frank breathed hard like he'd climbed a fucking mountain, nostrils flaring an' foggin up the metal on the underside a the barrel, an' he closed his eyes cause he didn't wanna see his finger pulling that trigger, see how old his skin looked up this close, when the fuck did he get so old --

An' something heavy hit him in the side a the head, right by the temples, something solid an' hard, an' it hurt enough that he wondered if he had pulled the trigger. He'd heard 'bout bullets bouncing off the inside of a fella's skull an' coming out the other end, but he hadn't heard nothing, hadn't felt nothin'.

The hard thing clattered to the floor and burst open, a tinkle a coins on kitchen tile. Frank'd pulled the gun outta his mouth by reflex, and blinked dumbly, sweat trickling into his eyes. It was dimes on the floor, dimes that'd split open the brown paper roll they'd been in and spilled out.

Old Man Hank McCarty stood in the doorway looking old an' sour an' resigned to something, leather vest an' ancient hat an' guns hanging at his sides slung low. He looked like he'd just walked in outta a hundred fifty years ago, an' wiped a little spittle off his mouth with the back of his liverspotted hand. "Best two dollars I ever spent," he murmured, nodding at the dimes. "That gun better be loaded, Frank. Might be we'll need it."

Frank shook his head, wondering just how drunk he was. "McCarty? What the fuck --" He rubbed his head where the dimes had hit. It fucking hurt.

"C'mon an' get in the pickup and buckle up. I'm too old to drive an' you're too drunk, so we're gonna have to hope we're vying con dios tonight. It's practically nine o'clock, boy. Cowboy up and hurry on, God damn it. Time's wastin'." That voice was strong even if the man didn't look it, a voice you didn't want to argue with and you wouldn't figure was gonna take no shit off you.

"Where we goin'?" Frank asked as he staggered to his feet.

McCarty split a grin, and it made him look fifty years younger, and Frank realized he'd probably been handsome once, one a them Kris Kristofferson types that some girls liked so much. "We got a jailbreak to put together."

CHAPTER TWENTY

Frank greyed out a couple times on the ride to Crestwood, the innocuous name they'd used to rechristen the San Pedro Home For Wayward Youth in the 1980s. The scary thing was when he came to, he was the one drivin'. McCarty weren't acting like anything was amiss, so Frank reckoned he'd been doing all right an' was just outta it from the whiskey. He'd popped some bennies when they got in the car, taken a long piss on the side a the highway almost soon as they left.

"So what the hell we doing, Hank?" he asked, not sure if he'd asked already. It was dark out, but a slow dark, a louring dark, and the pickup's high-beams seemed fuzzy in it, without the sharp lines you'd get south a midnight when the sky'd gone pitch.

McCarty grunted an' checked his guns for the fifth, sixth time since they left the house. "Breaking your boy out," he said. That voice sounded stronger an' more determined than Old Man McCarty'd sounded in alla Frank's days.

"But _why_?" Frank asked, feeling like an asshole for asking it. It made it sound like he wanted his boy in prison, but the thing of it was, maybe he did. Maybe he wanted him somewhere's it was harder to hurt anybody else, harder to get hurt.

"Town like this," McCarty said, "town this small, when it gets in your blood, you gotta choose Jesus or choose Hell, an' I guess I finally chose. I'll tell you something not many people know. I was born in New York City."

"Get the fuck outta town." McCarty more'n _had_ a New Mexico accent, he was the kinda yardstick you could use to measure anybody else's by.

"No," McCarty said, an' he seemed almost like in a reverie, like he was remembering something any other man woulda forgot by now. "Hard to believe myself sometimes, but it's true. When my father died, my Ma remarried an' we moved to Silver City, out in Grant County. McCarty's my Ma's name, I wound up going back to that. She died almost soon's we got there. Consumption. Not hardly nobody dies a that no more, this part a the world."

168

"Don't reckon they do. You were pretty young?"

"Fourteen," McCarty said. "Just a boy, just a little younger'n your Ricky. I got to thinking on that recently. An old man, he thinks on a lotta things, all them things he done good an' bad in his days. I was on a right hard path when I was Ricky's age. Kilt a lotta fellas. Some of 'em needed killin, yeah. Some of 'em I kilt 'cause we was at war. But some of 'em --" McCarty's eyes wrinkled darkly. "Some of 'em I jest kilt 'cause it's what I did."

"Well," Frank said. "We all been bad when we were young, I reckon." McCarty had a reputation for saying hard-to-believe things about his past, things he wouldn't elaborate on if you pressed the issue.

McCarty snorted. "Ain't the point. Point is that's why I needed that Halloween man a yours, that stranger with the yellow sign. Jack Dust, he was at the time. The first Jack Dust, greatest escape artist ever lived, the one that escaped death to become his own son. He's the one taught me how to get outta handcuffs. How to dodge a bullet. Some days I just about shit myself thinking about him. Some days last a good long while if I get to thinking too much, Frank."

"I know how that goes," Frank said, and McCarty snorted again.

When McCarty pointed out the turnoff he said, "That's why we gotta get your boy out, son. Ain't right a boy growing up like that, growing up hard. The two a you gotta get outta here, gotta get way the fuck outta here. Go to New York City, I dunno what it's like these days. Los Angeles where they got all them movie stars an' sunshine. Somewhere far, kid. Somewhere he ain't gonna come for you."

Frank thought about it, him an' Ricky on the road, on the run, family services an' the State a New Mexico prob'ly looking for 'em harder'n Josh Marlowe. "Frank Train would have to disappear," he said. "The state'd be after me forever. Ain't no statute a limitations on murder."

"Boy, who the fuck you think you telling that too?" McCarty muttered, as cranky and grumped up as he'd ever been.

They had the money. If they was just gonna disappear, they had the money to do it. If they weren't gonna pay the medical bills, the legal fees, shit like that, Frank had more than a hundred grand. He'd just have to get it quickly, which prob'ly meant he couldn't get all of it. Or maybe McCarty could get some of it to him. "The house sale," he said. "The money from it, an' from some other things, you could --"

"We'll get that settled," McCarty said. "Don'tchoo worry, I'll have your back. The important thing here is, can you cowboy up, Frank? Can you ride with me on this one and do your daddy proud? Are you on the hammer?" He checked his bullets again, spun the cylinders of his revolvers, holstered 'em. He looked like one a them "living history tour guides" at the Old West museums.

"Yeah," Frank said, and patted the Colt Series70 that'd been in his mouth less'n half an hour ago. "Yeah, Hank, Frank's on the hammer."

ooo000ooo

"So that's what you got from him?" Frank asked as they neared the facility, driving down the long driveway he reckoned was to make it harder for kids to run off, when there was so much open land to cross. "Escape?"

McCarty grunted. "Life. He ga' me life. And he took my will, 'fore you ask. I just ain't been the same since. It's like the old me just, well, dried up an' blew away."

And then they were there, pulling up to the guard's booth at the gate. "How much money you got handy?" McCarty asked.

"Uh, a lot."

"Gimme five hundred dollars to be safe."

"McCart --"

"Boy."

Frank reached in the glovebox, counted out five hundreds from one a the three envelopes in there. McCarty rolled down the pickup's window as the guard approached him, and grinned. "Hey there," he said.

"What can I do for you?"

"Well, we got a little delivery to make here, you know?"

The man glanced at his clipboard without actually looking at it. "What kinda delivery?"

"You know, a little under the table. One a the boy's father's, well, he's pretty well off. You know? Junior might be misbehaving, but he wants him taken care of." McCarty reached out like to shake the guy's hand, palmed him the five hundreds. "No big deal, right?"

"Yeah," the guard said after a pause. "All right. But I better see you backing outta here in fifteen minutes."

"The hell kinda delivery?" Frank asked as the gate opened.

McCarty shrugged. "Fucked if I know. Drugs, porn, whatever kids today get for Christmas."

Frank nodded, still cloudy. "Okay, what now? How we gonna find which room he's in?"

"Told you that already, kid. I called this afternoon an' found out. Now come on. You're gonna cover the front an' the path to the truck while I get the boy."

"Wait, why are you gonna --"

McCarty opened the door as soon as Frank came to a stop. "Cause I been shot before an' if it happens again I ain't gonna freak out and drop a brick in my britches. You, I ain't as sure about. Now leave the engine running an' make sure you know your pistol from your pizzle, an' we'll have this job done in two switches, all right?"

170

"Yeah, okay. Fuck. I'm just drunk."

McCarty eyed him when they got outside the truck, then came over and suddenly, roughly, planted a hand on his jeans and grabbed his testicles, squeezing hard right to the point that Frank yelped, then clamped his hand down on his mouth to muffle the sound.

"Feeling sharp, boy?" McCarty asked him. His breath smelled like Skoal an' Blackjack gum.

"Jesus," Frank breathed. The pain was like peppermint oil in your eye drops, but yeah, he felt awake.

"All right then. Here come a coupla guards. Let's try not to kill anybody, but try a little harder still not to get kilt."

McCarty didn't even draw his guns as he sauntered towards the two guards outside the entrance, who'd started approaching as soon as the truck stopped. "Evening, fellas," McCarty said, an' just like that he had one a their guns in his hand, and bung the butt of it into the other fella's head, then pistol-whipped the other till he fell down. Frank barely saw him move. Not that he was fast, exactly, just so smooth, no wasted movement.

The old man was a fucking hard case.

Frank helped him duct-tape their mouths shut and handcuff 'em, stowing 'em to the side a the door where Frank could keep an eye on 'em but they wouldn't be right there for everybody to see. "Don't draw your gun if you don't need it," McCarty told him before going inside with the guards' key rings in his hand, "but it's better'n not drawing it when you do."

He could imagine McCarty darting down hallways, prob'ly being taken for a janitor or something for being so old, till someone saw the leather vest an' hundred year old boots, the sixguns hanging at his sides that looked like they'd been used in a dozen wars in frontiers that'd long ago turned into suburbs. Asking McCarty what he'd got for his troubles, and what he'd given, made Frank wonder the same about hisself. He sure as shit didn't have nothing good to show for all he lost, but what he lost didn't seem like his soul, either. Leastways, not in any sorta literal sense. An' McCarty hadn't said nothing 'bout his family being killed off, one limb after another being sawed off the family tree.

The old man shot two a the guards who musta saw him on monitors or something, a bullet for each one just as he got to Ricky's room. Frank didn't know how he knew it, but he did, same as he'd known where the coyote with the ragged ear went the day a Mickey's funeral. Like daydreaming, doodling in his noodle, just led to seein'. Well, Frank thought, best be ready. Somebody'd hear them shots, an' it might prove tricksy getting outta here.

Not thirty seconds passed 'fore there they were in the parking lot coming at Frank from three sides, an' he was anxious to draw the gun, peg off a few shots, which was fucking stupid. They had him in a turkey shoot an' with shots already fired, he wasn't gonna have any hope a dry-gulching 'em. Besides which, he'd be using his bad hand. Why the fuck had McCarty shot 'em? God damn it.

"Easy there, boys," he said, hands not up but visible, 'cause up would imply he was acknowledging their control a the situation. "We don't wanna be getting into a mess. What seems to be the trouble?"

"Sir," one of them called over, "we're gonna have to ask you to put your hands on your head and get on the ground."

"This a bank robbery, Jasper?" Frank asked. "You want me to toss my wallet over next?"

A little shuffle a reaction at that, an' the man called over, "I know you, sir?"

"You know where your wife is?" Frank asked him. "You know where she goes when you work the night shift? Shouldna married a girl so young, Jasper. Practically robbing the cradle when you met her, and now, well, now she's too old to be too impressed by you but not too old to get bored waiting around for your sorry ass. Oh, you should see the things she wears for him, Jasper, things you ain't never seen her in. I'm talking 'bout that fancy up-class slutwear you buy on the internet, you know, 'less you drive up to Denver to buy it like she did that one time with her sister for that 'girl time' trip, you think maybe they double-teamed him? Where you think she is right now, Jasper? How far you think she got them honey brown legs spread, with that mole on her thigh bout three inches from her --"

Jasper fired a shot. It missed by a congressman's mile, hitting the cement walls behind Frank an' spraying the driveway with little bitty shards like you find alongside an old sidewalk. The other guards panicked at that, at Jasper opening fire an' maybe moreso at him missing, and that's when McCarty came out the door behind 'em, with Ricky at his side.

The boy looked steel-eyed but scared, like what he was scared of wasn't the guns or the guards but not knowing what was going on. That damnfool tattoo on his head looked rifuckindiculous with all its blue an' black lines tracing out the craters a the moon, the mares an' such like. "Nobody move!" McCarty barked. "Or I'll turn the boy's head into a fucking brain Slurpee right here an' now by God!" He poked his sixgun against the boy's ear, an' looked wild an' crazy, like some old-timer gone nuts on moonshine.

"All right, sir," somebody said when it was clear Jasper wasn't gonna step in, was in fact standing there mumbling to himself no longer paying no attention to what was going on, "just calm down now, let the boy go. What is it you need?"

"Ransom," Frank said, and McCarty nodded. "No need for anyone to get hurt, fella. Ransom straight up, the boy's mother's some stuck-up rich bitch who'll pay fifty thousand easy by mornin'. Nobody gonna get hurt. The boy'll be back for breakfast. Hell, no reason we can't all share." He tossed the rest a the money from the glovebox on the ground. They'd need more before they left, but that was doable. "No reason at all that I see, 'specially since them cameras ain't been working right since we got here, which is what you came out to investigate in the first place, right? But you didn't find nothing, an' that's what the report'll say."

"What about Theo an' Preston?" someone asked, and Frank snorted.

"What, I gotta do all your fucking work for you, Petty? Figure it fucking out. One of 'em shot the other cause they was gay for each other, take some a the porn from your locker an' stuff it in theirs. I don't fucking know. But him an' me an' the boy, we'll be going now."

"That's right," McCarty said, and his voice shook now for the first time, which Frank didn't like. "Nobody fucking move or the boy gets it."

Christ, Hank, Frank thought. We're kinda past that page in the script now.

He shook his head irritably and got in the pickup, not looking around to see who picked up the money, not needing to. Don't worry about getting a fancy gun, Jasper. Even a cheap bullet'll make its way through that cheating bitch's braincase.

ooo000ooo

"What the fuck's going on?" Ricky asked. They were long gone from Crestwood now, McCarty at the wheel of the pickup with a sixgun still in his hand, Frank riding with his back against the passenger side door looking behind 'em to see if any staties got on their tail.

"Jailbreak, boy," Frank said, and Ricky laughed, though he looked scared.

"Jesus fuck," he said, and McCarty slapped him, then immediately went pale.

"Don't blaspheme," he said nonetheless. "It's taken a lot for your Pa to get this thing done."

"We're gonna hit the road, Rick," Frank said, feeling like he was babblin'. He was sober as a bishop now, not that sobriety you reach far beyond the edge a drunk, but truly sober, steady an' clear. What the hell had all that been with Jasper? With Petty? How'd he even know their names? "You an' me, I guess it's like that vacation we'd talked about. Law'll be after us both, but you know what I say to that?"

"What?" It was so innocently asked that for a second there Ricky really did sound like a young teenager.

"I say fuck 'em in the ear," and Frank grinned from one side to th'other. "Right?"

"Fucking A," Ricky said. "Do I still get to do my art?"

Oh that wild look in his eye. Oh that wounded wild look, the way the coyote looked just before the accident. "We'll figure it out," Frank said, meaning fuck no you don't.

"All right," Ricky said, sitting back. "Where we going right this minute?"

"Mr McCarty's place," Frank said. "Down near the Widow's, south of Borachon."

"An' we're just about there," McCarty said softly. "Just about."

Frank looked out the windows. McCarty'd kept the high-beams off, just the regular headlights on, an' it was hard to see too far in fronta the pickup, but this didn't look like the man's driveway or even his road, although they were in the right area, they'd passed the Cinco y Dime a couple minutes ago --

The pickup started to slow down, though there weren't nothing around at all. "Hank," Frank said, an' the old man flipped the high-beams on as the truck came to a stop.

Them lights shone right onto a scarecrow hanging at the crossroads a Hosteen an' Texas.

McCarty turned the ignition to accessory, an' bowed his head like he was prayin'. "I'm sorry, Frank," he said. "He owns me." Hard to tell if the old man said <u>owns</u> or <u>owes</u>. "We made a deal a long time ago, and tonight's the summer solstice. Tonight's the night for bargains."

"Dad?" Ricky asked cautiously, as Frank opened the door.

"That's right!" the scarecrow called, waving its arms an' legs around like a spider that'd been tacked to a wall. "Tonight's the night for bargains, so <u>come on down!</u>"

Frank took a couple steps towards the scarecrow, far enough that he was blocking the light from the headlights, an' the man swallered into darkness. "What the fuck is this?" he asked. "What's the game this time, Marlowe?"

The scarecrow was wearing the same mask he'd been wearing when Frank first met him here on Halloween, an' grabbed the back a the post, lifting himself off it an' hopping down. "Same game it's always been, old pup, old son of a bitch." He shook himself like getting the cramps outta his muscles, an' pulled at his nose with his thumb an' forefinger. "Whoooeee! yeah. Same game we always been playing, you an' me."

McCarty almost ran to the scarecrow, looking like he was groveling, or 'bout ready to. "I done my bit," he said. "I brought 'em here just like you said, an' it ain't midnight yet!" He looked at his watch. "Eleven-fifty-three! It's eleven-fifty-three! I done what you said!" By that last sentence he was hysterical, no halfways or 'bout-tos about it. He was an old man gone fucking crazy with age. "It's been enough," McCarty said. "It's been too much. Release me like you said. Release me, Jack, gimme my pardon."

"Aye," the scarecrow said, and waved a hand at Ricky, who'd follered along behind McCarty. "Go wi' the Almighty, Henry McCarty," the scarecrow said. "Go wi' peace, an' be ye released this night the solstice, by the light a the midnigh' moon."

Snickersnack. That blade a Ricky's flashed between the headlights an' caught McCarty in the side, before the boy's hand twisted an' ripped. The look on his face was uncomplicated focus, just doing what he was good at.

The old man fell to his knees with the faintest a sighs, an' maybe he got what he wanted.

"God damn it!" Frank shouted, an' there was so much nothing around that it didn't even echo, just fell flat in the sand an' early summer scrub brush. "What the fuck's wrong with you, boy? That was a good man! He's likely killed now!"

"No likely about it," the scarecrow said, sounding amused. "Nothing much ever <u>was</u> likely 'bout Hank McCarty, an' I don't reckon his death should be the exception." He pulled off his mask, and Frank was actually relieved somehow, vindicated, to see Josh Marlowe's face staring at him, eyes a-twinkle. "Whooeee. This is exciting, ain't it?"

Ricky walked over to Marlowe, putting his knife away. "I still don't like it as much as when it's random," he said. "The art ain't there, it's just bullshit."

"But it <u>was</u> random," Marlowe said. "You just don't see the big picture yet, the chaos in the order a things. You'll grow into it."

"The fuck's wrong with Ricky?" Frank asked. He had his gun in hand, thought seriously about killing one or the other of 'em or both. "Why the fuck is he like this, what'd you do to him?"

Marlowe looked amused by that. "Well, the apple don't fall far from the tree, I reckon. The boy's just like me. Little boy blue and the man in the moon." He flicked a hand at Ricky. "Boy, go wait at the other corner."

"But --"

"Go."

He did, and Frank was impressed despite himself. "I'd rather he stayed," he said. "He's right in the thick a this."

"No, he ain't," Marlowe said.

"So, what then," Frank asked, itching on that trigger finger. "This about Kriste? About you an' her? You taking it out on me, some kinda jealousy, to get the boy from me?"

"Man," Marlowe said, shaking his head back an' forth. They'd both been stepping towards each other, and weren't more'n a coupla steps apart now, in the middle a the crossroads, with the pickup's headlights making a kinda corridor where they stood. "Why you gotta make this about a girl, Frank? This is about you an' me. Always was."

Frank shook his head, an' brought the gun up. "All this soul-selling business, it's bullshit, ain't it? You tried to get me to think of my soul as something <u>separate</u> from me. Something you could just take. That's like saying you're gonna take my mind an' leave me be, or take my palm an' leave the hand. It just don't work out, Marlowe. It just don't add up."

"Well, you're right about the palm an' the hand, but what you're missing is that don't mean I <u>didn't</u> take your palm, you damn idjit. It means you <u>gave</u> me the whole hand. So you gonna shoot me?" Marlowe asked mildly. "After everything Hank told you about me, I wonder what you think that's gonna do."

Frank shot him anyway.

The bullet caught Marlowe in the shoulder, knocking him down, an' when he got up, there was blood. Not dying blood, but blood, an' the man had to grit his teeth to fight down the pain. He stood up straight, though, 'cept for that shoulder. "All right," Marlowe said. "Feel better? Cause if you kill me, this ain't gonna work out for nobody. Ricky's still gonna have his problems, you're still gonna have yours, an' me, well, I don't reckon I cotton to being dead."

"Say it," Frank said, gun still aimed at him, the sight at the end a the barrel hiding Marlowe's forehead.

"We're running outta time, Frank." Marlowe actually appeared agitated a bit. "Say what?"

"Say you're Jack Dust. Say you're the Halloween man."

"Damnation, Frank. I'm Jack Dust -- both of 'em. I'm the Halloween man, the Hollow Man, the Bad November, Mr Bogeyman, Walter the Skinless. I can't remember 'em all, old pup, but that's a goodly list."

"Satan," Frank said. "The devil."

"I don't think there is a Devil," Marlowe said, an' pulled at his nose again. "If there's a Hell, I never been there, least not like they show it on TV. But the satan, mmhm. The adversary, Frank. The angel of opposition. And the Lord said unto the Satan, where you been, fella? An' the Satan answered the Lord, here an' there. I been around, doing your work, being your handyman. Why, whatcha need? Job one seven."

Frank put the gun down. "Why my boy?"

"I needed a son. Why'd <u>you</u> have one?"

"But he's so -- he's so God damn screwed up --"

"You just don't know how to handle him. Shit, old pup, kittens can't raise coyotes." <u>Kie-yotes.</u> Like Arthur Train Jr woulda said it. "He'll be fine under my hand, and you know that. Like you know Jasper's wife ain't gonna live to see tomorrow night. I just needed you to hang onto him for a while, till you were both ready. Looks to me like he is, looks to me like he ain't gonna do nothing but suffer an' cause grief to all them around him until he gets somewhere where folks know his kind, know his arts."

"And there's places like that."

"More'n you'd think, old son. More'n you'd think. Now hurry to hell an' take my hand. Right here in River City, old chum. Right here in the crossroads by the light a the midnight moon, if you love the boy you will take my hand and bleed with me, or I swear by Carcosa an' all that's come since, I swear in the names a all them I ever killed, it will go badly for both a you."

Frank took the offered hand with his bad'un, the one in the cast.

"Ricky!" Marlowe called, singsongy, an' raised his free hand. The boy tossed the butterfly knife, which whistled as it flew through the air, an' Marlowe caught it neatly, bringing it down hard on their clasped hands.

There was an instant of agony, enough to catch Frank's breath, an' then he flexed his fingers, which'd broken free a the cast where the knife had stabbed through it before piercing the web a flesh 'tween his thumb an' forefinger. No breaks. No busted bones, no torn-up tendons.

"You figured it out yet?" Marlowe murmured, like he didn't want Ricky to overhear. He sounded excited, thrilled, breathless. "You figured out what I gave you? You ready for Jasper to come to you, looking for help with a this or a that, 'cause he's got it fixed in his head you're the sort can do it? You thinking through all them Halloweens to come, all them solstices an' New Years?" Frank didn't say anything, and Marlowe grinned, still holding his hand. "Don't let us down, old pup. No matter what shape a cowboy's in when the world's done with him -- he's still there, all right."

Frank holstered the gun and picked up the burlap mask from where Marlowe'd dropped it, the rough old mask with the holes cut in it for eyes and a little slit for the mouth. The lights from the pickup fell as the engine cut out, an' the art teacher winked to him before leaning in to give him what they used to call a Judas kiss, just below the ear. The satan whispered something sacred that wasn't "Tag, you're it," but may as well have been.

ABOUT THE AUTHOR

Bill Kte'pi is the author of the haunted house novel *Low Country* and a number of short stories, some of which are available online and catalogued at ktepi.com. He lives too far north with his girlfriend and their three absurd cats.

39961395R00105

Made in the USA
Charleston, SC
21 March 2015